FINDING AMY

A Romantic Suspense Novel

by

Phyllis A. Humphrey

Published by Criterion House
Printed by CreateSpace

ISBN:978-1-884162-39-8 (Paperback edition)

ACKNOWLEDGMENTS

I very much appreciate the help given me by our British friends Jan and David Featherstone, who graciously answered all my questions about England and, especially, London which I threw at them when I first started writing this book so many years ago .

Chapter 1

As if Sabrina wasn't miserable enough sitting alone in her Chicago condo on a Saturday night, her father telephoned with bad news. "I'm afraid your grandfather has died."

She groaned. "Just what I didn't need to hear right now."

"You were thinking of Peter again."

"So what else is new?"

"It's time you stopped grieving for him."

"I have. I'm a strong person, never even glance at the gas oven."

He ignored her attempt at black humor. "Naturally the funeral is in London, and I think you ought to go."

"I haven't visited since I was nine. I shouldn't have waited so long." She sighed. In her experience, time had done a bang-up job of matching the speed of light.

"You must stop moping around feeling sorry for yourself."

"You're right, as usual. I'll go." Better than lying awake listening to mice chatting to one another in the walls.

"You haven't had a vacation in two years, not since your fiancé was killed in that car accident. Visit your cousins in England, go sightseeing. Look at this trip as a chance to renew your own life."

Of course, it was the worst possible time. Flying to London didn't solve Sabrina's business problem—to sell or not to sell: that was the question—and she doubted it would improve a life as dull as a mashed potato sandwich.

"When are you going?" she asked. "Can we fly together?"

"Tomorrow or the next day. I need to hurry back."

"And I'll need time to find someone to keep an eye on my business while I'm gone."

"Once in England, stay as long as you can. Maybe you'll meet someone over there."

"You're way too anxious to become a grandfather yourself. If that old mansion Granddad lived in is as spooky as I remember, I'm more likely to meet a ghost."

* * *

Three days later, Sabrina stood in the library of Gilmore Manor, its size and prominence reminding her again of *Rebecca*. Author Daphne du Maurier replaced Shakespeare in her mind. Since reading the book as a teenager, she'd always envisioned Manderly as her father's ancestral home, with a mysterious, handsome Max de Winter.

Now, however, instead of Max de Winter, a different handsome man stared at her and smiled. His slender build seemed every inch of six feet tall. His face, beneath a thatch of sandy hair, resembled that of a blond Hugh Grant: fair complexion, straight nose, firm chin, and eyes so blue and large one could almost drown in them. Had her father been clairvoyant about her meeting someone?

He spoke in a BBC-terrific accent. "I don't believe we've been introduced. I'm Hugh Pendleton."

She said the first thing that came to her mind. "Are you a cousin too? Did we play together as children?"

"No to both questions. I'm thankful we're not related."

Before she could discover what he meant by that remark, her cousin, Elmore Manville, ding-donged a little silver bell, her two widowed aunts pushed between her and Pendleton to take seats, and he moved to the end of the row of chairs in front of her.

Why did he not wish to be related to her? His smile assured her he hadn't meant it as an insult. In spite of running her business in Chicago, she'd skipped only a few Pilates exercises, let a professional work his magic on her long, naturally-curly hair when necessary, and her face hadn't scared anyone since the mask she wore at a Halloween party.

Another thought surfaced. If not a relative, why had he come to the reading of the will? Just her luck if it turned out the estate owed him money, and she had to pony up her share. Or, her thoughts of *Rebecca* fresh in her mind, did he harbor some mysterious secret, like killing his wife?

Elmore, obviously relishing the role of executor,

introduced another solicitor, a long-time family friend of the Gilmores, who had written the will, then took a seat with the others.

The man droned monotonously, and Sabrina found it difficult to concentrate on all the legal language. Instead, she remembered the last time she'd been in Gilmore Manor. The library took up a mere fraction of the three-story mansion nestling in a fold of the valley, and it brought back many memories. During that long-ago summer, she'd run across the broad, green lawns and waded, against Granddad's rules, in the lily pond. With her girl cousins, she'd climbed over the stone cherubs, giggling about whether the boy cherub was anatomically correct.

"–and to my granddaughter Sabrina," the solicitor read, "I leave the large blue trunk in the nursery."

That old blue trunk was her inheritance? As was becoming increasingly clear, her grandfather had died almost penniless. Gilmore Manor, apparently mortgaged clear up to its leaky third floor roof, now held only some furniture and the library's collection of books. They'd long since sold any objects of value.

Glancing again toward Hugh Pendleton, she caught him looking in her direction. As if embarrassed, he turned back toward Manville, but she'd detected a slight flush cross his face.

After a few minor bequests were read from the will, Elmore thanked everyone for coming and stood up to mark the end of the proceedings. Chairs shuffled against the fading carpet, and everyone ambled toward the doors leading to the drawing room. A hum of conversations began, mainly on the lack of anything worthwhile to inherit. The mortgage company would take over the house. The relatives, many of whom had journeyed some distance to London—none however from as far away as Sabrina—must content themselves with only some personal mementoes of the eccentric, reclusive Richard Gilmore. She sighed and rose from her chair.

"I say." The voice startled her, and she turned. Although she stood five-feet-nine in her heels, Hugh Pendleton's gaze lowered to look at her.

"I hope my remark earlier didn't offend you. I meant it as a compliment."

"That you'd rather not be a part of my family?"

He cleared his throat. "You have me at a disadvantage. I'm not saying this at all well. I meant I'd rather you weren't a cousin. That would be somewhat inhibiting."

Were all Englishmen so formal when starting an acquaintance with a woman? What a refreshing difference. Chicago men, at least many of those she'd met, were vastly different in that respect. Perhaps it explained her remaining single long after some of her friends were on their second, or third, marriages.

"What types of inhibitions are you concerned about?" She moved toward the Queen Anne desk.

He followed, circling the desk toward her. "Getting to know you better, of course." His smile revealed even, white teeth and made little crinkle lines at the corners of his eyes. "Mr. Manville indicated you're from America, and I wondered how you came to be a cousin."

"You said you wanted to know more about me, but

it seems you're more interested in my bloodlines." She enjoyed teasing him and edged away, putting the desk between them.

"But you're wrong. And your lines—" His gaze traveled over her figure. "—speak for themselves."

A warm glow stole onto Sabrina's cheeks, and she didn't answer. She noticed everyone else had already left the library, leaving them alone.

"I merely tried to get the polite generalities out of the way first," he continued, "and I have a natural curiosity besides, which is one of my better faults."

"You classify your faults?" She pretended to be shocked at the idea. "What are some of the worst ones, I wonder?"

"If I'm fortunate, there may be an opportunity to introduce you to one or two of those as well." He smiled again and continued his stroll around the desk.

Sabrina did the same and saw a twinkle flash in those electric-blue eyes. Contrary to what she'd heard, apparently not *all* Englishmen were stuffy and humorless.

"But you haven't answered my question." He edged his way around the desk.

Her pulse quickened. Yes, she was recovering from the death of her fiancé, and she not only liked Hugh Pendleton's looks, but loved mysteries. Yet, her two-week trip seemed inadequate for starting a new relationship.

"I'm the daughter of David Gilmore, Richard's youngest son. My father traveled to the United States where he met my mother and never lived in England again, although he visited from time to time. I visited by myself when I was nine."

"Weren't you a trifle young to travel so far alone?"

"My mother died, and father sent me here that summer while he put his life back together." Her throat choked for a moment. Her memory included the trauma of her own loss as well as the unfamiliarity of vastly different surroundings.

The smile left his face. "I'm most awfully sorry. How unfortunate. And your father–?"

"Never remarried, and is quite well, thank you." She went on quickly, to spare him the necessity of asking. "He came over for his father's funeral, but flew home yesterday to return to his job. I arrived this morning and am staying on until the tenth."

"I say, may we stop circling this desk? I shan't bite."

Sabrina realized with chagrin that she'd begun her third time around, always keeping the desk between them. She stopped moving and let him catch up. "I haven't been back since the summer I spent here."

"So long? What kept you from returning?"

"Life." She grinned. "You know, all those necessary evils: school, work." She moved away from him again, this time walking slowly about the library, looking upward along the shelves at the colorful bookbindings.

He followed her, the clean masculine scent of him mingling with the library's smell of furniture polish and old leather. "What work keeps you away?"

"I'm in business, and you don't really want to know the boring details."

"But here you are visiting Gilmore Manor once more." He paused. "Yet you did inherit something. A trunk in the attic sounds positively mysterious."

"You mean I might find an old skeleton inside?"

"Let's hope not, but aren't you anxious to find out?"

"Not much. Elmore hasn't led me to expect the Crown Jewels."

What *could* she expect? The mystery of the blue trunk suddenly intrigued her. She wanted to know what lay inside.

At that moment, Elmore entered the hall, and she used his appearance to say, "Excuse me," to Pendleton and head for the stairway to the upper floors.

* * *

Hugh didn't expect a conversation with Elmore, but the solicitor frowned and asked if he knew his way about.

"Yes, thanks. I'm just on my way upstairs."

"There's an elevator, you know, installed a few years ago. You'll find it behind the staircase." Elmore pointed briefly and walked off in the opposite direction.

Shrugging, Hugh watched Sabrina cross the Great Hall with its swords, shields and battle-axes fastened to the walls and colorful pennants flying from the rafters. She climbed the staircase, holding onto the polished bannister, while he stayed a considerable distance behind, yet close enough to catch her should she fall. Such gallantry was an ancient rite, but one all good English schoolboys learned early on. Modern women pretended not to want such courtesies, but he'd noticed they usually accepted them readily enough. The ones who insisted he not treat them so politely often failed to measure up anyway. A few appeared to have the brains of earthworms and the enthusiasm of your average brick. However, Sabrina seemed everything at once: an intelligent business woman—or so he'd surmised—and exceedingly feminine as well.

Admiring the elegant, if somewhat shabby, furnishings of the mansion, he paused at the second-floor landing. Sabrina, apparently not realizing he'd followed her, continued upward another flight. Although Manville had reminded Hugh about the elevator, he didn't mind walking up.

Besides, it gave him such a striking view of Sabrina's marvelous body, her trim waist, perfect hips, and legs that tapered to not-too-thin ankles. He'd never liked women whose legs seemed too spindly to support them.

He'd been attracted the moment he'd caught sight of her. Long curly hair framed her face and cascaded down her back. It's rich brown color, with a hint of red, made the grey eyes all the more surprising. Her rosy complexion, such a pleasant change from the pallor of many English women, together with a pert nose and generous mouth, made her absolutely delicious-looking.

He wanted to rush toward her but changed his mind. She might resent his following her without permission. She might wish to be alone while she perused her strange inheritance.

* * *

The nursery occupied the space at the end of the hall

on the third floor, and the mere act of approaching it set Sabrina's heart ticking like a fast-paced metronome. What sweet memories it evoked, remaining just as she remembered it: the wide windows overlooking the kitchen garden, padded window seats covered in faded chintz, the fireplace with its heavy metal screen. She patted the wooden rocking horse in the corner, saw low, scarred wooden tables and chairs. The shelves that once held children's toys and books now stood empty.

She paused at the doorway, drinking it all in, fighting the urge to cry. Had it been only three months she'd spent there? How, then, had it managed to color her entire life?

She crossed to the windows and looked down. The kitchen garden looked cared for, perhaps the work of the one gardener she'd seen at the reading of the will. Grandfather left him something, she supposed. Or did the cook, also present, plant those rows of parsley and chives?

She moved away from the window and spotted the blue trunk, its color faded, in the corner. Kneeling on the threadbare carpet, she pulled up the hasp. Inside she saw stacks of children's books and some old-fashioned clothes she'd once worn to play at being grown up. As she lifted a fringed shawl, she saw something in the bottom of the trunk. Amy! Her doll!

Tears sprang to her eyes. Her father had given her the doll when she started her solo journey to England as a child. But when she packed to return home three months later, she couldn't find it. Back in Chicago the twice-searched suitcases yielded no missing doll. Now it had turned up at last in the trunk she'd just inherited.

She picked up the doll and examined her. Almost twenty years before, Amy eased the loneliness of the long trip to London and served as constant companion, which made it all the more painful to lose her. Now, miraculously returned, Amy still looked almost brand-new, hardly played with. Perhaps she always lay in the bottom of the trunk and no one else ever removed the old clothes that covered her.

Amy's cloth face, with embroidered-on eyes, nose and mouth, smiled up at her. A short white apron still covered her blue gingham dress and, at the bottom of her cotton-stuffed legs, appliqued black cloth substituted for shoes. She had been neither expensive nor particularly pretty, Sabrina realized, but she meant more than any dolls she'd owned before or after. Was it because the black yarn curls resembled Sabrina's own long curly hair, or because she mysteriously disappeared, never having a chance to wear out or lose her appeal?

Yet, she felt heavier than Sabrina remembered. How odd. A cloth doll ought not to weigh very much. Furthermore, a doll ought to have seemed heavier to her when she was a child than now as an adult. The same way your first-grade schoolroom dwindled in size after you grew up.

Sabrina turned the doll over and inspected the closure of her apron. Obviously sewn together by a careless seamstress, the stitches didn't even match in color. Why had she never noticed it before? Even at nine, she hadn't been that unobservant.

She pulled at the threads with her fingernail, and

they came loose. The entire apron and dress opened. Beneath, on the cloth body of the doll, more clumsy stitches showed, and she tore those too, until Amy's back opened and her stuffing oozed forward. Sabrina probed inside, widening the opening. Something hard met her fingertips. She turned Amy upside down and the something dropped into her lap: an ornate jeweled necklace.

Chapter 2

Sabrina heard a noise in the hall and clutched Amy to her chest. Who else would venture up to the old nursery? A smidgen of fear slid up her spine. Not for her safety, but because of the necklace. She knew little about jewelry, but something told her it might be extremely valuable. What should she do with it?

For the moment, she decided, nothing. Until she knew its worth, who it really belonged to and why it had been hidden, she'd be cautious.

She jammed the necklace into the cavity inside the doll and pulled the dress and apron closed over it. Next she stuffed the doll down into a corner of the trunk. Just then the nursery door, which she hadn't completely closed, opened wider.

"Sabrina?"

"Hugh."

"I hope you don't mind my coming in. I've been told some of the old papers I inherited are up here, but perhaps they're in a different part of this, er, attic."

Sabrina rose from her place on the floor in front of the trunk. "You inherited something? Since you pointed out you're glad we're not related, I wondered how you came to be at the reading of the will."

"Richard Gilmore and I were merely friends. He left his old papers to me." A smile reappeared on his face, evidence he liked his own inheritance.

Sabrina thought about what he'd said. No doddering absent-minded professor, Hugh couldn't have been a contemporary of her grandfather. He looked not a day over thirty-five. His lean body appeared muscular beneath the summer-weight tweeds, indicating his exercise consisted of more than turning pages. And those eyes, not only heavenly in color, seemed alert and perceptive. Certainly the way he looked at her indicated a man who didn't spend all his time indoors with, as her father often accused her, his "nose in a book."

Sabrina realized Hugh was speaking.

"—and he knew of my interest in such things. Nevertheless, I was surprised as well as pleased he remembered me and put that bequest in his will."

She hadn't caught all of Hugh's explanation of how he became acquainted with her grandfather, but instead, she asked, "Are those papers you say you've inherited up here?"

"In an office safe on the second floor, I understand. And several boxes in this attic or possibly the garage."

She loved his accent, the way he pronounced "garage." In fact, so far nothing about him failed to please her. She supposed it came of living there the summer before she turned ten. Impressionable as a wet sandy beach, she had become a hopeless Anglophile: read novels by British authors (*Rebecca* three times), went to British films, and watched Masterpiece Theatre on her local P.B.S. television station.

"Is looking at old papers your career then?"

He grinned. "Not exactly. My father hoped I'd become a solicitor like Manville, your executor, but books interested me more, and now I look at them for business as well as pleasure."

Her heart sank. "You're a librarian?"

His laugh echoed. "No, although the occupation isn't considered so boring here in England as it may to you Yanks."

"I heard a rumor that librarians are all elderly ladies in high-necked dresses and thin-rimmed glasses."

"We have some of those as well. Actually, I teach history in a public school as well as pore over old manuscripts."

"What kind of old manuscripts?"

"I'm not terribly discriminating. I'll look at anything, but the older, the better. As I said, that's why I'm here."

Sabrina never expected to meet an exciting man in England, but a history teacher who liked old papers? He came farther into the room and strolled easily around, glancing at the children's furniture, before once more looking toward her.

She hadn't wanted him to come into the room, hoped to keep the mystery of the doll in the trunk to herself. "Shall we go back downstairs now?" She headed for the door.

"I prefer being up here, if you don't mind. There are too many people downstairs, whereas now I have you all to myself." He gave her that killer smile again.

The reaction she'd first experienced when she met him returned, and she couldn't think of a plausible reason for insisting they leave the nursery.

"You haven't yet told me what *you* do for a living."

"Nothing exciting. I'm just a business woman."

"You don't look it. I'd guess you to be something far more exotic. A model, or an actress or dancer. Yes, I can visualize you in one of those modern musicals. Perhaps in a leotard in *Cats*." He surveyed her figure again.

"I think my mother cherished that delusion for a year or so, but dancing lessons proved a waste of time." She wondered how klutzy she might have been if the lessons hadn't given her at least a smattering of grace.

"Any chance you don't have to return to the U.S. soon?"

"No, sorry." She moved away from the door to saunter toward the windows. "As I told you, I run a business."

He fell into step behind her. "What kind of business?"

"I own three shops, the kind that do fast printing."

"You own printing shops? How extraordinary!"

She smiled. "Yes, especially since you pictured me an actress or dancer."

He put out his hand. "How did you come to have such an unusual occupation?"

"I don't think it's unusual, even for a woman. We have thousands of such shops at home. They're very popular."

"Did your father start the business in America?" He

pulled out one of the small children's chairs and sat down, his knees poking up higher than his waist.

She grinned at the picture he made. "No, he became a commodities broker, sells sugar and coffee futures, pork bellies, things like that."

"How extraordinary!"

"You said that before," she reminded him gently. "At any rate—" She sat in another small chair at the little table. "—between semesters at college, I worked in a printing shop, and after graduation, I became the manager of one, and later bought out the business. Now I own three."

"A veritable conglomerate."

"Hardly. In fact, I took this vacation partly to come to my grandfather's funeral and partly to do some thinking about my next business options."

"Which are?" he prompted.

"To either open a fourth Copy Station, or else sell the entire business. I've had a very generous offer."

"Do you want to sell? You're successful, apparently, but it sounds dull, and I believe you said it's boring."

She leaned her arms across the table. "Not exactly dull—" as she'd once told her father, "—but very demanding. If I'm not filling out endless government forms for tax purposes, I'm trouble-shooting. A machine breaks down or an employee calls in sick, and I must find a replacement or work that shift myself." She shrugged.

He grinned at her again. "Personally, I think you should sell the business and move here."

She smiled at his obvious desire to see her again and

decided she might fall for his voice and his eyes even if the rest of him weren't terrific as well. At least during her vacation. Her heart tripped away in her chest as if she were a schoolgirl again, having her first crush. So what if it wouldn't last more than two weeks? Although she felt ready to put some adventure into her life, she questioned her eagerness. Would any attractive man have had such an effect on her, or only this particular one?

"You make it sound too easy."

Hugh rose from the tiny chair and advanced to the corner near the fireplace. "This seems to be a blue trunk."

He'd noticed the trunk. Just what she didn't want. She hurried toward him, but before she could say anything, he lifted the hasp and propped up the lid. "Children's books, I see." Bending over, he took some out, stacking them in neat piles beside him.

"Nothing important, really. I've already looked." She stood next to him and touched his arm. "Shall we go now?"

He squatted near the trunk and examined some of the books closely. "You may have a first edition or two here, I think."

"Really? I thought they made certain nothing of value escaped the bankers." She tried to think of a way to get him to leave without sounding rude.

"More likely they didn't know. Books are my field, however. Most of these are quite worn, but when there's only two or three copies of something in existence, it can bring a high price, even without the original dust jacket and perfect cover."

"I wouldn't sell them anyway."

"I thought not." His voice, close to her ear, as she bent next to him, carried understanding and concern. He seemed to realize how much they meant to her.

As he pulled out the pile of folded garments from under the remaining books, he broke the mood. "What have we here? Don't tell me you actually wore these?" He held up a yellowing lace dress of ancient vintage and a man's black cutaway coat and striped trousers.

Sabrina couldn't help laughing. "Of course I did." Perhaps if they concentrated on the clothes, Hugh wouldn't find the doll. She took the dress from his hands, and held it against her body. The hem came only to her ankles, but she remembered how it once dragged on the floor. "I'm not an actress, but I did love to play dress-up. Isn't it gorgeous?"

He took to his feet too, shrugged out of his coat and slipped into the cutaway, his shoulders stretching it taut.

Falling in with his mood, she removed her own pink linen jacket, which matched her sleeveless summer dress, and pulled the musty lace over her head, ignoring the dust settling on her hair.

"Music, we must have music." Hugh looked around the room. An ancient gramophone sat on a bench nearby, and he turned it on and put the needle onto the one record which still remained in the machine.

A scratchy tune emerged, one Sabrina didn't recognize, but Hugh began to hum the melody and took her in his arms. They glided effortlessly over the floor to a slow ballad.

The feel of his arms around her waist tore Sabrina's thoughts away from the doll and brought her most definitely into the moment. She enjoyed being in his arms. He might be the handsome man she imagined in those long-ago summer days when she put on the old clothes and pretended to be at a fancy dress ball. How delightful that he seemed to know instinctively she had played the phonograph and danced in this lace dress, one hand holding up the skirt and one on the shoulder of an imaginary partner.

Now her hand touched a real partner, a man whose admiration shone clearly in his eyes. His arms moved farther across her waist, pressing the length of her body to him, her thighs against his thighs, feeling the next step he would take in the dance. Her arm slid across his shoulders and rested at the far side of his neck, her fingers along the fine blond hairs.

The music came to a screeching halt, as if the needle had been dragged across the record. Instinctively they broke apart and looked around, but no one had entered the room. The record had apparently been damaged long before.

Sabrina pulled the dress over her head, letting her curls spring back into place without smoothing them, and folded the garments carefully. The action gave her an opportunity to recover from the unexpectedly strong emotions he aroused in her during that brief dance. She liked him, but falling for a man she'd only just met simply would not do.

He removed the tailcoat and replaced it with his own jacket, and she decided that, whatever his thoughts, they differed from hers. *He* wasn't in a strange country, reliving old memories. Besides, she needed to stop fantasizing, keep the doll hidden and get Hugh out of the room.

Instead he knelt on the floor, replaced the clothes in the trunk, and lifted out a fringed shawl. "Did you wear this shawl, too?" Without waiting for an answer, he reached under the shawl and held up the doll.

Sabrina rushed to him and snatched Amy from his grasp. She hugged the doll to her chest, as if finding her only that minute. "It's Amy. I thought I'd never see her again." She looked at Hugh but went on hugging the doll, as if she were nine years old again. "You can't imagine what this means to me."

She plopped down on the floor next to him, hoping he hadn't noticed the doll's unusual heaviness during the brief time he held her.

Hugh put his arm around her, comforting her as if she were still a child. She leaned against him, feeling the strength in his broad chest, hearing the heartbeat beneath his shirt and coat. In a few moments, she feigned recovery, sighed, and pushed herself away. "I didn't mean to get carried away by a sentimental moment."

"No apology necessary. Even we Brits, who pride ourselves on correct behavior, have our sentimental moments."

She stood up, still clutching Amy, and thrust out her free hand to him. "It's been nice meeting you."

He scrambled to his feet and took her hand. "I say, that's awfully abrupt, isn't it? I rather thought we were getting on famously. Might we at least have dinner together? Somewhere seriously public if you like."

She hesitated. She felt strongly attracted, too strongly. If she saw him again, if their relationship continued the way it seemed to be heading, would she be able to return to Chicago without regret? Still, hadn't she wanted adventure?

"Well, all right." She paused. "But not tonight. I'm still suffering from jet lag. I'd probably conk out and end up with my face in the soup."

He laughed. "Tomorrow then."

"That's fine. I'm staying at a bed-and-breakfast on Devonshire Terrace."

He wrote down the number she gave him and grinned as if he'd just won the Irish Sweepstakes. "Now I believe I'll go and see about my own inheritance. I'll collect you tomorrow at seven."

"Very well." Still clutching Amy, she watched him go. By the next day, she hoped she'd have done something with Amy. Yet, what would she do? She frowned. How could she learn the meaning of Amy's mysterious contents?

Chapter 3

Sabrina closed the lid of the trunk and left the children's nursery. She wanted to hurry away with her new-found treasure, but returned to the drawing room to say goodbye to the rest of the family. Some sat on the three sofas in the room, others stood about in small clusters.

Elmore greeted her, once more acting as if the Great High Poobah had put him in charge. "Ah, Sabrina, there you are. We wondered where you'd gone off to."

"I went upstairs to see what I'd inherited."

He frowned. "Rather a let-down, I imagine. But then, none of us has inherited anything much. The remaining servants received a few hundred pounds each, but the rest of us— well—"

She didn't tell him she'd found something which might be worth considerably more than a few hundred pounds. When she visited before, it seemed the family employed lots of servants and had plenty of resources. She often wondered if her father made a mistake by going to America to work for a living. She'd gladly have adapted to being called "heiress" in the tabloids.

"This is my son Zachary." Aunt Charlotte took her arm, and Sabrina looked up to see a tall, muscular man in his early thirties with dark hair, brown eyes and a stubble of beard on his chin. Unlike everyone else, he wore casual clothes.

"Cousin Sabrina, is it?" Zachary took her free hand in a strong grip, while his gaze roamed over her figure. "I'm Zach."

She smiled but pulled her hand free. "Have we met before?"

"No, I was a bit late showing up for the festivities." His voice, low and husky, sounded disdainful, although the rest of him showed a certain rugged handsomeness.

"I meant when we were children and I visited here before."

"No. I didn't live here then. You probably played with Aunt Mary and Uncle Philip's children. I came to live here when my father died and mum asked my grandfather if she could come home."

"I see. So you live here now?" Sabrina asked.

"Us and Uncle Philip's family. But we may all be chucked out on the street now the bankers are going to inherit the place."

"I'm sorry." Sabrina's brain tried to sort out the circumstances. She hadn't realized anyone else still lived in the mansion besides her late grandfather and Philip's family. Of course, as Zachary said, soon no one would.

Where would they all go? A sudden sadness struck her. During those years in which she grew up in Chicago, she'd occasionally felt deprived of the life she might have lived had her father stayed in Gilmore

Manor. She'd imagined herself prevented from becoming a wealthy Gilmore. Instead, her current better financial situation overshadowed those of her cousins.

Zach moved closer. "Let's get together while you're here, shall we? I can take you around town. I know all the best night spots."

She'd just bet he did. "Thanks." She didn't follow up on his invitation, "I must go now. I flew in this morning, and I'm afraid jet lag is catching up." She said goodbye and headed for the door.

In the large entry hall Elmore shook her hand, and Thomas, one of the remaining servants, called a taxi for her return to London. After a short ride, she entered the bed-and-breakfast on Devonshire Terrace.

From street level, forty-nine steps led to the small suite on the top floor, and, when she arrived in London that morning, she suspected the landlady gave her both bed and sitting room for the price of a single because she looked young and healthy enough to survive the climb.

Little did the landlady know. Interminable working days, and commuting between her three printing shops, had nevertheless not kept Sabrina in condition for marathon stair-climbing. She wondered how exhausted she'd feel were it not for her exercise class. In the end, she blamed her fatigue on having slept little during the long flight from Chicago. Breathing heavily, she slumped into the small love-seat taking up most of one wall in the tiny sitting room.

A knock at the door brought her to her feet.

The landlady, Mrs. Carruthers, came in, arms full of

clean towels. "I didn't expect to find you in. You weren't gone long." The woman set the towels on the edge of the small chest of drawers and rubbed her hands along the green apron tied around her ample waist. "Been shopping, have you?" She nodded toward the doll Sabrina had placed on the seat of the antique sofa.

"No, I've come from the reading of my grandfather's will."

"Your grandfather passed away? I'm sorry to hear it. But as you're an American you can't have been very close." Mrs. Carruthers had obviously failed the British reticence test.

"No, I hadn't seen him for almost twenty years, not since I was nine and spent a summer here." For the third time that day, the memory seemed as vivid as if it were twenty hours instead.

"You're not staying with the family?"

"No, the house is— er— sold." Sabrina decided not to mention the foreclosure and risk having it bandied about all over London in case Mrs. Carruthers liked to share everything her steady questioning uncovered. "Everyone is moving out. I don't really mind. And this is closer to town for sightseeing."

"Rather a long way to come for a doll, I'd say."

"I never expected to receive anything of value." Inheriting something hadn't been the reason for flying to England. Besides the urging of her father, she recognized the need to get away from the demands of her business. She needed to revitalize a life as exciting as watching paint dry.

"Nonetheless, a doll must have come as rather a

surprise."

"Very. On the other hand, it used to be mine."

"Left in England since you were nine? Well, you can give it to your own children now."

"I haven't any yet. I'm not married."

"Oooh, and with your looks and figure? American men must be blind." A sincere smile accompanied her words.

Sabrina laughed. "I've been too busy to look at them."

"Well, now you're on holiday, you can make up for it. Lots of men here would jump at the chance to meet you."

"Thank you." Sabrina remembered Hugh Pendleton's attentions and her own reaction to them. A vision of his face suddenly hovered in her mind's eye, and she almost wished she'd agreed to see him that very night instead of the next, jet-lag or not.

Mrs. Carruthers departed, and Sabrina closed the door after her and returned to the love-seat. She pulled the doll onto her lap and once more pulled out the necklace.

Bits of cotton fluff clung to it, dimming the brilliance of the stones—mostly diamonds, a few emeralds—that is, if real. Sabrina never cared very much for jewelry, and she couldn't have told genuine from fake if her life depended on it.

Yet, who would hide real jewelry in a doll? And why? Why leave it to her in such a strange way? Even as a little girl, unlike most of her friends, jewelry never interested her. She remembered her cousin Elmore saying, before the reading of the will, that everything except personal mementoes belonged to the bank. So if the jewels were real, hiding the necklace might have been a ploy to cheat the bankers. She dismissed the thought. Her grandfather wouldn't cheat anyone.

Too beautiful to be real, the necklace must be costume jewelry. After all, she'd found it in a trunk in the nursery. Although she never played with it, perhaps some other child wore it with the dress-up clothes. But why sew it up inside a doll? Still, if not part of the estate, merely a memento, Grandfather Richard could dispose of it as he pleased. She shook her head. She could find out. Elmore would know. Or, if she preferred not to ask him, and he seemed too preoccupied to be bothered about something unimportant, she could ask to see a copy of the will.

She should have it appraised. If costume jewelry, she could stop worrying about it. Placing the necklace on the bed, she searched the room for a box or sack to carry it in. Nothing. Her purse was too small, but her tote-bag too large. Plus she'd have to remove all the travel gadgets she carried in that. She put the necklace back into the doll. Having already lost any veneer of sophistication when she carried the doll in the taxi that brought her from the Manor, what was another half hour, more or less?

On the ground floor, Sabrina found the landlady arranging flowers in the public sitting room and asked her for directions to a jeweler's shop.

"Mr. Kendall has a shop two streets over—" She pointed with a sweep of her hand. "—number fifteen it is. A very nice man. Been there ever so long."

Sabrina thanked her and left the inn. She went down the steps and along the clean, narrow street, past other Victorian-looking houses, all three or four stories high, mostly white, with columns in front and tiny squares of grass or flowers next to the stairs leading to shiny—mostly black—front doors.

She turned the corner at the end of the street, but as she walked, a chill slid up her spine. Someone was following her.

She turned her head around quickly, but saw no one nearby. She told herself not to be silly and forced her feet to resume walking. She soon saw neat-looking ground-floor shops, and number fifteen occupied a location in the center of the block. Although smaller than she expected, the shop interior contained several glass jewelry cases and velvet-covered chairs in front of low antique tables.

No one greeted her on entering, but a bell over the door jangled, and soon a velvet curtain at the back of the shop parted and a bespectacled, white-haired man emerged. At first Sabrina thought two men entered. She glimpsed another man who was taller, younger, and dark-haired, behind the older one. However, he receded into the shadows of the back room, leaving the curtain gaping slightly.

"Good afternoon. I'm Mr. Kendall," the older man said. "How may I help you?"

"Good afternoon." Sabrina paused, embarrassed to reveal the way she carried the necklace. She wished the younger man had pulled the curtains tightly shut. The fewer people who saw this, the better.

"I have something I'd like you to appraise." She placed Amy, face down, on a low table, just under a circle of light. While the jeweler looked on, she removed the necklace from the opening in the doll's back and laid it on a velvet-padded square on the table.

Mr. Kendall accepted the unorthodox method of delivery without comment, put his jeweler's glass up to his eye and bent over the necklace.

"What do you think?" she asked. "Is it worth anything?"

"I believe that it is, but I would like some time to evaluate it thoroughly. There are so many stones."

"I see. How long?"

"A day or two." He glanced at his watch. "It's near closing time, but I'll see to it first thing tomorrow."

"You want me to leave it?"

"I shall keep it quite safe in my vault. To be honest, I must say many items I appraise turn out not to be genuine, merely clever reproductions."

Sabrina squelched the doubts creeping into her thoughts. Mrs. Carruthers recommended the man, and the sign on his door announced he'd been in business forty years. Besides, the necklace might have no value. Nor belong to her. And, since she seldom wore jewelry, except for her watch and, on a few occasions, some pearls, she convinced herself it didn't matter.

"Of course," she managed to say at last, noticing Mr. Kendall already writing out a receipt. She gave him her name and her London address. "I'll come back tomorrow then."

"Late afternoon, if you don't mind. I should have finished by then."

Sabrina retraced her steps to the inn, but she hesitated before entering, standing next to a solitary tree growing from a round circle cut into the narrow sidewalk. The forty-nine steps loomed before her, and though she intended to mount them eventually, she realized she'd had no tea, the dinner hour had arrived, and she had nothing edible in her room.

She disliked eating by herself, a definite drawback to traveling alone. At home she never went into a restaurant without a friend or date. But she had no choice. She must go somewhere for dinner or wait to eat until breakfast.

Deciding she'd rather not carry the doll around with her, nor go up and down those stairs again, she returned to the public sitting room, which, fortunately, Mrs. Carruthers had vacated. Planning to pick her up later, Sabrina tucked Amy behind two fat books on the lowest shelf of the bookcase and went out again.

Daylight fading fast, she surmised only another hour remained before darkness settled completely, enough time to find a restaurant or pub. She headed in the direction of Bayswater Street, and another block took her to a busy intersection with a pub on the opposite corner. As she started to walk over to it, a chill slid up her spine again. Someone stared at her.

She whirled her head around but saw no one.

She told herself it was nothing, but the feeling persisted. Her heart trip-hammered in her chest, and she had to fight to keep from turning around again. Increasing her speed, she almost ran into the building.

The pub's dark interior made Sabrina pause near the door to adjust her eyes. A few customers sat at tables, and a long wooden counter, which looked old enough to have been there since the time of the Celts, ran the length of the far wall. Behind it, a stout, balding man in a white apron, wielding a wicked-looking knife, invited her in.

"Special tonight is baked 'am, but yer can 'ave the roast beef, if you've a mind." He gave her a toothy smile.

Sabrina forced herself to approach the counter. The warmth of the room and the smell of hot food eased her panic. Still, she couldn't quite shake off the earlier mood. She decided, suddenly, not to stay and eat there, but to take something to her room. That way she'd be back before total darkness. She ordered a ham sandwich to take out and watched its preparation.

"A few crisps?" the man asked, and without waiting for a reply, put a small bag of potato chips on top of her paper-wrapped sandwich in a sack. "Something ter drink?"

"No thank you."

He took her money, made change, and gave her another broad smile. "'Night."

Sabrina stepped out on the sidewalk and at once the feeling of being watched returned. In spite of the short time she'd been in the pub, the sky had become noticeably darker, and she congratulated herself for making the decision to take her simple dinner home with her. Still, her stupid fear haunted her.

Again she looked around the street. A few cars drove past, but the only pedestrians seemed relatively far away and paying no attention to her whatever. She saw only a young couple, an older woman with a dog that resembled a walking dustrag, and two young boys. But the buildings, set at odd angles, cast shadows on one another. Then she heard footsteps behind her.

Chapter 4

Sabrina took to her heels, running, making noisy beats on the pavement. Barely above panic, she finally arrived at her door, and, inside, leaned against it and let out the breath she'd been holding. She climbed the stairs to her room, trying to analyze her strange feelings. Although she lived in Chicago—a city many foreigners still equated with Al Capone and other gangsters—she seldom felt afraid there, not even after dark. She never felt the need for a man to protect her. Yet, she wished she had one right now. Hugh Pendleton came to mind.

* * *

She woke to sunlight streaming through her window and felt much better. In daylight, she convinced herself her fears of the evening before were groundless. No one followed her. Nothing happened.

Ready to go sightseeing, she put on her good pair of jeans, a cotton top in shades of blue, and athletic shoes. Her one suitcase didn't allow for many choices. She locked her door and started down the sixty-two steps to the bottom floor. The ground floor was only forty-nine steps down, but below that, what had once been the servants' domain now housed the kitchen and the guests' dining room.

Mrs. Carruthers greeted her with orange juice and soon brought tea, poached eggs, bacon and toast. Sabrina enjoyed the breakfast and ascended to the ground floor where she let herself out through the glass-paned doors. A discreet sign indicated the doors would be locked at midnight unless other arrangements had been made with the staff. Sabrina grinned. Just like a college dormitory.

As she stood on the sidewalk in front of the tall, Victorian-era building, shivers started up her arms. The air chilled her, in spite of the sun, and she decided to return to her room for a sweater.

Once more she tackled the steps and, as she rounded the turn at the second-floor landing, the foreboding of the night before returned in full force. Someone was watching her.

Her fists clenched over wet palms. Although she feared the rose-colored carpeting might muffle their footsteps, no one else appeared to inhabit the stairway. She leaned against the balustrade and peered up the stairwell. Nothing.

Heart pounding, she nevertheless started up again. The darkness made its own scary rules the night before, but she wouldn't let those unreasonable fears intimidate her in the morning. She decided the mystery of the necklace turned everything into a Hollywood horror picture. But morning sun shone, and the inn bulged with people. Surely no harm could come to her.

At the next landing, she glanced upward again. No one. Only one more flight led to her rooms and, except for hers, no guest rooms on that floor. She remembered two other doors in the hallway. One led to her bathroom and the other read, "Employees Only." She assumed it belonged to the staff, or perhaps stored linens or old furniture.

The next stair creaked and Sabrina paused and looked up again. The hallway, so friendly and safe when she came running in from the threatening dark street the night before, now became menacing itself. Scenes from old movies sprang to her mind, scenes where the heroines always walked boldly into haunted houses in the middle of the night, something she groaned over, something she would never do. In those films, otherwise-bright women suddenly came down with a severe case of stupidity. And yet now she walked upstairs in a strange house just to get a sweater.

However, this was different, not some creepy, cobwebby house with candles instead of electric lights, and morning besides. Still, she sensed eyes staring at her and remained standing like a petrified tree.

"I say, is that you, Sabrina?"

Her head snapped upward, and she saw Hugh Pendleton leaning over the railing. With a rush of air into her lungs, her fear evaporated.

"Hugh. You frightened me half to death."

"Frightened you? I say, I'm dreadfully sorry. When I inquired for you, the girl downstairs sent me here. I'd about given up when I heard someone on the stairs.

Afraid I'd missed you."

"You very nearly did." Sabrina came up the remaining steps and stood in the narrow hallway facing Hugh. He seemed taller, no doubt due to her wearing walking shoes, and even handsomer than she remembered. An open-necked short-sleeved shirt the color of his hair revealed tanned muscular forearms lightly dusted with blond hairs. Brown slacks fit snugly over his trim hips.

Sabrina remembered their parting the day before. "I seem to recall our making plans to see one another tonight."

"I couldn't wait."

Glad he'd persisted, considering the spooky feelings attacking her, she relaxed.

A broad smile lit his face. "Attractive women don't make a habit of dropping into my life. I might be a feeble old relic before this opportunity occurs again. Teaching is rather limiting in that respect."

"To say nothing of browsing among old papers."

"Exactly."

Sabrina's earlier fears turned into something very different, a desire to spend time with him, get to know him very well.

As if sensing she had capitulated, he added, "At the very least you might let me give you a tour of the city."

"I planned to do that myself. As a matter of fact, if I hadn't come back upstairs to get a sweater, I'd have been on my way." She fit her key into the lock. "I'll just be a moment. Have you had breakfast yet?" She called the last over her shoulder and went through the sitting room and into the bedroom to fetch the sweater.

Hugh came as far as the sitting room and looked around it. "Yes. I'm an early riser. You've had yours?"

"Just now. Frankly, I don't like to go sightseeing all alone. Although, this being England, I can at least ask directions if I get lost." Draping the sweater over her shoulders, she came out of the bedroom.

Hugh leaned against the door jamb and watched her, as if appraising her looks. "Then you don't believe we're two peoples separated by a common language?"

She grinned. "You forget I once lived here for three months."

"That doesn't count. It was a long time ago, and you've acquired an American accent."

"I find some old expressions creeping back into my mind. And perhaps I'll adopt an English accent while I'm here."

"Don't bother on my account. I find yours utterly charming."

Sabrina felt warmth steal onto her cheeks. They would spend the morning together, viewing London. She couldn't think of anything she'd rather do. The memory of her fright on the stairs returned, but she'd been foolish to worry. That was only Hugh waiting and watching above. But what about last night? Did someone follow her then? If so, who?

"Hugh?" She moved past him into the hallway again and paused while he pulled the door shut and locked it with her key. "Did you come here last night?"

"No, of course not. Why do you ask?" He moved ahead of her to the stairway and, descending slowly, glanced at her again, his expression one of concern.

Sabrina started down the steps, hoping he wouldn't realize how frightened she'd been. "I only wondered."

"We're not far from St. Paul's Cathedral. Would you like to go there first? It was designed by Sir Christopher Wren and is quite famous."

"I know." Sabrina turned her face to Hugh. "I'd love to go there."

They followed St. Paul's Cathedral with visits to Westminster Abbey, the houses of Parliament, Big Ben, and, after lunch at a charming cafe, Trafalgar Square.

Using Sabrina's small digital camera, as well as his own, Hugh snapped pictures of her feeding the pigeons, and she giggled over one in which he caught a pigeon in flight just in front of her face.

They ambled through the National Gallery, Sabrina lingering over Van Gogh's painting of sunflowers, and after a stop in a tea room for scones and jam, he suggested a boat trip up the Thames.

"Sorry. I've done enough for one day."

"Do you mean you'll let me escort you tomorrow as well?"

"Can you take the time off?"

"Of course. It's summer, and I'm not teaching now."

"I'd love it then, but I've walked my feet off today. And there's still this evening."

"I promise not to make you walk anywhere for dinner." His remarkably blue eyes seemed to penetrate hers.

"I'll hold you to that."

With a broad smile, he escorted her across the street. A large red double-decker bus slid to a stop in front of them, and he ushered her upstairs where they sat in the front seat.

"This is delightful." She remembered their conversation the day before. "Did you find the papers you'd been looking for yesterday?"

"Yes, your solicitor, Elmore Manville, showed me the boxes of ancient records stored on the third floor."

"I guess I've always known part of that floor is used for storage in addition to the play room."

"Manville is your cousin?"

"Yes. My Uncle Philip's son."

"Then his name should be Gilmore, should it not?"

"He used it for awhile, then changed it. You see, he isn't Philip's real son, but his wife's by a previous marriage. Uncle Philip adopted him, but after he went to school he took his former name back again, didn't care to be known as Elmore Gilmore. I can't think why, perhaps a British idiosyncracy."

Hugh laughed at her joke. Then he took her hand in his, the long slender fingers stroking her palm and sliding up to her wrist where the pulse beat strongly. "Technically, then, he's not related to you." His voice became soft.

"You seem excessively interested in relationships. Why is that?" His touch made her quiver, as if an electric current passed between them. She felt caught in one of those rare moments when two people share an instant chemistry, with both aware of knowing the others' feelings.

"Merely trying to eliminate the competition." His eyes sent messages to her as plainly as those he'd spoken.

"Elmore is hardly competition." She paused, wondering if she'd been too direct with Hugh, sounded too eager to let something happen between them. Yet why else would he look at her that way, and why let his hand caress her arm? As much as she enjoyed his touch, she needed to back away from such thoughts.

"When we were children, I'm afraid I never liked Elmore."

"However, he seems to have become very successful. What dreadful things did he do, steal your sweets or pull off butterfly wings?"

"How did you know?" Hugh hadn't been serious, Sabrina decided, but she was. "Worse than that. He wouldn't share anything. I was an only child, but I knew how to share."

"Did his being adopted, having lost his real father, have anything to do with his behavior, do you suppose?"

"Perhaps." She paused and looked away. "You make me feel guilty. I should have thought of that myself."

He shrugged. "One can generally find an explanation for every action."

"You may be right, but I never forgave him for tormenting the animals."

"He was a child then. Don't most boys play pranks? He's grown into a successful solicitor and might be embarrassed to find you still remember the past so vividly."

"Perhaps I do because the summer I spent here became very special for me. We owned a comfortable home in Chicago, but that summer I came into a world I'd seen only in motion pictures. Gilmore Manor, you must admit, is grand by most standards: twenty-two rooms, greenhouse, stables, on I've forgotten how many acres of land."

"It is nice, isn't it?"

This time Sabrina laughed. The English understatement. A comfortable silence settled between them, and she wondered where he lived. An estate like Gilmore Manor, *un*mortgaged?

"Where do you live, by the way?" She tilted her head to the side so she could look at him.

"I have a flat here in London, and the family owns a country house in Durham. My older brother lives there."

"The oldest inherits the land, is that it? Sounds positively feudal."

"Actually, we worked it out between us. The old house is charming but too far away from London for my taste. He's married as well, and has children, so he needs the space. I did teach at the university there for a short time, and took the opportunity to look at some of the marvelous illuminated manuscripts dating back to the fourth century. However, I prefer living in town these days." He paused. "Would you like to see my flat?"

Sabrina laughed. "In the U.S., a man would suggest the lady look at his etchings."

"Then they've stolen the saying from the British. At any rate, I prefer not to use trite and perhaps unnecessary excuses."

"Do you mean you assume I'm aware of your designs on me?"

"I thought I'd established that at the outset. Of course I have designs. I had the moment I laid eyes on you."

Sabrina remembered his arms around her while they danced in the nursery, and afterward. For the moment, she settled for letting his hand capture hers, while she looked out at the London traffic.

"Do you always spend your summers seeing London? How very boring for you, having lived here all your life."

"Natives seldom appreciate their own surroundings, but a visitor who wants to 'do the city' forces us to look at them again with fresh eyes. I've enjoyed today."

"Suppose I hadn't turned up this year. What would you be doing?"

"I'd visit my brother in Durham, perhaps. Afterward I might go abroad for part of the time. I like Paris and the French countryside." He paused. "I've been to the U.S. too, you know. Not Chicago, but Miami, New York and a few other cities. I liked San Francisco, which seems very cosmopolitan."

"I must say I agree with you. I liked it much better than any other city I visited in California."

"This summer," he continued, "I suppose I'd have spent a great deal of time poring over the manuscripts Richard Gilmore left me."

"Have you looked at those papers already?"

"I've moved some of them to my flat, but the boxes in the attic will have to be shipped by a transport company."

"Does that restrict you?"

"Not at all. Although I'm anxious to delve into the seventeenth century, I'm enjoying reading the more recent papers I've found."

Sabrina expected his remarks to be somewhat over her head, but wanted to be polite. "How recent?"

"Some of them are from the 1940s, World War II documents, in fact."

"Really?" That *was* interesting.

"Yes, written in German as well. I've translated a few of the letters and they're exciting, even mysterious."

"Mysterious? In what way?"

"A letter written by a German says your grandfather came into possession of a very valuable jeweled necklace."

He stopped and Sabrina felt as if someone had put rubber bands around her throat.

He added, "The necklace had been stolen."

Chapter 5

Sabrina's thoughts flew to the jeweled necklace she'd found in her doll, the necklace which now resided at a jeweler's shop being appraised. She tried to remain calm and kept her voice low. "Who had the necklace? The German or my grandfather?"

"That's somewhat unclear at the moment, or else my German's simply not good enough. Yet the language implies your grandfather is involved in either its theft or its recovery."

Recovery. Perhaps Hugh spoke of a different necklace. "My grandfather certainly couldn't be involved in a theft." Nevertheless, Sabrina found that a good excuse to remove her hand from Hugh's. Besides, her nerves had made her palm wet enough to sprout alfalfa seeds.

"Of course not." Yet he sounded more polite than convinced. "However, I'm sure you're aware the Nazis stole considerable amounts of jewelry, art and antiques during their occupation of European countries."

"That makes the Nazis thieves, not my grandfather."

"I believe sometimes Allied forces discovered caches

of stolen property when they advanced during the last
days of the war. And sometimes the items never found
their way back to their proper owners."

Sabrina straightened in her seat. "I'm sure my
grandfather could never do anything illegal."

Hugh reached for her hand again, and put his other
arm across he back of the seat, near her shoulders. "I
hope not, but I wouldn't judge him too harshly, in any
case. And not without more evidence. I've many more
letters to translate. I'm sure I'll clear it up soon."

But Sabrina couldn't look into his eyes, lest he see
the doubts there. She knew her grandfather had served
in Europe during the war, and furthermore, she knew
about a necklace. Could there be two of them?

She supposed it was possible Richard Gilmore
somehow acquired it during the war and forgot about
it, or, due to the deterioration of his health afterward,
neglected to do anything about returning it to its rightful
owners, if he even knew who they were. She simply
refused to think he kept it out of greed. Surely, if he
meant to take advantage of its value, he would have sold
it long ago rather than put a mortgage on Gilmore
Manor.

A strong temptation to tell Hugh everything then
and there seized her. He appeared to like her for herself
and not because he knew anything about her necklace.
Still, it wouldn't hurt to wait a little longer, until he
translated more of the letters. Perhaps he'd solve the
mystery by then. And yet, one more obstacle remained:
did the necklace belong to her, to the bank or someone
else?

Hugh dropped her at her rooms, promising to collect her again at seven. She sensed that, if she encouraged him, he would put his arms around her and kiss her right on the front stoop. In a way, she wanted that to happen. He held her close when they danced the day before, but what would his lips feel like against her own? Smooth, warm, fresh with a minty flavor, perhaps, from the peppermints they shared after the tea and scones. Soon, she promised herself, she would know for certain. He would probably kiss her that very evening. She shivered in anticipation.

She waited in the hallway, watching Hugh's retreating back through the glass, reminding her of old Cary Grant movies. The actor also walked with a slow, smooth lope. When Hugh disappeared from sight, she stepped outdoors again and hurried two blocks in the opposite direction to the jewelers' shop in Bayswater Street, feeling romantic, guilty and confused all at once.

Mr. Kendall spoke the moment she came through the door. "You've come about your necklace."

"Have you finished appraising it?"

The jeweler paused before speaking, rubbed one hand across his chin and looked out of the windows. "The stones alone," he finally said, each word coming in a slow and deliberate manner, "might not be genuine, the entire necklace not worth more than two hundred pounds."

Sabrina felt her throat tighten. After Hugh's comments, she visualized, hoped, to be truthful, the necklace would turn out to be valuable. She felt as if she'd been deceived.

"The setting," Kendall went on, "Makes one expect it to be an antique, but, by today's standards, of course, it's simply old-fashioned. Although I've seen similar settings in the past, I'd need some other opinions to give you a complete appraisal."

Sabrina sat down. So it wasn't valuable after all, perhaps not even worth two hundred pounds. No doubt about it now: Obviously it was not the same necklace Hugh spoke of.

"May I have it, please? I don't believe it's necessary for you to go to any further trouble."

"No trouble at all. I won't charge you for the extra time," he added. "You see—"

Sabrina interrupted. "No, I'd really rather you didn't."

"I can't return it just now. You see, it's not on the premises."

Sabrina lapsed for a moment into silent surprise. "Not on the premises? But I don't understand. You appraised the stones here, didn't you?"

"In a manner of speaking." Kendall seemed at least as upset as Sabrina herself. His face turned red and he looked everywhere in the shop except into her eyes. "I'm terribly sorry. You'll just have to forgive me and be patient. I promise I'll have the necklace for you tomorrow."

"Do you mean the necklace isn't in the shop?" The same uneasiness returned in full force. It was beginning to get monotonous. "You can't return it to me now?"

"Regrettably, Miss Gilmore. But I do promise—" Beads of sweat formed on the man's upper lip, and

Sabrina couldn't help feeling sorry for him. Still, what should she think?

She glanced at her watch and saw she had an hour left before dinner with Hugh. "If I wait, can you get the necklace from wherever it is and return it?"

"I'm afraid not, but I will have it tomorrow."

"Then where is it now? If you know you can give it to me tomorrow, you must know where it is right now."

Mr. Kendall dropped his eyes and wiped his face with one hand. "I'm sorry. It's closing time now, so you'll have to go, but tomorrow afternoon I shall have the necklace for you."

She debated with herself about whether she should threaten to call the police, but saw no reason to believe doing so would help. If Kendall didn't have the necklace on the premises, she couldn't have it. In spite of the circumstances, she remained convinced of his honesty. Besides, apparently the necklace was no more than costume jewelry, as she originally suspected.

She said "good day" and left the shop, and, all the way back to her rooms she pondered the strange turn of events. Yet, nothing had been normal since her arrival in London. She thought she saw the same integrity in Hugh Pendleton, but honesty forced her to admit she could be wrong. She had only his word he found some papers which implicated her grandfather in a theft. She didn't really know him, nor were they related. What if he had a secret agenda of his own? At any rate, there seemed nothing to do at the moment but wait and see.

She returned to the inn and climbed the stairs. In

spite of the long shadows cast on the walls, she felt no fear that time. And yet, suddenly, when she'd reached her own landing and stood in front of her door, it returned.

Pulling the key from her bag, she inserted it into the lock of her bed-sitting room. Before she could turn it, the door swung open of its own accord.

Panic grabbed her, clutching at her insides, taking away her breath. The darkening room yawned like an abyss, but she forced herself to reach in and find the wall switch. Bathed in weak light from two low-watt bulbs in the overhead fixture, the sitting room stared back at her, its former tidiness only a memory. If a tornado had gone through the room, it could not have created much more of a mess.

Pictures were tilted on the walls, books and knick-knacks lay in toppled heaps, the cushions from the loveseat lay scattered on the floor. Through the connecting door, she saw utter chaos in the bedroom: clothing everywhere, drawers gaping open, spilling their contents. Her suitcase, which she'd stored in the closet, stood open on a chair. The bedcovers lay in a heap beside the window, and the mattress hung partly off the bedsprings.

Her body bathed in perspiration, she grabbed the doorjamb to keep from slumping to the floor.

Chapter 6

Sabrina wanted to run downstairs and tell someone, anyone. She wanted to demand to know who had done it, to force someone to put it to rights. The impulse passed. She knew perfectly well who'd done it: a person who wanted the necklace, a person who knew its value. Despite what Mr. Kendall had said, she suspected from the first that someone other than a child had hidden it in the doll. That someone now wanted it back. But who?

Since her arrival, no one but Hugh Pendleton had made any effort to get close to her. She first thought of her step-cousin, Elmore Manville, the executor of the estate, but so far they'd held no more than normal, polite conversations.

In addition to Richard Gilmore, the family consisted of his two sons, Uncle Philip and her father David, two daughters, Mary and Charlotte, now widows, and Philip's wife Frances. Next came the cousins: Elmore and his half-brother and sister, Edward and Penelope, Charlotte's son Zachary and the children of Mary. If she remembered correctly, they were Franco, Jr., Deborah and Hildegard Poldoro, all of whom lived in Italy.

However, names had never been her strong point. She often joked, "I never remember a name, but I always forget a face."

All but the Italian cousins attended the meeting at Gilmore Manor the day before, but not one of them showed the slightest interest in her beyond the expected friendliness on seeing an almost-forgotten American cousin. They inquired about her flight and insisted they must all get together again. However, having apparently considered their duty fulfilled, made no further effort to contact her.

Well, Zachary suggested they go night-clubbing, but she suspected that was more predatory than anything else. She'd met men like him before, always assuming their steroid bodies made them irresistible to women. If he'd been an actor, he'd spend the greater part of a film with an AK-47, eliminating the rest of the cast.

To be fair, she hadn't spent much time in the Manor or at her bed-and-breakfast to receive anyone's calls, nor did she plan to leave town soon, so all of that might change. Nevertheless, having met them, even briefly, the day before, she couldn't imagine any of them either hiding the necklace or turning her room upside down to find it again. And yet, appearances could be deceiving. Con men, and women too, were *supposed* to be charming, weren't they, while they caught you off guard and robbed you of all your worldly goods?

She sighed and began to put the room to rights, while sifting through her mind for anyone else she'd met since her arrival in London. She could eliminate her landlady, Mrs. Carruthers, since she knew nothing about the Gilmore family. To her, Sabrina was just another paying guest.

And Mr. Kendall. Ah, now there was a possible suspect. He knew the value of the necklace, and when she tried to retrieve it, he gave her no real excuse for not having it available. That bubble burst at once. For the very reason he hadn't returned it, she couldn't suspect him of searching her room to steal it. Leaving only her British cousins and Hugh.

Minutes later, one of the suspects turned up in person, standing in her doorway. She'd forgotten she'd left the hall door open when she entered.

Hugh, hands in trouser pockets, said, "I believe you've a worse mess in here than in the sitting room, and that looks as if a bomb went off."

"You noticed." Seeing him made her face hot and tingly, and turned her voice cold. "Tell me, when did you do it? Did you come back after you dropped me off and take advantage of my absence, or did you have someone do it for you while you dragged me through all the tourist traps?"

"Dragged you through... ? Just what are you talking about?" His turn to be annoyed, it showed in the frown creasing his forehead and the sparks shooting from his eyes. "Took advantage of your absence? I don't know what you mean."

"I mean you're responsible for this." She picked up yet another piece of her filmy lingerie from the floor, stuffed it into a drawer and slammed it shut.

"I'm responsible?" He leaned toward her, glowering.

"You don't think I enjoy living in such chaos, do

you?"

"Of course not, but how does that make me responsible?"

"I've just told you. You searched my rooms." She closed the suitcase and, grabbing the handle, threw it back into the closet.

She stooped to pick up a blouse and when she straightened, Hugh stood next to her, glaring down. "Stop that for a moment, Sabrina, and tell me what this is all about. Who did this?"

"That's what I want to know, or haven't you been listening?"

"I've been listening, but you're not making sense. I gather you suspect me of trashing your room. Well, I didn't. Why don't you explain what happened?"

He grasped the handles on the mattress and shifted it back into place on the bedsprings. Then, putting his hands on her shoulders, he pushed her down so they both sat on the side of her bed.

Sabrina couldn't discuss the situation so calmly. She jumped up, but he pulled her down again.

"Sit still and talk to me."

Her distrust of him evaporated quickly. How could she suspect him when he seemed so surprised by it all? Perhaps she should get everything out in the open.

"After you dropped me off, I went out again for a short time." No need to tell him why just yet. "When I returned about an hour later, I found this."

"Someone's been searching your rooms, is that it?"

She did a Henry Higgins imitation. "By George, I think you've got it."

"Forgive me. My penchant for detail. Now, why would anyone search your rooms?" He answered his own question. "For money, of course. I regret to say London has its share of thieves and pickpockets, and tourists are fair game."

"You think someone came all the way up here to do it? If I were a thief I'd pick a lower floor."

"Perhaps they did. Have you enquired? Have you called the police?"

Sabrina answered in a low tone. "No."

"Why not? What's missing?"

Her voice dropped to a mere whisper. "Nothing."

Hugh released some of the pressure he'd been using to hold her down, and instead held one of her hands in his. "Just what is it you're not telling me, Sabrina?"

She didn't answer, couldn't. She still viewed him with suspicion. He'd been with her when she found the doll. What if he knew what it contained? After all, someone knew about the necklace, and until she became certain Hugh was not that person, she'd probably better keep her own counsel.

He shrugged. "Well, if nothing's missing, I suppose it means the thieves couldn't find anything they wanted. I suppose your cash is all in travelers checks which you carried with you."

"Yes, that's true." In fact, as he talked, she began to feel she might have overreacted. Thieves could very well have caused the mess, although she thought it a colossal coincidence thieves would choose the rooms of someone who just found a valuable necklace. Yet, stranger things had happened, she supposed.

"Did you leave any jewelry lying about?"

At the word "jewelry" Sabrina's heart pounded like a piston, but again she answered "No." She found that a good excuse to remove her hand from Hugh's. Besides, her nerves made her palm moist again.

"So, it's not so awful, is it?" He rose from the bed and helped put the bed covers and pillows back in place. "Nothing damaged?"

"No. Things seem to be all right, just rearranged." Her natural sense of humor returned and she even let a smile lift the corners of her lips.

"Well, then, if you're not going to call in the Bobbies, let's straighten this place and go to dinner. I'm famished, and so must you be, after all this exercise."

"All right." Feeling somewhat ambivalent, having accepted Hugh's claim of innocence and his logical explanation, she put him to work straightening out the sitting room while she changed clothes in the bedroom. He was right, fretting would accomplish nothing, and she was hungry enough to eat the wallpaper. She slipped into a moss-green summer dress and matching jacket.

Hugh preceded her down the stairs toward the street a few minutes later. "Why is it you look so beautiful in everything you wear?"

Sabrina liked nice clothes, but never thought of herself as beautiful. "You're not doing justice to English girls. They have beautiful complexions, and are all so marvelously cool and elegant."

"Cool is the right word." He opened the ground floor door for her. "Even when you're wearing a cool color, you look warm and, well, vibrant." He laughed at himself. "Dear God, I sound like a blasted commercial."

She didn't reply because they'd reached a gleaming black Jaguar parked at the curb and he stopped next to it.

"Your car?" she asked, not moving.

"Yes. One of my few indulgences." He opened the car door.

Sabrina adjusted her perception of Hugh. At first, she thought him a penniless professor, whose brother got the family mansion, him merely a small flat in London. And the sightseeing that day, all done by buses or on foot, hadn't changed her opinion. Until now.

Well, he must be in his thirties, she surmised, stooping and slipping into the leather seat, so he'd probably saved rather a long time for it. She'd have preferred, one of her fantasies, actually, to meet a wealthy Englishman. However, rich men in any country were relatively scarce, and she preferred this one, whose blue eyes and charm made her knees go soft, to someone with nothing going for him but a lot of money.

Unless, of course, this one turned out to want to steal the necklace.

"I don't drive it in town much. It's rather a bother." Hugh started the car and steered it through the city traffic. "Most of the time I use it to drive to Durham for occasional weekends with my brother."

"Have you any other family?" Sabrina relaxed and concentrated on finding out as much as possible about her escort.

"No, and I've never been married."

"Why did you say that?" Sabrina assumed he read

her thoughts, but pretended otherwise. She needed to know a great many other things, as well.

"Have you?"

"What?"

"Been married?"

"No, I was engaged once, but...."

"But what?"

Sabrina didn't want to go into details and have him feel sorry for her. "It just didn't work out. Since then, I've been too busy running my business."

"I find it hard to believe you've avoided it. Men must ring you day and night, or camp on your doorstep."

Sabrina found herself responding to his charm again, decided it wouldn't hurt to flirt a little. "I appreciate your compliments, but many men are intimidated by a business woman. Until they're in their thirties, they're insecure around someone with ambition. And by then, they're already married."

"All of them?"

"Or divorced. Not that I have anything against divorced men, unless they're still carrying torches, or carrying grudges, or carrying hand grenades."

He grinned at her remark. "You make me think there aren't any eligible men at all."

She laughed. "I'm sure they're out there. I really haven't looked. No time." She turned toward him. "What about you? You're not married, either. What's your excuse?"

"Oh, I have tradition on my side, you know. Englishmen tend to marry late. We have so much precedent to live up to: Edward the Eighth, Prince Charles, James Bond." He laughed. "Well, here we are, 'Rule's'."

"Rules? You've taken me to a schoolhouse?"

Hugh turned off the ignition and handed the car keys to an attendant. "It's the oldest restaurant in London, and if we're very nice, the *maitre d'* may let us look upstairs."

"To see the ghosts of customers past?"

"Almost. You see, Edward the Seventh, while still Prince of Wales, used to bring the actress, Lily Langtry, here. They required a private table, even a private entrance so they wouldn't be seen."

"Color me impressed." She let him help her out of the car, and they walked the narrow pathway to the old building. Although showing its age, it was well maintained, and the dining room provided an elegant, yet warm, atmosphere. Drawings, paintings and cartoons depicting the colorful people who had come to dine, as well as the events of all the years, covered the walls. And, as if that weren't enough, she adored the food.

When the waiter brought coffee, Sabrina thanked Hugh for bringing her. "I'd never heard of Rules, but I was told once to be sure to go to the Post Office Tower."

"To patronize the revolving restaurant on top?"

"On the top of the post office?" she repeated. "I know of a restaurant on top of the John Hancock Building in Chicago and I've even been to the Top of the Mark in San Francisco, but the top of the *post office*?"

"Quite nice, actually. Splendid view. Unfortunately, at the time, the IRA threatened to blow up the tower."

"Really?" Sabrina decided he was joking with her. "Isn't that a rather extreme reaction to bad food?"

Hugh laughed, but turned serious again. "As the center for telephone as well as postal service, they couldn't afford to let anything happen to it, so they closed the restaurant and the observation deck."

The serious turn of the conversation reminded Sabrina of the mystery of the necklace, and she changed the subject to something more pleasant. "What do you recommend for dessert?"

He paused, while his eyes scanned her face. His voice came across the table, so softly she could barely distinguish the words. "I hesitate to say. My mind is misbehaving, I'm afraid, imagining the sweetest dessert would be kissing your lips and your eyes, the tip of your nose."

Sabrina didn't answer but ran her tongue across her lips, which had become dry. Her pulse beat a tattoo in her throat.

He grinned. "The trifle is good, or the strawberry tart with Devonshire cream."

She found her voice at last. "I've heard about Devonshire cream. I understand it's so thick it stands up without having to whip it. And, I'm sure, has a calorie count as high as the Himalayas. I must watch my figure."

"I'll watch it for you tonight, and you can enjoy yourself."

"You're teasing me." She wondered if the feeling building within her was hunger for the dessert or desire for him. She ordered the tart and changed the subject.

They drank coffee and talked until the waiter cast annoying looks in their direction.

They returned to her rooms at a very late hour. Desire or not, she couldn't let Hugh come up. She still considered him a suspect in her own mystery. She remembered the sign on the door stating it would be closed and locked after midnight.

As they walked from his car toward the building, she said, "I forgot all about it. I should have told Mrs. Carruthers I'd be late. Now I'll have to ring the bell and wake her."

Before he could stop her, she pressed the bell and they heard it clang somewhere within.

Hugh waited with her, not speaking, until Mrs. Carruthers appeared, hair in curlers, wearing a blue chenille robe. The woman held open the door, letting Sabrina step across the threshold, but frowned when Hugh attempted to do the same.

She looked at Sabrina instead of him. "You could have unlocked it with your room key, you know."

"Really?" Sabrina's voice sounded as innocent as she could make it. "I'm terribly sorry."

"All right, dearie." Mrs. Carruthers turned and started down the hallway.

Hugh dug his hands into his pockets and stayed on the sidewalk. "I'll say goodnight then, but I'll see you tomorrow."

"Yes, all right." Sabrina smiled and started up the stairs, leaving him at the open door.

***

Hugh closed the door of the bed and breakfast inn and listened to the latch spring into place. So she wanted to get rid of him. Did she fear he'd attempt to seduce her? Surely he hadn't given that impression. Attraction, yes. Desire, yes. But tasteless adolescent groping? Never. Still, something about him still bothered her. Such as the nonsense about suspecting he ransacked her rooms. But perhaps she was just upset and lashed out at the first person to come by. She didn't seriously believe that. Yet, had he inadvertently given her any reasons to be suspicious of him? He hoped not. That would upset his plans.

Chapter 7

Sabrina thought she must have worn a path to the jeweler's shop, having made a third visit in as many days. A fiftyish woman with a hairdo plastered in place with lacquer sat at the counter while a clerk showed her diamond cocktail rings. In less than a minute Mr. Kendall came from the back room, and, seeing her, smiled. Some of Sabrina's tension melted. He must have good news for her this time.

"Ah, Miss Gilmore, here is your necklace, just as I promised." He lifted a square of velvet cloth from a cabinet and unfolded it. The necklace lay there, more beautiful than before, polished and shiny.

"I believe I may say with confidence that this is worth about two-hundred-and-fifty thousand pounds."

Sabrina gasped. "Yesterday you seemed sure it was a fake."

"I'm happy to report better news. May I have the receipt?"

Sabrina surrendered the paper and watched while the jeweler entered his fee for the appraisal and returned it to her. She paid what she considered a fair sum, then leaned forward and looked into Kendall's eyes, her voice only a shade above a whisper. "Have you told anyone else about the value of the necklace?"

He walked to the end of the counter, as far from the other customer as possible, Sabrina following, and spoke in an equally soft tone. "No one."

"Your other clerk?" she persisted.

"My only clerk is trustworthy and discreet. His references are impeccable." He glanced toward the other man in the showroom.

Again she whispered her words. "This is your only clerk?"

"Yes."

Her unease returned. "But, when I brought the necklace here three days ago, I saw someone else, a younger man, dark-haired."

Kendall's face took on a pink color, as if caught in a lie. "I beg your pardon," he said at last. "I did have another clerk, but I had to dismiss him. I assure you, he knows nothing about the value of your necklace. I never discussed it with him. I dismissed him for... er, unrelated reasons."

Sabrina had to admit Mr. Kendall appeared as honest and trustworthy as ever. She felt compelled to believe him. Besides, he had returned the necklace to her.

She brought forth her doll—which she found that morning right where she'd left her in the sitting room bookcase—and began to put the necklace into her back. But Mr. Kendall took it from her hands, wrapped it in a square of velvet, and returned it to its former hiding place in Amy's body. And never cracked a smile.

Sabrina retraced her steps to her rooms, clutching Amy tighter than before, feeling as if she carried a million dollars in her arms. She came very close to losing the doll already, remembering how someone had searched her room. As it happened, even the doll had been elsewhere at the time. She left it behind some books on a low shelf in the downstairs sitting room the night before and—after returning from dinner with Hugh—once more she put on jeans and forgot all about it until morning. She wondered what would have happened if the doll had been upstairs. Would it have been taken, and her belongings not thrown about?

Although glad to arrive safely at her rooms, she realized her problem lingered unsolved. Hugh would pick her up any moment, take her for a drive through the Cotswold area and then up to Stratford-on-Avon. Afterward, she wouldn't have time to take the necklace to the bank before it closed for the day. Yet, she couldn't leave it in her rooms in case the thief returned. She had only one choice: she must wear the thing.

As she'd already discovered, London weather varied considerably from Chicago's in the summer. Some days could be very warm, but others were foggy and cool, that day being one of the latter. Slipping out of the dress she'd chosen that morning, she once more removed the necklace from the doll's back and held it against her throat and chest. The diamonds seemed to glare at her as if resenting having to lie against a lace bra instead of a ball gown. Nevertheless she fastened the clasp in back. Tearing her gaze from the glistening stones, she pulled a sweater from a drawer and drew it over her head.

That would never do. The necklace showed, no doubt of it. The clingy knit outlined the shape of the stones. She pulled off the sweater and this time put on a blue print jersey top from the closet. Much better. A large red scarf would do the final bit of concealment, she decided, and she folded it into a triangle and tied it behind her neck, letting the fullness cover the upper part of the blouse.

When Hugh arrived, he commented on her choice. "This is summer, Sabrina. You mustn't believe people who say England is cold and damp."

"Oh, but I like cool weather. I mean, I'm glad it's not hot or anything." She stopped again, wondering if she'd given herself away. She hoped the necklace remained hidden. Feeling as if she wore Hester's bright red "A" instead of a designer scarf, she murmured, "Let's go, shall we?" She almost dragged Hugh from the room and down the steps to his car.

As the Jaguar wove its way through London traffic, Sabrina made what she hoped were discreet references to Hugh's translations of Richard Gilmore's papers. She ached to know if he'd discovered anything new in them, anything pertaining to the stolen necklace of course. He said he hadn't had time. She resigned herself to playing the role of tourist all day, a subject not difficult for her since she loved sightseeing, and they spent the remainder of the morning at it.

After lunch of tender chicken sandwiches and cold drinks at a pub in Stratford, they visited Shakespeare's home. Relying on Hugh's familiarity with the area, she gave herself up to enjoying the sights and sounds and smells of England. The moors were just beginning to turn purple with heather, and great fields of yellow mustard made bright splashes of color against the grey skies. They observed herds of sheep and cows and once passed a row of British soldiers who, judging by the sound of shooting in the distance, and the signs which prohibited their entrance into certain areas, were headed for target practice.

Dinnertime found them back in London, and Hugh stopped at an inn whose excellent food included mutton, Yorkshire pudding, braised celery, and blueberry tart. Sabrina enjoyed everything, especially the mutton, which tasted like the youngest, tenderest lamb, and called the tart a pie, in spite of Hugh's laughter at her American term.

"Actually, we ought to skip dessert. We won't have time."

"Time for what?" She smiled, anticipating something interesting.

"I have tickets to a play. We'll just make it if we hurry."

He took her to Agatha Christie's *The Mousetrap*, a classic which had been performed in London for more than forty years. Sabrina loved mysteries and had read most of Agatha Christie's novels, so she found it a special treat. Yet, the coincidence was not lost on her. A mystery of her own dominated her life at the present time.

After coffee at a shop in Soho, they returned to Devonshire Terrace. This time Sabrina unlocked the front door with her key, and Hugh insisted on going upstairs with Sabrina "to be sure you're safe."

That part suited her just fine. Since she wore a very valuable necklace under her blouse, she liked having him escort her to her room. However, once there, he sat down on the loveseat in her sitting room and drew her down to sit next to him.

Under other circumstances she would have enjoyed being alone with him, close, her head on his shoulder perhaps, his kisses on her lips. But not just then, with the necklace hidden under her blouse. What could she say to make him leave? Her mind went blank. His arm went across her shoulders and he pulled her toward him. Well, perhaps just a kiss and then he'd go. She lifted her face to him and his lips found hers, his fingers twining through her long curly hair.

Centuries passed. His mouth felt soft at first, then became firm and, soon, demanding. Her lips parted under his and she felt his arms around her back, pressing her to him. One of his hands stole upward, fingers twining through her thick curls. Sweet desire filled her body, and her own arms went around him.

His body pressed inexorably, albeit without haste, toward hers and she leaned back into the corner of the loveseat, the weight of his hard, lean frame coming forward onto her breasts. The delightful sensation blotted everything else from her mind. Her body throbbed. His hand left her back and traveled sensuously upward along her arms, then to her face. His thumb at her chin, he caressed her cheek, his mouth moving over hers, a small moan escaping. Or was that *her* moan?

When his hand rested on her neck, and at the same time his other tangled in the knot in the scarf at her back, she came out of her trance. Good grief, he'd discover the necklace.

She pushed him up with both hands, breaking the kiss.

"Oh, uh, I mean, I think...."

"Sabrina, what's the matter?"

"Nothing." Her voice came out high-pitched and squeaky.

"Well, then." He resumed his position and pressed her to his hard body again, caressing her back. He kissed her cheek, the side of her neck, nudging aside the collar of her blouse.

She brought her hands up between his, forcing them apart.

Once more he backed off for a moment. "Am I rushing you?"

"No. I mean, yes. We haven't known each other very long."

"Only forever." He leaned into her again, his strength more than sufficient to have his way if he wanted. And worst of all, she wanted. She hadn't felt this way about a man in years, never experienced such an overpowering desire to make love to him, to caress every inch of him and let him caress every inch of her. Only, not now.

He kissed her ear, the tips of his fingers along her ribcage, creeping upward toward the curve of her breasts. She pushed his hands down.

What if he were indeed after the necklace? Did he know it lay against her skin just millimeters from his hands? Was that why he wanted to make love to her? Would he take her to bed and then vanish with the spoils? She found it too complicated and wished she'd never found the necklace. Wished she'd never come to London.

No, not that. No matter what happened, she'd always be glad she came. And maybe Hugh knew nothing about the necklace at all. But just for tonight she'd have to assume he mustn't find it on her. They'd have a time and place later to sleep together, wouldn't they?

His fingers returned to her waist, caressing the soft flesh beneath her blouse.

She shoved them aside. "I'm sorry."

He pulled away from her and straightened. Standing, he looked down at her. "I'm sorry, too, Sabrina. I'm afraid I assumed you felt the same way toward me."

"I do," she blurted out. "I mean, I will. But not tonight."

He looked at her as if she made as much sense as the Queen of Hearts in *Alice in Wonderland*. Then he laughed. "Sabrina, if all American women are like you, it must be a very captivating country. It's perhaps as well you kicked the British out."

She stood up at once, so as not to give him an opportunity to put her in a vulnerable position again. "I don't think I'm typical. In fact, I'm sure I'm not. I'm just...." Damn! What could she say? Her mind went blank. "I'm just nervous."

"I understand." He stared down at her for another moment, looking as if he'd lost a cricket match to a bitter rival. "I say, have you considered moving from here? Perhaps if you took a room at a regular hotel, where there's a staff of people available at all hours, you might feel safer."

"What a good idea." She grasped at his suggestion like a drowning swimmer to a lifeboat. "I'll do that."

He took her hand in his and squeezed it with a gentle, yet sensuous, pressure. "Good night, Sabrina. I'll see you tomorrow. Ready by eleven?"

"No, not so early. I have to, er, do an errand." She realized she almost said she planned to take the necklace to the bank.

Hugh only grinned, backed out and closed the door behind him.

Sabrina took a deep breath. She wished she could take him into her confidence. Before he decided some village was minus its idiot.

Chapter 8

The next morning, Sabrina packed her suitcase and travel tote, paid Mrs. Carruthers for her stay and then took a taxi to Gilmore Manor. While she waited for someone to open the door, she looked up at the huge mansion, three stories high, its stone walls covered in many places with ivy. She admired the tall mullioned windows, with their decorative designs above and below, the many chimneys and roof-line crennelations. She wished there were more houses that looked like that in the Chicago suburbs.

Thomas let her in, greeting her with a smile, and then Aunt Frances, as perfectly groomed as if expecting the Queen, met her in the cavernous, echoing hall. "Come into the sitting room. It's cozier than the drawing room and there's a fire laid there already."

Sabrina didn't wonder about lighting a fireplace in the middle of summer. That house was always a bit cold, as if the stones absorbed winter's chill and refused to let it go, lest it take the mortar with it. During that summer of so long ago, she noticed it at night when she preferred to sleep under a down quilt. During the day, she played with her cousins, indoors or out, too busy to notice the weather.

"May I offer you some coffee or tea?" Aunt Frances asked, then added, "I've put out tea already in the sitting room."

"Then tea will be fine."

The sitting room, although smaller than the drawing room across the hall, nevertheless held two sofas, three overstuffed armchairs, a desk, and a walnut cabinet on one wall which also housed a large-screen television set, now dark. She sat on one of the sofas, and Frances joined her and poured tea from the silver service on the coffee table in front of them.

"Milk and sugar?" Frances asked.

"Yes, please. I've never got over the habit of drinking tea. It's a nuisance sometimes, though."

"How is that? Do you mean because everyone in the States prefers coffee?"

"Partly. They don't make it the same. And sometimes you can't get tea at all. Where offices and banquet rooms used to provide coffee or hot water for tea, now they provide two kinds of coffee: regular or decaf."

"Pity."

"Is anyone at home today?" Sabrina asked, "or are they all working at their jobs?"

"Everyone's here but Elmore. He's so conscientious, always working, it seems."

"You must be very proud of him."

"We are. Although we do wish he'd marry. He's thirty-four years old. High time."

Sabrina remembered her conversation with Hugh on

that very subject. "I have it on good authority that British men like to marry late." She sipped her tea.

"That's true. But Philip and I were married by the time he was forty, in spite of having delayed marriage because of his having served in Korea."

"But you'd been married before. My father told me," she added.

"Yes, one of those youthful mistakes that didn't work out. Philip adopted Elmore after we were married, and then we had two more children of our own. Of course you remember Edward and Penelope?"

"Although they were older than I was, I remember playing with them as well as Aunt Mary's girls, Deborah and Hildegard."

"They were all here that summer you visited, but they didn't come this time. Jobs and families, you know."

"Of course."

"Edward has come because he's between jobs at the moment, and Penelope will be leaving tomorrow to go home. She's married, naturally."

"Of course." Sabrina realized she'd said that twice, but this time, Aunt Frances's saying "naturally" annoyed her. As if society accepted the idea of men postponing marriage, but women should do so while they were young. She, as the entire family no doubt knew, was nano-seconds from thirty and still unmarried.

While she struggled to find a different topic of conversation, Aunt Charlotte entered.

"Ah, Sabrina, how nice to see you again, my dear. We shall have to have you for dinner one day while you're still in town."

"I was about to ask her that very thing." Frances turned to Sabrina. "You will come, won't you? Tomorrow, perhaps. I shall ask cook to make something special."

"That would be fine." Sabrina looked first at Frances and then at Charlotte, who had taken a seat on the other sofa, where she made a big deal out of straightening the little matching covers over the arms. It didn't take a rocket scientist to realize that the women held a mild dislike toward one another. Perhaps Charlotte, a recent arrival according to Zach, tried to act as if she belonged there, and Frances, after so many years of being the sole manager of the household, resented the interloper.

The door opened and Edward came in. He wore white trousers and a tennis sweater and, although still in his twenties, his blond hair seemed to be thinning already. He hesitated and then acknowledged Sabrina. "Oh, hello there. Nice to see you again."

"Do keep Sabrina company, dear," Aunt Charlotte said. "I've some things to do."

She stood and headed for the door, and then Frances, perhaps fearing that Charlotte's "things to do" might encroach upon her own duties, followed her out.

"Well." Edward helped himself to some tea and one of the scones from a platter. "How are you? Everything fine at home? I hear you have a business."

"Yes, I own some copy shops."

He looked surprised, as if he thought she'd been going to say she sold cosmetics door to door. She smiled, hoping to put him at ease. "I joke sometimes that I put in an application at Gucci and while I was waiting to hear from them, I got restless and started my own company."

He managed a grin at that. "That's the way to go." He seemed to recover some of his nonchalance. "Jolly good to own your own business."

Sabrina preferred to take the spotlight off herself. "Your mother says you're between jobs at the moment."

"Yes, but I have an interview Monday next and that ought to be the end of that. I have tons of experience."

"And that would be in...."

"Insurance. Actuarial tables, things like that. Quite complicated, in fact." He paused. "Of course, I'd love to have my own business as well, but it takes capital, you know, to start up. How fortunate your father could help you with that."

"Yes." Sabrina kept to herself the fact that most of the money that she used to buy her first shop came in the form of a loan from a bank, as well as her own savings. She began to sense that her English relatives had been unused to working or otherwise taking charge of their own lives, as if someone had slipped them all some bad affirmations. Then, when Richard, the head of the family, became unable or unwilling to manage their money, everyone suffered. Once more she felt sorry for them.

She especially hated the fact that this lovely house would soon be taken over by outsiders, who might turn it into a home for aging pensioners. A hundred years ago, it might have been a home for unwed mothers, but nowadays unwed mothers no longer hid from society.

She'd even heard of a society called "Single Mothers by Choice," whose members sired their babies via sperm banks found on the Internet. In future, psychiatrists would be kept busy teaching them how to cope.

"Do you plan to stay long?" Edward asked.

"I'm taking a two-week vacation."

"Then we have a chance to see more of you."

"Your mother invited me for dinner tomorrow night. I'm looking forward to that."

"Capital." He paused. "I say, you'll have to excuse me. I'm just off to play tennis with a chum." He put down his teacup and rose from his chair.

Sabrina got up too. "No problem. I really came to find out if I could move some things."

"Some things?"

"Yes, the blue trunk in the attic that I inherited. I'm moving from my bed-and-breakfast into a hotel."

"Of course. Just ask Thomas. He does everything around here: butler, handyman, runner of errands, driver of guests. He'll take care of it for you."

"Thanks."

She followed Edward into the hall and made her way in the direction of the kitchen. Sure enough, Thomas sat at a table, chatting with the cook. When she explained what she wanted, he said he'd have it taken care of, if she would just give him the name of the hotel.

That errand over, Sabrina started down the hall again and almost bumped into Zach, who came out of the dining room.

"Oh, wow!" he said. "Just the person I've been wanting to see."

"Really?" She doubted very much that he'd even thought of her since the reading of their grandfather's will.

"Absolutely. Who could forget those lips, those eyes."

"You sound like a bad song lyric."

"Well, why not? Music is what I do."

"Don't tell me you're a singer."

"No. I mean, I do sing, but not alone. These two other chaps sing with me. We have a band. Maybe you heard of it: Barking Dogs. We put out two CDs. Didn't make the charts though."

"Barking Dogs? Why not something more pleasant?"

"You're right, of course. We're thinking of changing it." He paused. "You're very perceptive. We should have had you pick out a name for us. What would you suggest?"

"I've never heard you play, so I'm afraid I couldn't help."

"You could hear us right now. I have a music studio up on the third floor, and I can play one of our CDs for you." Without waiting for an answer, he took her hand and led her toward the grand curving staircase that dominated the end of the hall.

"No thanks." She tried to pull her hand free, but, his strength overpowering hers, he didn't release her. "Please. You're hurting me."

"Sorry." He let go then. "But I'd really like to show it to you. You'd be impressed."

"On the third floor? You mean near the old nurs-ery?"

"Opposite that. Rooms that once housed servants. I had it made into a music studio, soundproofed and everything."

"Maybe some other time." She headed for the door again.

Again he took her hand, but dropped it as soon as she turned toward him. "Look, I didn't mean for us to get off on the wrong foot. I'd really like to get better acquainted. You know, go dancing, the pictures, stuff like that."

Sabrina smiled. She had no interest in him, but she always felt flattered when someone found her attractive. "I don't think that's a good idea. In the first place, I won't be in town very long, and in the second place, since we're cousins, I don't believe—"

"That's an old-fashioned attitude, don't you think? A shame to let it keep us from having some fun."

"Thanks for the compliment, but no thanks. I'll stick with just being your cousin, if you don't mind."

"Well, I do, there's a fact, but... Well, you win some, you lose some."

"I'm glad you have a sense of humor about it."

He followed her toward the door. "Personally, I think you'd change your mind if I had a pot of money. Birds like a bloke with plenty of cash on him."

She turned and tried to keep her face from showing her distaste for his comment. "I told you why I don't want to go out with you. Money has nothing to do with it."

He shrugged and, this time, he didn't follow her. Thomas did. "Miss Sabrina, may I drive you to the hotel? We can put your trunk in the boot and that way you shan't have to take a taxi or wait for the trunk."

Sabrina grinned. "Why, thank you, Thomas. That would be very nice."

"You wait here, Miss, and I'll just bring the car 'round."

In less than ten minutes a black Bentley rounded the corner and stopped in the gravel driveway. Thomas leaped out and opened one of the back doors for her. "Your trunk is already inside, Miss."

She got in, feeling a bit silly to ride in back, but she hadn't expected a limousine. If the last of the Gilmores were penniless, how did they happen to have such an expensive car?

As if answering her thoughts, Thomas turned and spoke to her.

"It's an old car, been in the family for years, but I take good care of it. Don't know what will happen to it now. I just hope they don't go squabbling over it, like some folks do when there's a death and things get parceled out."

"I hope you're right."

She wanted to ask Thomas some questions but thought better of it, and he—apparently feeling he might have said more than a servant should—looked straight ahead and didn't speak again until they arrived at the Cavendish Royal Hotel.

She checked in at the desk and had the jeweled necklace, now in the velvet bag, put into the hotel safe. Thomas arranged for a bellman and porter to see to moving the trunk, and when she arrived in her room, found it waiting for her.

The room was large and bright, with cream-colored walls, pale beige draperies and carpet, and white-and-gold French Provincial furniture. Besides a queen-sized bed, she saw a triple dresser, cabinet topped with a television set, desk and chair, and a *chaise longue* under a good reading lamp.

She unpacked and then knelt down in front of the trunk and opened it. The sight of the old clothes brought a flush to her cheeks and she remembered being with Hugh when she last saw them. She remembered how he'd looked at her when she pulled on the old lace dress and shawl.

Wait just a minute. She'd have to stop those feelings. Sure, he was handsome and they were attracted to each other, but reality told her she had only a two-week vacation planned. Like it or not, she'd go back to Chicago and he'd stay in London, and that would be that.

She sighed and closed the lid, but not before remembering that she had found Amy in the trunk and Amy had spawned a mystery. Who owned the necklace and how had it got inside the doll? More important, who apparently wanted it back now and was rash enough to search her room for it? She liked detective stories in books and TV shows and sometimes even guessed who was the villain early on, Hollywood writers' attempts to fool her notwithstanding.

Stretching out on the chaise, she played detective. Who were the suspects in this case? She hoped it wasn't Hugh, but he couldn't be ruled out yet. His obvious interest in her could be a disguise for his real interest: the necklace. And his telling her about a supposedly stolen necklace could be a ruse to get her to tell him about what she'd found so he could take it away from her.

And yet, she couldn't quite accept that scenario. Sure, it was possible he was the culprit, but was it probable? She'd always thought of herself as a pretty good judge of character. After all, she'd had to hire people to work in her shops, to handle money and care for valuable equipment, not to mention satisfy customers. She could think of only one instance where she'd been fooled and had to fire an untrustworthy employee. No, she decided, if someone she'd met this week were guilty, it wasn't Hugh. She might have to leave town without their ever starting a love affair, but it would be knowing he was innocent of any wrong-doing.

Just that day, she'd talked to two other men who might have reasons to want the necklace because they needed the money. Edward had hinted he could start his own business if he had enough capital. Zach's band earned very little, apparently, and soon he'd have to leave the Manor, including his soundproofed studio, to live elsewhere. For that matter, perhaps everyone who lived in the mansion could be considered a suspect. All of them were about to lose the home that had been in the family for hundreds of years.

She shook her head: not even Kinsey Milhone had cases with so many suspects.

Chapter 9

Once again Sabrina looked forward to an evening with Hugh. However, being a person who believed in traveling light, she'd brought only one flight-attendant-size suitcase and she'd already worn most of the clothes she managed to cram into it. Certainly all the "dressy" ones, fit for fancy restaurants or other posh occasions. She had only a long, navy blue skirt and "mix-and-match" blouses left. Well, that would have to do.

After showering and drying her hair, she chose the print blouse in colors of navy, purple and rose, with its three-quarters-length sleeves and boat neckline. Her go-everywhere navy wool blazer would keep her warm on the way to a restaurant.

Hugh arrived promptly at seven, spent a few minutes admiring her hotel room, and escorted her down the hall to the elevator and then to his Jaguar.

She slipped into the passenger seat. "I thought you didn't like to drive in the city."

"I don't, but this time we're just going home, and I can park it in its usual slot."

"Home?" Sabrina's heart began to quiver. Did he

intend to push their relationship further? She tried for
a flippant tone. "Is it those etchings after all?"

He laughed. "Not quite. I thought you might prefer
a home-cooked meal for a change."

"You cook?" She couldn't keep the surprise out of
her voice.

"Dear me, no. But my man does, and quite superbly
at that."

"Your 'man'?" This was getting more mysterious by
the minute.

He steered them through traffic, his eyes focused on
the road. "Yes, Leonard has been with me for years.
Couldn't do without him."

When she didn't respond, he elaborated. "He's my
valet: keeps my clothes in order, cleans my flat—well,
he hires a woman to come in and help—serves my
meals. Leonard also cooks, which is a plus. Other valets
must order in from nice restaurants." He glanced at her.
"Most men have valets, you know."

"No, they don't," Sabrina said, "not in Chicago,
anyway."

He looked at her for a second, before returning his
gaze to the busy street. "I'm sure some do. Perhaps you
just weren't aware. Perhaps most wealthy American men
have cleaning persons and cooks, and only hire a butler
when hosting a party."

Sabrina didn't know what to say. She obviously
moved in the wrong social circles. Sure, she'd dated
some men she assumed were quite well off. However,
since she never accepted their invitations to visit their
apartments or houses, she didn't know if they had live-in

servants or not. Most men she knew seemed uncomfortable in a room without either a wet bar or futons.

"Here we are." Hugh pulled up in front of a gorgeous, tall, white building which resembled the one in *Upstairs, Downstairs*. By the look of it, as well as the other gracious homes surrounding them, she decided he lived in Belgravia, an exclusive area of London she'd read about.

"Let's just go in, shall we? Leonard will park the car."

She tried to keep the awe out of her voice. "He parks cars as well as cleaning, serving and tossing off the occasional gourmet meal?"

Hugh laughed again in that wonderful way he had, making Sabrina's pulse do a little jig. "Of course." He helped her from the car, took her arm and led her up the four steps to a shiny black front door that opened at once in front of them.

"Good evening, sir." Leonard was almost as tall as Hugh, slender, gray-haired and wearing some sort of black uniform.

Hugh introduced them, then said, "Thank you, Leonard,"and led Sabrina into a large vestibule. He helped her remove her jacket and hung it in a closet, then led her down a long portrait-lined hallway and into a sitting room with blazing fireplace, silver sconces on the walls, and furniture so sleek and pristine Sabrina almost felt afraid to sit down.

"What would you like to drink?"

"I... I don't know." She perched on the edge of a peach silk covered chair. "Whatever you're having."

He lifted the top of a cabinet and up out of it sprang a shelf containing cut-glass decanters and a swarm of different sized glasses. He poured pale-looking fluid into two flutes and she assumed they'd be drinking champagne. He brought the glass to her, then sat opposite in a matching chair.

"You really live here?" What was she thinking? She wished she'd bitten her tongue before saying that, but it was too late now.

"Actually seldom in this room. It's strictly for show. I spend my spare time, what there is of it, in my quarters upstairs. A very plain bedroom and an office. Quite different, I assure you. Messy, even, especially right now, when I have some of Richard Gilmore's papers strewn all over my desk."

Sabrina sipped her wine. "Teachers in the U.S. don't get paid enough to afford places like this."

"Nor do they here, I'm afraid. However, I love to teach, and, since I have an independent income, I can afford it." His smile turned into a small frown. "The Gilmores had an independent income, as well, had they not? Do you know what happened to it, why, as your cousin said, the bank will foreclose on the Manor?"

"I have no idea. I've just always assumed they were my rich English relatives, and I envied them. Elmore says he's convinced Granddad made some bad investments. He tried to advise him, but Grandfather rejected his suggestions."

"What a pity."

Leonard came into the room, this time wearing a small black apron over his clothes, and announced dinner was ready. Sabrina and Hugh followed him out of the sitting room, across the hall and into a spacious dining room.

For a brief moment, she wondered if they were going to be seated opposite one other at the ends of a football-field long dining table and they would have to communicate via satellite. But then she saw two place settings resided next to each other, one at the very end, one next to it on the side. She sat in the heavy brocade chair that Hugh pulled out for her, and they waited in silence while Leonard returned bearing soup bowls and a tureen. He served them both, left the tureen on the table and disappeared again.

Sabrina tasted the soup and recognized it as Potato-Leek, or, as the French called it, *Potage Parmentier*. She'd made it herself a few times, when she took a French cooking class one summer between semesters at college.

"Leonard is an excellent chef," she told Hugh.

"I agree."

The silence stretched, and she searched her mind for a topic of conversation, but nothing but Leonard's expertise and versatility came to her mind. "And he does all those other things besides."

Hugh looked up. "You acted surprised when I said Englishmen always had valets."

"I'm afraid so. I've read Jane Austen's novels and other books by British writers, but apparently they never felt it necessary to point that out."

"Took it for granted, I suppose. You're aware of course we have this blasted class system in England. Wealthy families required dozens of servants and never did anything for themselves if a servant could do it. Even when they went to war, the men took their valets with them. After all, someone had to see to their uniforms and polish their boots, didn't they? Naturally, they were always the officers and could get away with it."

"You sound as if you don't approve."

"We still have a monarchy, and there are still Lords and Ladies and all the rest of it. I hate it." He frowned. "Why can't we all just be Miss and Mister as you are in America?"

His words surprised her. "You hate it? But you're part of the, er, upper class."

"I know, but what can be done? It's very hard to change a centuries-old tradition."

"I read they're changing Parliament to be more democratic."

"Only time will tell how far they go. As long as the country still supports the royal family and all that it entails—" He waved his hand in a circle.

Leonard reappeared again, this time bringing the main course of roast beef, tiny peas and a sculptured mound of something orange-colored that tasted delicious, no matter what it was. He followed it with a tossed salad, pineapple sherbet, tiny petit fours and coffee.

By the time they finished, Hugh had changed the subject, reverting to the plight of the Gilmores and his inheritance of all of Richard's papers.

"Why do you suppose my grandfather left them to you?" Sabrina asked.

"We met at a dinner party some years ago, and, when I said I researched old documents, he said he possessed tons of old family papers and would give them to me when he died. I never believed he was serious though."

He rose from the table, and this time, instead of returning to the sitting room, he escorted Sabrina to a small room with the usual fireplace, plus walls lined with books, a brown leather sofa and a console with a combination television/stereo set.

Sabrina sat on one end of the sofa. "Was that the only time you ever saw him?"

Hugh sat next to her and took one of her hands in his. "No, he came to my school several times, and we chatted in my office for about half an hour. It was then I began to notice he seemed, er, out of it. His conversation would wander off the subject. Sometimes he'd just sit and stare straight ahead without saying anything. I wondered if he might have Alzheimers."

She left her hand in his, enjoying the warm feel of it, trying to ignore what his touch did to her senses and still carry on a proper conversation.

"According to his children, he was always a bit strange after the war. I'm not sure what he did. I don't think he was one of your upper class set who traveled with a valet. Whatever, it supposedly scarred him for life, leaving him with a loose grip on reality. If he seemed lucid in your early talks with him, he must have been having a few good days."

"Perhaps. I'm very sorry about what's happened, but I hope to learn more as I go through his papers."

"I don't see how that would help. The man must have frittered away the family fortune quite legally. However, you may find copies of his bills and the mortgage on the Manor."

"We'll see, won't we?" He put his arm around her shoulder and drew her close.

She looked forward, not at him, afraid if she turned her head, he'd be kissing her. Well, what did she expect? He'd kissed her before and now they were in his house, where he might have something more elementary in mind.

She got up. "What about those papers? May I see them?"

After she spoke, she realized her request might take her out of the frying pan and into the fire. After all, the office with those Gilmore papers strewn over the desk resided upstairs, along with his bedroom. Would he be able to maneuver her from one room into the other? She'd just have to chance it.

"Righto." Hugh took her hand once more, led her out of the library, up a broad staircase and into a wood-paneled study. More books lined the walls, leather chairs sat in corners and there were two desks, one behind the other. After Hugh turned on some lights, Sabrina went to the first desk and looked at the piles of documents, which were not very messy at all, but apparently sorted into some kind of order.

Hugh came to her side and pointed. "These are from the seventeenth century, these from the eighteenth and these from the nineteenth."

"My, the piles get larger with time, don't they?"

"We are a planet addicted to the use of paper. It's a wonder there are any trees left in the world. Every time some invention comes along that's supposed to free us from paper—the telephone, telegraph, computers—we end up using even more of it."

"And therefore, this largest pile—"

"Is the twentieth century."

"Show me some of the letters you found."

"You mean the ones that mention the stolen necklace?"

She hadn't wanted to come right out and ask about it, for fear she'd give anything away, so she just smiled. "And other things."

He pulled some thin sheets out of the stack and showed them to her, but, being written in a spidery German hand, she learned nothing.

"You translated them, didn't you?"

"Yes, although my German isn't what it used to be."

"And the papers told you my grandfather might have stolen a necklace?"

"As near as I can determine, that seems to be the gist of it. Someone who knew about it chides him for not returning the necklace to the rightful owners."

"Did that person know who the rightful owners were?"

"Perhaps."

"Does he name them?"

"No, but there may be more letters, and one of them may tell. I haven't read everything yet."

"Do you know who wrote the letters? Can we contact that person and ask him?"

Hugh grinned. "What an optimist you are. The letter is dated 1947. The man is probably long dead."

"Maybe not. My grandfather didn't die until this month."

"The letter is unsigned and there's no envelope."

Sabrina fingered the edges of the paper. "They say modern forensic techniques can determine who manufactured a certain kind of paper and where it was sold."

"You want to play detective? Why do you find it important to know who wrote the letter?" She didn't answer and he continued. "Oh, I see. It's the necklace that interests you."

She scrambled for a plausible reason for her concern. "Well, this letter-writer did imply my grandfather stole it, and I don't believe any Gilmore would have done that."

"Not even a gentleman suffering from some kind of mental problem contracted in his military service?"

"Not even then."

"Well, it happened a very long time ago, and I don't believe any Bobbies camped on his doorstep demanding the return of the stolen property. Certainly none are there now." He shrugged. "It's all just a story from the past and probably untrue."

Suddenly she wanted to tell him he was wrong. There not only was a necklace, but she had it. Yet her need to keep it private for now clicked in. "I suppose you're right."

Hugh set the paper down and put his arms around her. "I suspect it's because you're a woman that the story fascinates you."

"What do you mean?"

"Women love jewelry, don't they?"

Sabrina didn't care much for it, but she accepted his explanation without really lying. "Most of us do." She smiled up at him, then turned so that his arms dropped away from her shoulders. "I must be going." She went through the door and walked briskly toward the stairs.

"As long as you're up here, don't you want to see the rest of my digs?"

"You mean your bedroom? I think not."

"Sabrina, I'm not a rapist. To be honest, I'd like to make love to you, but if you say 'no,' I'll respect that. However, I rather thought we were getting on exceptionally well." His arms went around her again and this time she didn't move out of them.

Yet, her voice came out high-pitched and soft. "In only three days?"

"It seems more. I do know that, ever since I met you, I've developed a tremendous desire to hold you and smother you with kisses." He began by kissing her cheek, her ears, her neck.

Eyes closed, she savored the warmth of his mouth on her skin, the delicious sensations coursing down her back. She desired nothing more at that moment than to taste those kisses, feel his body against hers, as it had been in her room the night before. This time, no necklace lay hidden under her blouse to inhibit her, and his bedroom was behind a door only a few steps away.

"No." The word came out before she could stop it, as if it came from some woman who lived in 1947 and couldn't let herself be carried away by passion because, in those days, it "simply wasn't done."

He let her go, then started down the stairs, looking back once as if to be certain she followed. She did, although, under the long skirt, her legs trembled.

"I'll have Leonard bring the car around, and I'll take you home." He disappeared down the hallway.

She'd made him angry. Tears gathered behind her eyelids at the thought of her foolish rejection. He was the most handsome, charming man she'd ever met. To say nothing of intelligent and rich, as well. What on earth was the matter with her?

They'd reached the first floor, and Sabrina felt a wild desire to run after him and tell him she'd changed her mind. The idea died almost instantly. She'd feel even more like a fool.

He returned in moments, brought her blazer from the closet and held it while she slipped her arms into the sleeves. Then he turned her around, held her in a tight embrace and kissed her soundly, before again letting her go.

"Hugh... I..."

"I'm seeing you tomorrow. Your Aunt Charlotte called and invited me to dinner, and we're going sight-seeing by day. Shall I pick you up at eleven?"

She let out the breath she'd been holding and it came out like a sigh of relief. Which it was. She hadn't driven him away. She'd see him again the next day, and maybe by then she'd have sorted out her feelings and decided who was in charge: some 1940's person or the twenty-first century modern woman she called herself.

Hugh stopped the Jaguar in front of the hotel,

helped her out and then waited until the doorman held the door open for her. "Until tomorrow." Then he turned and left.

Sabrina went up to her room and, after hanging up her clothes, fell across the bed. Why, oh why, had she stopped him? He wanted to make love to her, and she wanted that too, so? Her past history with men surged into her mind. After her mother died, she and her father became especially close. She idolized him—still did—and none of the boys in high school stood a chance. They even nicknamed her "The Ice Princess" and said she was stuck-up and thought she was too good for them. She didn't feel that way at all, only that they seemed so immature compared to her father.

In college, she dated a steady boyfriend in her junior year, but, although he'd promised to visit her over the summer, he never did, nor did he even call. Bitter, she seldom dated afterward, and soon she became a businesswoman with a shop to manage, then two, then three, and no time for men. Except one. They met at a business conference, quickly became intimate and planned to be married, until the night he died in a car accident. No one had taken his place so far.

Used to being alone, she liked her privacy, enjoyed independence, with no one to answer to. She could go where she wanted, eat whatever food she desired, read all night in bed if it pleased her. She grinned, remembering something she'd read: "Agatha Christie has pleased more people in bed than anyone else."

And yet, something was missing. She was normal, after all. And normal people needed love and companionship. Normal women wanted a man in the bed with them, possessed an innate desire to "nest" and to nurture children. She was almost thirty and her biological clock didn't tick: it thundered.

However, Hugh was British, not American. Not her type, really, and she not his. This relationship was, perhaps, one of those "opposites attract" things. His American Express card was probably Platinum, his British Airways card Supreme Premier Class, and his personal banker—he surely had one—probably bowed to his Exaltedness. He would marry a cool, English blonde, with money of her own, a fancy English boarding school background and maybe a title somewhere in her family's past. No, he was merely toying with Sabrina, having a fling before settling down—and not until he was forty or so—with someone else.

In a way she felt relieved to get that settled. Being a twenty-first century woman, she could have an affair with him if she liked and then leave him wanting more, while she went back home.

Still, when she crawled into bed and sleep came, she dreamed of Hugh holding her naked under the covers, while their children slept in the nursery upstairs under the watchful eye of their very expensive nanny.

Chapter 10

The next day Hugh took Sabrina to Hyde Park, where local artists hung their paintings on the outside of the black iron fence that surrounded it.

They walked the entire distance, pausing now and then to admire a particular painting, and Sabrina discovered Hugh's taste in art reflected her own. He offered to buy one, done in the Impressionist style, that she particularly liked, but she refused.

"I can't take it home on the airplane."

"You could, but why don't I keep it here for you, and you may come and visit it every now and then."

"A tempting thought, but so far my visits to England have been once in twenty years."

"Or I could take it to Chicago."

"And just how often do you make the trip across the Atlantic?"

He grinned. "Starting now, you mean? You might be surprised at how often I'd show up on your doorstep."

She let that linger in her thoughts. So far no man had even traveled from Indianapolis to Chicago to spend an occasional evening with her, much less six thousand miles. But then, Hugh wasn't serious. Two weeks after she returned home, he'd be saying, "Sabrina who?"

On the far side of the park, the paintings being exhibited became more modern, abstract, and somewhat incomprehensible. Hugh tilted his head to one side. "I believe this one has been hung upside down."

Sabrina rushed to his side and whispered. "Be careful. He might hear you."

Hugh straightened and shrugged. "Sorry." Then, once far out of earshot of the artist, Hugh said, "That last one looked as if it might jump off the canvas and do something disgusting on the pavement."

They entered the park and strolled along, watching children sail tiny boats in the pond. They sat on a park bench and talked about not only their taste in art, but music, films, television and, especially, books. Both read a great deal, and Hugh wanted to know all about her school days and afterward.

"You were engaged once," he said.

"Yes, for a very short time."

"What happened?"

"He was killed in a car accident."

"Whilst driving?"

"No, he wasn't driving. A friend drove. Thinking he had a green arrow, he made a left turn into oncoming traffic and was broadsided by an SUV."

"How terrible."

"Peter, of course, occupied the passenger seat which got the full impact of the crash. He died instantly. His friend survived."

"You must have been devastated, and the friend who drove, as well."

"His friend's father happened to be in the back seat, the men having been to a hockey match, and he died of his injuries a week later."

After a long silence, Hugh said, "The driver... I suppose losing both his father and a friend..."

"He stopped driving altogether, later moved away."

Hugh squeezed her hand. "Tell me about growing up in Chicago. Are there still gangsters?"

Grateful for a new topic, she cleared her throat and grinned. "Of course not, not anymore. On the other hand, my mother went to high school in Cicero for a short period of time, and walked past the very home Al Capone once lived in."

"Al Capone was a gangster, wasn't he?"

"Yes, but he'd long since gone to prison. He didn't live there when she passed the old house, but she said she used to walk on the opposite side of the street, just in case."

Sabrina plied Hugh with questions about his growing up in Durham. He told her of some of the pranks he and his brother perpetrated, then about attending a public, what Americans would call a private, school. He also spoke about his university days and how he came to teach history, the subject that interested him most.

She drank it all in, visualized him as a boy, then a young student, crossing the quad at university, with a black robe floating behind, as she'd seen in films. She also pictured him dressed in tweeds, perhaps with reading glasses hiding those marvelous blue eyes, addressing a class of rapt students.

Hugh interrupted her thoughts by suggesting lunch. She rose from the bench, and they found a quiet dining room where they talked even more, annoying the waitress who no doubt wanted to clear their table. Next, they walked back toward the Mall.

"Will I get to see the changing of the guards at Buckingham Palace?"

"It's not the right time of day," Hugh told her, "but I'll buy you some Belgian chocolates to make up for it."

"You're spoiling me."

"You don't smell spoilt. You smell like gardenias."

She laughed with him and they boarded a bus to go back to her hotel.

"I have some news for you," he said.

"What kind of news?"

"About the stolen necklace."

Sabrina began to perspire, wondering what he'd reveal, but she tried to sound only mildly interested. "Oh?"

"This morning I translated another of the German letters and now I can answer the question you asked me yesterday."

"What question?"

"About who the necklace might have belonged to."

"That's wonderful. Who are the rightful owners?"

"The family of a Count de Villot in Paris. The Nazis stole the necklace along with other jewels, money and works of art."

"See, the Nazis stole it, not my grandfather."

"But the letter writer believes your grandfather had

the necklace, if not the other items, and urges him to return it."

"I can't believe my grandfather would keep something valuable if he knew who the rightful owners were."

"Perhaps he tried to trace them and failed, so he couldn't return it."

"Perhaps."

"Even if he did have it," she added, "what happened to it? Where is the necklace now?" Considering the value the jeweler placed on the one she found, she knew exactly what happened to it, but she wanted to know what Hugh knew before telling him.

"That's a mystery, I should say. You wanted to do some sleuthing yesterday. Here's your chance."

"If my grandfather had it, and if it's really valuable, why wouldn't he have sold it and used the money to pay off the mortgage and save the Manor from foreclosure?"

"Perhaps he did sell it, but, like the rest of the Gilmore fortune, lost the proceeds through bad investments."

Sabrina thought that a possibility, except for one thing, knowing for sure that it didn't happen: the necklace was still in his possession. Or, at any rate, still in the mansion until she found it in the doll and took it away. Perhaps, now that she knew the name of the original owner, she should try to find him and return it.

They reached the hotel and this time Hugh came up with her. They sat on the chaise, still talking, as if each needed to tell the other everything that had happened in the years before they met.

Darkness settled over the room when at last he put his arms around her and kissed her. She held him close, savoring his touch, his scent, his sheer masculinity. Her resolve of the night before returned, and she let him caress the underside of her breasts, kiss her throat, and undo the buttons of her blouse. The pressure of his body sent her backward, so she lay on the chaise with him over her, murmuring soft words in her ear, kissing her exposed flesh. Her muscles throbbed with desire, and she knew the magic moment had come.

Then, suddenly, he pulled away and stood up, taking her with him. Arms still around her, his face close to hers, he kissed her. "Sabrina, my sweet angel, I want you very much."

"I know."

She expected him to lead her to the bed, but instead, he dropped his hold and ran a hand through his hair. "We have a dinner engagement in a few hours. I'll just pop home and change clothes. I'm sure you want to change as well, and then we'll go to the Manor. But, afterward—" He came close to her for his final words. "—we'll take advantage of the time and place, and I won't have to leave you if you don't want me to."

He headed for the door, not even saying goodbye, because this was merely *au revoir*. She threw off her clothes, showered and dressed again in the long blue skirt, but this time with a low-cut silvery blouse that revealed plenty of *decolettage*. She would make him yearn for her, and later tonight they'd spend hours together, naked in the bed, just as in her dream.

* * *

Sabrina found dinner at the Manor to be as formal as she expected. The two aunts, Frances and Charlotte, fussed over every detail, including how long the cocktail time should last and who would sit where. Aunt Mary only smiled at the other woman's quest for oneupmanship, and Sabrina hoped they wouldn't come to blows.

All the ladies wore long dresses, and Philip, Elmore and Edward, like Hugh, wore dinner jackets. Only Zach looked out of place, with his open-necked shirt, although at least he'd exchanged jeans for dark trousers. She wondered that he even attended the dinner party. Candles and crystal adorned the dining table, and five courses appeared. Sabrina sat opposite Hugh, so, although she hoped they might touch one another during the meal, she contented herself with just looking at him most of the time, licking her lips and holding her wine or water glass close to her breasts so he might become aroused.

Conversation ranged from the weather—unseasonably warm: good heavens, it hadn't rained in days—to the abysmal state of the world, but mostly about the Gilmore family problems.

Elmore expressed his severe disapproval of Richard's having put them all in their current predicament. "If he'd only taken my advice," he said more than once. "And not just about this house. The family originally owned property in other towns, as well as in the nearby village. He seems to have lost everything."

"He wasn't a well man," Uncle Philip said. "Perhaps we should have arranged for a conservatorship."

"Yes, Philip," Aunt Frances said. "You ought to have done so. We all knew he wasn't himself these last few years: going about in his pajamas all hours of the day and night, walking out of doors in the rain, bringing stones from the lily pond into the house and leaving them in our rooms as gifts."

"It's water under the bridge," Philip said. "I'm sorry I didn't act sooner, but nothing's to be done about it now."

Edward spoke up. "Easy for you to say. You're retired anyway, with a pension from the government. You and Mother can live well enough somewhere else. What about the rest of us? We have to start over, as if the Gilmore legend, and its fortune, never existed."

"And lose this house," Elmore added.

"It's true your mother and I will not live in poverty, but don't think I'm not aware of what this means to you young people." He cleared his throat. "If Father had not been so careless with money." Bitterness clung to his words. "He never took advice. On his death the property should rightly have come to me and then to you. I'm more sorry than you can imagine that it won't happen."

"And this beautiful house," Charlotte said, "where we've lived for so long, gone."

Sabrina remembered that Charlotte only recently moved back into it because of the death of her husband but said nothing. She also wondered which of his sons Philip referred to when he said the property would have passed to them. Elmore, who was the eldest, but adopted, or Philip's biological son Edward? Perhaps, if his choice might provoke a family feud, it was just as well it couldn't be passed on. She'd read about wealthy families who squabbled so much over their inheritance that only the lawyers ended up with anything. Perhaps, after all, it was better not to be rich and therefore have few expectations.

Thomas served after-dinner coffee in the drawing room, and this time Hugh made it a point to be near Sabrina. He sat next to her on one of the long sofas, and his knee pressed against her leg so often she wondered if anyone noticed. As soon as a polite interval passed, he suggested they leave. Sabrina hugged her three aunts and thanked them for a lovely evening.

"When do you fly home?" Aunt Frances asked.

"Next Sunday. I still have another week."

"I would like very much to invite you here again before you go, but I'm afraid that won't be possible. We've been instructed to begin packing at once and vacate the premises before the end of the week."

"I'm so sorry," Sabrina said. "How dreadful for you."

"Gilmores have lived in this house for centuries," Aunt Charlotte added. "Unless a miracle occurs, I don't know what we shall do."

Uncle Philip gave Sabrina a kiss on the cheek and everyone said goodbye. Sabrina and Hugh departed in his Jaguar.

All the way back to her hotel, Hugh talked about the Gilmore problem, saying he believed, as she did, that the situation would test the ability of family members to recover and build successful lives.

She, on the other hand, felt like the heroine in a romance novel. She would take Hugh to her room and let him make love to her. They only met four days ago, but, quicker than you could say, "Barbara Cartland," she was in love. Oh, last night she argued with herself that he merely toyed with her and she would do that as well, take what pleasure she could and then leave him hungering for more. Yet now, after another day of his company, feeling as if she knew everything about him, and all of it wonderful beyond belief, she knew that their lovemaking would be exquisite and make their parting unbearable.

The silent ride up to her room in the elevator reminded her of a scene from the old Cary Grant movie *Indiscreet*, shown often on the movie channel at home. He and Ingrid Bergman went up to her room in an elevator and carried on an affair that seemed doomed not to end in marriage. Now Sabrina was about to start an affair of her own, and she feared nothing lasting would come of that, either.

As she put the plastic card into the slot in the door, her hands trembled, and Hugh steadied her, then pushed the door for her. She snapped on the light switch. And froze.

The room looked as if a missile struck it. The bed resembled a hastily created pile of sleeping necessities —-coverlet, blankets and sheets tossed aside and the mattress pulled halfway off the box springs. The drawers of the chest lay on the floor, her clothing strewn about, the chaise, on which they'd almost made love that afternoon, overturned and the bottom slashed open.

Chapter 11

"Omigod." Sabrina choked out a gasp, and stopped on the threshold.

Hugh pushed past her and also stopped, his gaze scanning the scene. Then he turned to her, his voice firm, but not unkind. "What the devil is going on?"

She couldn't answer. Hot tears filled her eyes, her throat closed. She checked a scream from rising. Fear and anger waged a battle for her emotions. Yet Hugh stood before her, and she had no time to find the perfect answer. She barely understood the situation herself.

Obviously, whoever had broken into her rooms on Devonshire Terrace two days before had also broken into this one. She'd been right: someone wanted the necklace, knew she had it and took this extreme means to get it back.

"Sabrina, answer me."

She closed the door behind them and moved into the room, picking up her lingerie from the floor. She cleared her throat and strengthened her voice. "I don't know."

"The other time, well, I put it down to thieves looking for cash, but twice in a row is too much of a coincidence. Something's going on. You must tell me what it is. Who did this?"

She shook her head, not trusting herself to say more just yet. And what could she say? Although she believed she knew why her room had been broken into, she hadn't a clue about who had done it. She longed to tell Hugh the truth, but, whether her feelings for him were genuine love or not, he might still be behind the break-in. He knew about the necklace. He knew she inherited some old things, including a doll, in the trunk and, smart as he was, might have deduced she had the necklace.

Of course, he couldn't have broken in himself—after all, they'd been together all evening—but he could have arranged for someone else do it, his "man" Leonard, for instance. Leonard would do as instructed, no questions asked, loyal as a St. Bernard.

Hugh's voice became firmer. "Stop that. Don't pick up anything. I'm going to call hotel security, and we want them to see what's happened." He moved to the telephone at the side of the bed and made the call.

Sabrina stumbled to the desk and sat in the only chair still upright, clutching her silk underwear in her hands and staring at the design in the carpeting beneath her feet.

Hugh didn't speak to her again but went to the door and—moments later, it seemed—the doorbell rang, he opened it and two men in plain clothes entered. Both were medium height, medium-build and dark-haired, nondescript, as perhaps hotel detectives ought to be so they could blend, unnoticed, into the background. They stood still in the middle of the room for a moment, then the taller man asked questions. When had she been in the room last? How long was she gone? Had she assessed the damage? Was anything missing?

She answered their questions honestly, still trembling and clutching a half slip to her chest. Then, at their last question, she went into the closet, where her clothes now lay in a heap on the floor, and looked them over. She pulled out her suitcase and tote bag and looked in them, but, except for the cotton bags in which she packed her shoes for traveling, they were empty as before. Even Amy, although no longer on the shelf, lay on the closet floor. The wider hole in her back indicated someone poked beefy hands inside.

While the two plainclothesmen watched, she checked over the garments, but nothing was missing so far as she could tell. And who would want her underwear, scarves and belts anyway? The fact they looked inside the doll told her they knew what they wanted. The contents of her large handbag—she'd taken a tiny evening purse to the Manor—lay on the floor near the bed, but the travelers checks remained, along with her pocket calendar, cosmetics bag, pen, breath mints and packet of tissues.

The men helped Hugh return the mattress to the bed, and they looked over the bedding as if to make sure nothing hid in the folds of the blanket and sheets.

They asked her to check the bathroom as well, and she found her nightgown and robe still hanging from the hooks on the back of the door. Her toothpaste, toothbrush, dental floss, small plastic bottles containing shampoo and cleansing lotion had all been taken out of the travel bag she carried them in and lay loose on the bathroom counter.

"Nothing missing?" one of the men asked again.

"No, I don't think so."

"Money, credit cards?"

"I have a small billfold with money and two credit cards, but I put them in my evening bag when I went out."

"Very wise," the man commented.

"We're terribly sorry," the other one said, "for your inconvenience. We'll send up a maid immediately to put things to rights. Of course, we shall notify the police and report the incident. They may want to question you further."

"Naturally," the first man said, "the hotel will compensate you by eliminating all charges. You will be our guest for the duration of your stay."

"And," the other added, "we will post a guard in the passage to watch your door."

Sabrina felt overwhelmed by the lengths they would go and assured them she didn't consider herself in danger.

"Probably it was just thieves preying on a tourist such as yourself, and we shall make every effort to catch and bring them to justice. But in a large hotel like this, it's not possible to patrol every area at all times."

Her confident tone helped to calm her even more. "I understand. Nothing's been stolen, it seems, and I'm sure it won't happen again. Thank you."

The men left, and Sabrina continued to pick up her things and put them where they belonged. Every action took more of the anxiety away and made her stronger. She rehung dresses and blouses, and, when she came out of the closet, she found Hugh had returned the drawers to the chest and the chaise to its upright position.

He came to her and placed his hands on her upper arms.

"You didn't tell them this happened to you before."

"Nor did you, and thank you for that."

"I didn't feel it was my place, but why not, Sabrina? Why not tell them your other rooms were broken into? Someone is stalking you, and the police need to know. This is a very dangerous business."

"No one is stalking me, and I'm not in any danger. Don't you see: I'm never home when they strike. They don't want to harm me."

"Then they're looking for something."

"I think that's a reasonable explanation."

"But when they didn't find any last time, why would they do it again? And how would they have known you moved here in the first place?"

"Since they couldn't have known I moved, it's just what we said before, a coincidence." Her mind quickly conjured up a reason. "They're not the same thieves at all. One haunted the bed and breakfast inns and this one likes big hotels." She paused. "London is a huge city. It's probably crawling with thieves." She pulled out of his grasp and sat on the edge of the chaise.

He sat next to her, but the mood had changed

dramatically since dinner. His body language told her he didn't intend to make love to her just then, and she didn't want him to. Fear gripped her for a moment. She'd lied to the officers about not being in danger, but now she realized she might be. She almost wished she hadn't put the necklace in the hotel safe. Better to let whoever wanted it so desperately find and take it. Instead, if that person or persons still believed she had it, their next step might be to confront her and try forceful means. She shivered.

Hugh's frown indicated he still puzzled over the matter. "I'm not sure I can buy your theory that thieves are so rampant in London you can be a target twice within a week, but, I confess I'm at a loss to come up with a reasonable explanation. You seem like an ordinary—no, not ordinary, beautiful—lady with nothing to hide. But, *do* you have something to hide, Sabrina? Is there something going on that you haven't told me about?"

She hated lying, but, what the heck, she'd done it a few other times, so what was once more, especially considering the importance of keeping the secret of the necklace at least a little longer? "No."

"Well, I'm not letting you stay here one more day, even if they post a dozen guards at your door. You're coming home with me." He paused for a second. "I have a guest room."

"No, I can't do that."

"Why not? Look, I won't seduce you. You'll be under no obligation. I just want to keep you safe."

"I am safe. I will be."

"If you won't come to my place, then at least let me stay here with you tonight. I'll sleep on the chaise."

She laughed, and it eased her tension, but she still needed to reassure him. "I have a terrible headache from all this, and I want to go straight to bed. I'll see you tomorrow. All right?" She got up and went to the door. She opened it to let him out and saw a hotel maid standing there, one arm holding clean linens, the other upraised and about to knock.

Sabrina decided that, as a proper English gentleman, Hugh probably felt he had no choice but to obey her wishes.

"Are you sure you'll be all right?"

"Positive. And you know there will be a guard on the door tonight at least. I think I see one in the hall now."

As the maid slipped past them and hurried toward the disheveled bed, Hugh kissed her forehead. "Tomorrow then. Think about what I said, that you should stay with me. Will you do that?"

"I'll think about it."

He said goodnight. The maid finished the bed, checked the bathroom and left, taking the wrinkled sheets with her.

Sabrina had wanted desperately to confide in Hugh, but something told her not to just yet. Even if he had nothing to do with the necklace and the break-ins, she couldn't tell him, because if he knew nothing about it now, he'd be better off not learning of it. Although he wanted to get involved, put her under his roof, that would only put him in danger. Yes, she felt threatened, but she wouldn't risk his being in danger too. This wasn't his problem. She'd handle it herself.

She knew what to do, something she should have done long ago. In the morning, she'd retrieve the necklace from the hotel safe and take it to someone in authority, the police perhaps. She remembered her cousin Elmore was a solicitor, and he would know what to do. He'd help her, and soon this nightmare would all be over. She'd tell him about the letters which said Count de Villot owned the necklace and they could set about returning it. Then, if Hugh hadn't been involved in the break-ins to steal it from her, they could pick up where they left off. Assuming either of them still wanted to.

Did she? Before they returned to the hotel, she'd been certain she'd fallen in love with him, but should she start an affair? And why did all this have to happen to her anyway? Why did her mother die at such a young age? Why did her fiancé get killed in that accident? Why did she fall in love with a man she couldn't have? Why must she love him and lose him and go back to Chicago with a broken heart?

Okay, she was not a perfect person. She'd made mistakes. Her bedroom was often a mess and, without her accountant, she might owe back taxes high enough to solve the national debt crisis. But if this was what life was supposed to be like, could she please exchange it for something else?

The fresh pillowcase became stained with tears before she fell asleep.

Chapter 12

Sabrina woke the next morning in a better mood. Doing something positive always had the effect of putting the past behind her and helping her move forward. What's done was done and she had to accept it and carry on. Her father once called it his "Well-that-crisis-is-over,-how-can-I-mess-up-now?" syndrome. The thought made her smile.

She put on pants, tunic and cardigan and then retrieved her doll from the closet. She looked about for something in which to carry the doll, spied the shiny gold bag with little handles which once held the box of Belgian chocolates from Hugh and put Amy inside.

Then she took it, along with her handbag, and left her room, making sure the lock clicked into place. She saw no policeman or house detective on that floor and assumed, even if one stayed overnight which she doubted, he'd gone now to other duties.

Once in the lobby, she stopped first at the accommodations desk where she asked for the item she'd placed in the hotel safe. The attendant requested her claim check, went behind the partition for a few minutes and returned with the necklace in its velvet bag.

After thanking her, Sabrina retreated to a side hallway where rows of telephones and a bench or two took up space between doors marked "Ladies" and "Gentlemen." Seeing no one else there to observe what she did, she pulled Amy out of the gold bag, once more inserted the necklace into the opening at the back of her body, and returned her to the bag.

She sighed. For a person who never cared much for jewelry, she had more of it than she wanted. At the same time, she realized it made her vulnerable, and she'd have to get rid of it as soon as possible.

However, assuming offices weren't open for business yet, she went into the dining room for breakfast, placing her handbag on the chair next to her. She put Amy's bag in her lap and ordered orange juice, eggs, toast and coffee. While she waited, she scanned the few other patrons in the room: a family of four, several middle-aged couples, and a few single men reading the morning newspapers. None seemed at all interested in her or even looked in her direction.

A tiny glass of orange juice arrived first, and she drank half of it at once. A waiter hurried to her side and spoke in a quiet tone. "Miss Gilmore?"

"Yes."

"You're wanted on the telephone."

She got up, retrieved both the bag and purse, and followed him into the hallway, wondering who wanted to talk to her. Hugh? Or perhaps the police. The hotel detective had said they might want to question her about the break-in. The phone lay on its side on the narrow counter and she picked it up and said, "Hello," but no one answered.

She repeated her word, but the line went dead. Puzzled, she walked back to the dining room. Hugh would not have hung up before she answered, but perhaps a police officer might, especially if some emergency called him away.

When she returned to the table, she found her breakfast in place already and she ate quickly, anxious to get on with her errand. She would have to contact Elmore and get directions to his office, at which time she could leave the necklace for him to care for.

After signing the bill and adding her room number, she got up and headed once more for the hallway with the telephones, but a wave of dizziness engulfed her. Her vision blurred. She shook her head, trying to clear it, closed and reopened her eyes, but nothing helped. The problem got worse.

She needed to sit down and wait until the strange sensation passed. She recalled seeing benches in the hall and decided she'd sit there rather than go back to her room. In fact, she doubted she could get to her room at all. The dizziness worsened. Black spots appeared in front of her eyes, the walls seemed to quiver and the floor to undulate. She staggered to the nearest bench, and by the time she dropped onto it, her sight had completely gone, and her body felt limp and useless.

A voice spoke in her ear, a woman's voice. "Permit me to help you. Take my arm."

Incapable of taking anyone's arm, Sabrina felt a hand on each of hers just before the blackness took over completely.

* * *

She woke to more blackness. As consciousness returned, she remembered her eyesight disintegrating in that hallway. Was she blind? Had some horrible disease attacked her without warning? A sharp pain began in her midriff and climbed into her head. Blind? And she was still less than thirty. Could she endure being blind for the next fifty-odd years? She shook herself out of that scenario. Medical science did wonders these days. They'd fix her eyes.

However, she'd need help until then, and the major question was where was she now? The dizziness had gone, and she realized she lay on something soft. A bed? She moved her arms and legs in tiny circles. Yes, they worked fine. She sat up and that movement seemed normal as well. Whatever had caused the blindness didn't seem to have affected any other part of her body.

But blind? Her mind kept rejecting it. Maybe only temporary blindness. Her optimistic spirit wouldn't let her believe it was a permanent condition. She had excellent health, always did. She joked to friends that if she were any healthier, she'd outlive Styrofoam.

Yet, such things did happen. What if she would be blind for the rest of her life? She shivered, then took a deep breath and tried to calm down. If this thing lasted—and she just knew it couldn't—then she'd cope with it. Somehow.

She'd start by getting off this bed. But, not being

able to see made it hazardous. Perhaps she'd just have to wait until someone came to help her, a nurse or doctor, assuming they had taken her to a hospital. Yet it didn't smell like a hospital, with its antiseptics and cleaning agents. Perhaps she was still in the hotel, and they had moved her to some anteroom until paramedics could arrive. She'd have to let them know she was awake now.

"Hello," she called out. "I'm awake. Hello."

No one answered. In fact, her voice seemed to echo, as if she were in a cave. Her heart pounded like a drumbeat. Where was she? Why didn't someone come? Who had brought her to this place, whatever it was?

"Hello!" This time she screamed the word, but still nothing happened. The silence was almost as frightening as the darkness. And then she realized it didn't smell like the hotel, either. It smelled like concrete and dust and mold. She shivered again.

She would have to find someone on her own, get off this bed and go out of this room—it must be a room, not a cave—and get help. But first she'd better find out how high the bed was off the floor. She didn't want to fall and possibly break something, not now. She swung her legs to the side and met a wall. Okay, the bed sat against a wall. Try the other side. But her legs didn't drop to the floor, they stretched out *on* the floor.

She paused and assessed the new information. The bed lay on a floor. She used her hands to feel the surfaces around her. The soft thing she lay on was some sort of quilt rather than a mattress, like a sleeping bag perhaps. Not that she knew much about sleeping bags.

She never went camping, or wanted to. Her friends who did often described the experience to her, but, to her mind, it sounded like camping was just being a glorified homeless person.

Next she touched the floor under her legs. Smooth and cold to the touch, like concrete or some other hard substance, not wood or carpeting. She felt all around the perimeter and then, near the top of the quilt, her hands met an object. Gingerly, she explored it with her fingers. Not very large, round like a cylinder. She picked it up, touched its sides. A knob. She pushed it and a beam of light glowed in front of her. She held a flashlight and she could see. She wasn't blind at all.

The sudden happiness of having sight dissolved into fear of another sort. The same questions flooded her mind. Where was she? Who put her there? What was going on? But at least now she could see. She flashed the beam around and saw four walls, none of them very far away. Across from the makeshift bed stood a chair, but she could make out no other furniture. She scrambled to her feet and explored the space.

First the bed. Yes, over a thin pad lay a sleeping bag, dark blue or black, with a red and blue plaid lining. Aiming the light along that wall, she soon came to a corner and there stood a stainless steel wastebasket, complete with lid that opened when you stepped on the lever. As if brought from someone's kitchen, the thing held a plastic garbage bag inside and on top of it sat a roll of bathroom tissue. Her stomach tightened. Was she supposed to use that? Why? Again the question returned. Where was she?

She turned away and flashed the light along the next wall. Nothing. Another corner. Then she faced the wall opposite the sleeping bag/bed. The chair, a plain wooden one with arms and back and casters so it could roll around, held a medium-sized cardboard box.

Deciding not to see what the box held just yet, she continued her tour of the room and next saw a large plastic bottle which appeared to contain about a gallon of water. Another corner. She saw a light switch. She flipped it up but nothing happened. She flashed the light toward the ceiling about ten feet above. No light fixture anywhere. The switch on the wall might operate an electrical outlet, but no lamp was plugged into it. She flashed the light back to the wall. A door. Thank goodness, a way out.

Well, there had to be a door, didn't there? She saw no windows, but she didn't get into that place by osmosis. She moved closer to it and saw it was a heavy wooden door and locked. She turned the knob, even tried to shake it, but it didn't budge.

Why was she not surprised to find it locked? Because, ever since she found the flashlight, reality had come seeping into her brain. She'd been kidnapped. Drugged first, which explained her dizziness and blacking out, but how, when? Probably the telephone call had been a ruse. And when she returned to her table her coffee was already there, coffee which tasted funny at the time, but she had put down to the British not knowing how to make American coffee. Almost anyone could have passed her table while she took the bogus phone call and dropped something into the coffee. But why would they do that? Of course she already knew.

A final sweep of the light brought her gaze to the head of the bed and there, against the wall, lay the gold bag that held Amy and the necklace. The bag was empty now: no necklace, not even Amy. After all her precautions, someone had stolen it from her after all.

A smidgen of hope sprang up. Perhaps the doll and her precious cargo were still there, if not in the bag, then in the cardboard box on the chair. She rushed over to it but found the box contained food: several sandwiches wrapped in plastic film, little bags of potato chips—with the word "crisps" in red letters on the side—an apple, an orange, a banana. She put the box on the floor and sat in the chair to think.

She'd been drugged and kidnapped so someone could steal the necklace, but whoever it was didn't intend to harm her. They'd provided a bed, food, water, even a "portapotty." They were amateur thieves, otherwise normal folks who just wanted the necklace and found a way to do it without anyone getting hurt. Probably they would come back and let her out later that day. She'd just have to wait. If it weren't for the necklace, she'd think this was just a harmless prank.

Wait? No, she didn't have to wait, because, besides the flashlight and gold bag, her purse also lay on the floor next to the "bed." She picked it up from its place on the floor, and, returning to the chair, rummaged through it. Another sign her kidnapper possessed a benevolent side: nothing appeared to be missing, just as the night before when he'd searched her hotel room. That morning she had replaced her cash and credit cards into the handbag, and they were still there, along with her cosmetics bag, comb, pen, notebook and sunglasses. Even her cell phone, but, of course, she found no service in her concrete prison.

She turned off the flashlight. No use wasting the batteries when she didn't know how long they might last. Yet, she couldn't bear the oppressive darkness and turned it on again. She'd never been so completely alone in her life. She'd always had her father, then classmates at school. After college, she moved into her own apartment, complete with a radio, television set and computer. On rare occasions when the power went out due to a severe snowstorm, she could at least go out of doors, or talk to neighbors. Sometimes, in spite of local outages, a nearby restaurant or movie theatre would have power, and she'd go there until the gas and electric company restored her own. Still, none of that was available to her now.

She chided herself for being a wimp who couldn't stand silence for a few hours or days. What did prisoners do when locked in solitary confinement? She drew upon her memory of books and films. Some recited poetry they'd once memorized, some made up stories in their heads, some wrote on bits of paper. Well, she did have toilet paper, assuming she wanted to use it that way.

Another thing: prisoners scratched marks on the walls to indicate the passing of days. That reminded her. What time was it? How long had she been out? She flashed the light on her watch. Two o'clock. Assuming it was the same day, she'd only been unconscious for a few hours. She decided it couldn't be a different day or she'd be hungry. Instead, she still felt full from breakfast. As for scratching days on the wall, what could she use for that?

Aha! Her cosmetics bag. She unzipped the small bag and let the contents spill into her lap: lipstick, eyebrow pencil, mascara, tiny hairbrush, tweezers, nail file.

Nail file?

Her nail file had a sharp point. She could scratch a line in the wall to mark off the days. She smiled at the thought, not believing for a moment she'd be there that long. She remembered the voice of the woman who spoke to her just before she blacked out. A normal, even kind voice, someone concerned for her welfare, perhaps the person who provided the food and other amenities. However, she'd have to remember to be careful opening the sandwiches—assuming she was there long enough to eat them—so the police could get fingerprints off the plastic wrap. Yet, if the thieves were amateurs they might have no police record and that wouldn't help.

Wait a minute. The nail file had a sharp point which might be good for something besides scratching marks on walls, something like picking the lock on the door. She grabbed it and stuffed the rest of the items back in the bag, dropping her purse on the seat of the chair. She put the end of the file into the keyhole and wiggled it. Nothing. She tried to turn the file in the slot but nothing happened then, either. Back and forth, around and around, in and out. No maneuver she made caused the lock to yield.

But it had to. People always picked locks, so there must be a way. After all, if a million monkeys tapping on a million computer keys could eventually reproduce all the works of Shakespeare (but the Internet proved *that* false!) then somehow she could, by persistence and sheer dumb luck, open the damn door. She put her purse on the bed, rolled the chair in front of the door, and sat down. She turned off the flashlight, left it in her lap and tackled the lock with a vengeance.

Hours passed, and hunger and darkness plagued her. She gave up the job for awhile. Her fingers already hurting from the effort, she turned on her meager light and opened one of the sandwiches: turkey, lettuce and sprouts on whole wheat bread. Her captor was health-conscious. Nevertheless, he or she forgot to provide a cup or glass for the water, and Sabrina was forced to pick up the heavy bottle and try to drink from it without spilling any. The thought amused her. In one moment, she knew she would soon be rescued, and in the next she wanted to conserve water as if it had to last across the Sahara.

After resting and massaging her hands, she again turned off the flashlight and attacked the door lock. This time, she sang songs out loud to keep herself company, and was amazed at how many she remembered, mostly from her childhood. Anyway, who was there to hear her sing old nursery rhymes and Beatles' songs?

Hours later, hands sore and aching by then, and no closer to opening the lock, she again retreated to the other side of her prison cell. She ate two more sandwiches—ham and Swiss in one and cheese and tomato in the other—as well as the banana.

She realized she was cold. She wished she wore a heavy coat instead of just a sweater, anything more than what she'd put on that morning. She almost always traveled with a cashmere sweater, because they were light but warm and took up very little space in a suitcase. When she packed for the trip, she'd promised herself she'd try to buy another one while in England, because they were cheaper there than at home. Yet, she was grateful she at least had this one with her. And the sleeping bag.

She kicked off her shoes and crawled into the bag to get warm. She'd tackle picking the lock again when she awoke. And maybe she wouldn't need to. Maybe someone would free her. Meanwhile she could sleep. After all, she hadn't slept much the night before. She thought of the other things she could be grateful for: the food and water, the flashlight, her purse.

That was all well and good, but she resented being locked up for God only knew how long. She wanted to tell whoever had done this that she'd gladly have given them the necklace if they just asked instead of leaving her in a locked room.

She wanted to shout, "I don't care who you are. Just let me out!"

Who were they, or him or her? All the people who might have wanted the necklace came into her mind: Philip, Elmore, Edward, Zach, but not her aunts, surely. Yet, those were her very own relatives. Relatives wouldn't do this to her, would they?

That left only Hugh. Once again, tears dribbled down her cheeks before she slept.

Chapter 13

When Sabrina awoke, she found the pitch blackness remained and had to train the flashlight on her watch to learn the time. Six o'clock. She lay still in the sleeping bag, hoping to doze off again, so she wouldn't be able to think about her predicament. That didn't happen.

She thought of Hugh. He wouldn't have done this to her, couldn't. Oh, how she wished now she had taken him up on his offer to stay in her hotel room that night. They would have had breakfast together, and even if someone had managed to slip a drug in her coffee—and how could they?—he'd have been there to take care of her until she came out of it.

Besides, she thought she'd fallen in love with him, and no one she loved could be so vile as to lock her up in a black dungeon for days. She'd already decided she was a good judge of character, and therefore she couldn't be so wrong about Hugh.

Yet, in that case, why hadn't she confided in him at the outset? First, probably the fact of so valuable a necklace coming into her possession so oddly had made her more than unusually suspicious. After all, nothing in her life so far had prepared her for such a mystery. Second, he had talked about the necklace, said he read about it in her grandfather's old letters. That could be true, but, since she couldn't read German herself, she had only his word for it that he read it there and not that he had plied her with that so-called information to get her to reveal she had the necklace.

On the other hand, he was not a relative and, except for the papers, had no prior knowledge of it, or its value or any claim to it. And, finally—and the impact of her next thought made her so excited she sat up in the bed—he was independently wealthy! He had no need to steal anything. He could no doubt buy a dozen such necklaces without jeopardizing his home in Belgravia, dismissing his man Leonard or causing a panic in the London stock market!

Why hadn't she thought of that before? Of course, she hadn't known of his wealth until two nights ago. By that time, she'd already made up her mind to tell no one of her find. As for the last time they were together, she had begun to care for him so much that she worried for his safety. If the person who wanted the necklace were to become violent—and at that time she didn't know he, she or they were as benevolent as they turned out to be—she didn't want Hugh to become a target.

The last time they were together, or rather, the time before that, they had lain on the chaise in her room and he had kissed her with intense desire. Her wanting him to take her to bed and make love to her played like a video in her head, and she closed her eyes and tried to imagine the rest of it. He'd have removed her clothes gently, sensuously, and she'd have helped him with his, marveling at the muscles in his upper arms and back, the taut abs. They'd have slipped into the hotel bed with its fresh clean-smelling sheets, and he'd have caressed her naked body while kissing her passionately. Then he'd have massaged her breasts, her inner thighs, bringing her to heights of desire, before beginning the ritual of entering her body, moving rhythmically, bringing her to a climax of ecstasy.

She didn't feel cold anymore.

Thinking wouldn't make that vision come true. She had to act. She crawled out of the sleeping bag and turned on the flashlight for a few moments. Everything looked the same as before. No magic genie had appeared in the middle of the night and transported her back to her hotel or even unlocked the door. The cold remained and she decided some warm-up exercises might help. Remembering the stretches and other exercises she'd done in her Pilates classes, she began to move, first slowly, then more rapidly, getting the circulation going. Arms up, arms down, reach for one side, then the other. She stretched her legs into various positions, then bent down to brush the floor with her fingertips several times.

Ten minutes later she felt better, ready to again tackle the job of escaping from her prison. First, breakfast. She ate the orange and apple, rolled the chair into position and inserted the nail file into the door lock. Click. The latch released.

She screamed. What had she been doing wrong all that time the day before? What did she do right now?

She had no idea, but she didn't care. She turned on the flashlight and looked at the door, turned the knob. It opened. She stood up, grasped the knob and tried to pull it toward her, but it stopped. She yanked as hard as she could, but the door refused to open more than a few inches. Something held it. What?

She directed the flashlight's beam into the crack and peered into it as well as she could. The doorknob on the other side was wrapped with a wire and attached to the wire was a thick piece of rope. Whatever held the rope refused to budge.

Although she couldn't squeeze through the opening even if she'd been all skin and bones like one of those anorexic teens or a victim of the Holocaust, she could at least see a tiny bit of what lay beyond the door. Another room, cavernous, echoing, but somewhat lighter than her dungeon, as if windows somewhere let in morning sunshine. She could also see a large pillar, around which the rope that held her door was wrapped and tied. A thick rope, tied to a thick wire wound around the doorknob. She might as well not have bothered to try to pick the lock. She was still trapped.

* * *

Hugh dragged himself from bed and bounded down the stairs to the kitchen. Leonard was preparing break-fast, a short white apron over his dark trousers, his jacket off, revealing white shirt sleeves.

"Good morning, sir," Leonard said.

"Have you heard anything? Did she call?"

"No, sir. Nothing. You know I'd have awakened you if she had."

"You wouldn't have had to wake me. I've barely slept."

Leonard stopped beating eggs in a small bowl and looked worried. "Is there anything I can do?"

"I wish there were. I tried everything yesterday, haunted the hotel, even went back to her bed-and-breakfast in case she returned, called almost every other hotel in the city. Unless she's using an assumed name, she isn't anywhere."

"Surely, sir, she's at Gilmore Manor then."

"I called there too, but no one has seen or heard from her."

"I'm sorry, sir, but people don't simply vanish."

"I even called the airlines thinking she might have gone home, but they have no record of her either."

"Her father in Chicago then."

"I don't know his address or telephone number."

"Perhaps the other relatives can provide it."

"You're right. That's a good idea. I find it hard to believe she would decide to rush home, but I can't afford to leave any stone unturned."

"You're very worried, aren't you?"

"Yes, I didn't tell you, but night before last, someone broke into her hotel room, and before that, her bed-and-breakfast."

"I say, that's very mysterious. Have you called the police?"

"My friend at Scotland Yard is looking into it for me. And checking hospitals and other hotels too."

Leonard put down his spatula. "Shall I lay out your clothes, sir?"

"You're a mind reader, Leonard. Yes, I have no appetite. I'll just take a shower and set out again."

While he showered, he replayed in his mind's eye the time they had lain on the chaise in her room, how much he wanted her then, but had decided to wait until after the dinner party. That way they would have had all night to make love, not a mere hour. Yet even an hour would have been better than nothing.

It was all his fault, not just deciding to postpone the moment, but, afterward, when they returned to find her room tossed. He should have stayed then. What a fool he'd been. She was upset and he had accused her of hiding something from him. Perhaps that explained why she ran away.

What if she didn't run away? What if something terrible had happened to her? He fought down the idea. He would find her if it was the last thing he ever did.

He drove the Jaguar to the hotel first and learned Sabrina hadn't been seen since breakfast the previous day. He asked if he might question the waiters, in case they noticed something suspicious. One, upon seeing the picture he had snapped at Trafalgar Square, admitted he had served her.

"And she was all right then?"

"I would say so."

"She sat alone? No one spoke to her?"

"No one. Oh, she had a telephone call, went into the passage to take it."

"Would you have any idea what that was about?"

"Oh, no, sir, but I do remember she didn't stay away very long. She was just heading in that direction when her food came up and I debated not putting it on the table lest it grow cold, but she was back again quicker than a wink. Like for a wrong number. So I brought her order to her."

Hugh thanked the young man and pondered the information: a telephone call so brief she was back at her table in seconds. What did it mean, if anything?

At Gilmore Manor, he met the same blank looks and negative answers as before. Sabrina's cousin Zach, who had disappeared soon after dinner two nights before, came bounding down the steps of the staircase to ask what all the fuss was about.

"I'm looking for Sabrina. She's been missing more than a day."

"That so? Maybe got a bloke on the side, good-looking bird like her."

Hugh, more frustrated than ever, wanted to punch him in the nose, but restrained himself. "I'm the only bloke she's seeing. She was to meet me yesterday morning and never turned up."

Zach tossed his long hair back, tucked his hands into his jeans pockets and put on a more serious expression. "Mystery, is it? Well, this old house might hold more than its share of mysteries. See those swords and battle-axes on the walls? Probably lots of knights got killed here in the old days, and ladies got carried off." He grinned.

Carried off was just what Hugh feared, but where and by whom? He should never have left her alone that night no matter what she said. He was certain she was hiding something, and now he was being proved right. In addition, whatever she knew had placed her in mortal danger. He slammed his fist down hard on the newel post.

"Feel free to look about," Zach said. "Maybe someone's hiding her in a dungeon. Except we don't have one of those here." He grinned again. "You're welcome to look in my rooms if you like. I've a studio up top, too." He waved a hand and headed off down the passage.

Hugh was tempted to search every room in the old house, but he'd come just to learn David Gilmore's address and telephone number in Chicago. Frances, who'd been running the Manor for many years and seemed as efficient as a spreadsheet, found it for him almost at once.

"You're welcome to call him from here, if you like. Before the telephones are shut off, in case Richard didn't pay the bill." She smiled. "We're all packing, as you see. Everything is quite a mess, but the bankers are getting anxious." She turned to leave, then reconsidered and said, "Mind the time difference. You don't want to wake the dear boy."

Hugh, figuring out the time in Chicago, picked up the telephone to make the call, but the line was being used. He recognized Elmore Manville's voice on an extension, so he put it down and went back to his car where he'd left his mobile phone. Connected finally, Hugh introduced himself, but Sabrina's father—whose voice showed very little of an American accent—declared he hadn't heard from her.

"I ought to have stayed there after my father's funeral, but I had an important obligation. I insisted Sabrina should go as well, for the reading of the will and to visit with her cousins. For once she agreed to take a holiday."

"Is there anyone else in London whom she might have gone to visit?"

"Not to my knowledge. I have no idea where she could be if not right there at the Manor or the hotel."

After promising to keep in touch, Hugh sat still, pondering his next move. Zach's having talked of dungeons in medieval houses made him wonder. Suppose Sabrina were locked in a dungeon? Not that any of her cousins had put her there, of course. But, suppose she'd been exploring this old place and accidentally opened a door to a hidden room and got herself locked in? These two-foot thick walls might muffle her calls for help. Or she might be incapacitated, knocked unconscious so she couldn't cry out. He chided himself over the preposterous idea, but stranger things had happened. He remembered a newspaper article about a man who'd been shot in the head with an arrow from a crossbow and not only lived to tell about it but walked into the doctor's office under his own steam.

What about this old house and its secrets? He'd been given access to all Richard's papers, some still stored there. Could one of them be a plan used in building it? Could there be secret staircases and hidden rooms? He should find out right away and at least cross that possibility off his list. The trunk in the attic, Richard had said, contained the "really ancient" stuff.

He started up the stairs and encountered Elmore rushing down. "I say, Mr. Manville," Hugh began, "I hope you won't mind if I look about."

"Sorry," Elmore said, "I really haven't time to talk now," and he hurried away.

Hugh shrugged and continued upstairs. Until he thought of something else, or the police or Leonard gave him news, this search was all he could do. He could only hope it would provide answers.

Chapter 14

Sabrina ate the last sandwiches and drank some water. With the light from the crack in the door, her prison became somewhat lighter than before, and she kept the flashlight turned off much of the time. However, her frustration and depression deepened. She'd worn her fingers into blisters trying to pick the lock—which miraculously yielded after a night's sleep, as if timed to do so—only to be met with rope and wire she couldn't possibly cut. Nothing in her cosmetics bag could handle that kind of work.

Or could it? She picked up the nail file again. Its pointy tip, which finally touched the right tumbler, or whatever lived inside key locks, had two rough sides. Could that surface, which whittled down her fingernails, saw through rope? The wire would be impossible, but the rope consisted only of fibers twisted together. The individual fibers were thin and easily breakable. What if she rubbed the sharper side of the nail file on it? Would that gradually cut through the rope? Maybe, but the rope was outside the door, between the doorknob and the pillar to which it was tied, and the space she could work in incredibly narrow.

Still, she must try. She rolled the chair to the door again and slipped her hand through the crack. She could just touch the rope. So far, so good. She withdrew her hand, grasped the nail file and slipped it through again. By holding the door open with her left hand as widely as she could, she kept the rope taut and vigorously rubbed the side of the nail file against it. After awhile her right arm began to ache and she stopped to give it a rest.

She aimed the flashlight at the rope to see if she'd succeeded in breaking any of the strands but couldn't tell. She stretched her arm, rubbed her shoulders and then started in once more. She sang aloud again, using the rhythm of a song her mother used to hum, along with the rhythm of her sawing motion against the rope.

"I will survive..." She sawed aggressively. "I will survive..." And she sawed some more.

When she thought her arm was numb and about to fall off, she again trained the flashlight into the crack. The rope was definitely fraying. If she just kept on, this might work.

For the next hour she alternately sawed at the rope with her nail file and massaged her arm and shoulder. She even tried switching hands, but even if she'd been ambidextrous, it didn't work. The door opened to the left so only her right arm was in a position to do the job.

Some time after it grew dark even in the room beyond her prison, she lost her grip on the nail file. It fell with a tiny "clink" onto the concrete floor on the other side of the door. She stooped down and tried to retrieve it, lay on her stomach and pushed her entire arm through the opening, but the file remained just out of reach. She screamed out loud, and tears coursed down her face as they always did when she was angry or frustrated, and this time she was both. Then she crawled in the sleeping bag and repeated every curse word she knew. She'd have stayed awake longer, except, her vocabulary never that picturesque, she ran out of words and gave up.

* * *

After a fitful night, Sabrina awoke, trained the flashlight beam on her watch face and saw the hands pointing to only a little past four in the morning. She lay still in the sleeping bag, thinking of Hugh, wondering what he might be doing.

They made plans to meet and she didn't show up. Did he worry, or had he forgotten her already? The thought he might not care that she'd disappeared made her angry and kept her from going back to sleep. She decided it was still too early to get up, but what did it matter since, day or night, her world remained almost totally dark and she had nothing better to do than try to escape? Her thoughts flew to the problem of the night before: how to retrieve her nail file and saw through the rope holding her prison door from opening.

She was tired of being alone, angry at whoever had done this to her and frustrated by her helplessness. She was also hungry and out of food. What if the kidnappers never returned with more? She didn't like to think she'd be found there months from then, shriveled into a skeleton. Even if they did return before that happened, might they decide to kill her rather than risk she could identify them later?

She had to escape first. She left the bed and drank some water, deciding that, even without food, she might live for days, maybe weeks, as long as the water held out. But she would give a year of her life for some toothpaste and a brush just then. She exercised her cramped muscles, then tried once more to stretch her arm through the crack of the open door and reach the nail file. As her arms had not mysteriously lengthened during the night, she still couldn't reach it.

She remembered a scene from a film in which a character used a piece of paper slipped under a door to retrieve a key, but she had no paper firm enough to do the job. Wait, maybe she did. She carried a pocket calendar with pages she could tear out. Would that work? Then a better idea came along. She went to the cardboard box which held the rest of her provisions and pulled out the bag which had contained potato chips. Composed of sturdy paper, coated and slick, with, perhaps, enough salt or oil on the inside, the nail file might stick to it.

She tore the bag open, folded it inside out and pressed it flat. Then she lay on her stomach again and slid her makeshift device out toward the nail file. There, she touched it. There, she just pushed it farther away.

She forced herself not to scream or cry again. She must find a way that didn't involve having to retrieve the file. She went back to her purse, but nothing else there or in her cosmetics bag contained a sharp enough edge to finish cutting through the rope on the door. A small mirror once lived in that bag, one whose edges, if broken, might have been able to cut through the rope, but not anymore. She must have left it on the counter in the hotel bathroom. Still, perhaps she had something almost as good.

She pulled out her lipstick and removed the cap. At the open end, the edges of the metal case were smooth. But maybe she could roughen them, make them sharp. Once, a long time ago, when she'd broken a nail and had no file with her, she rubbed her fingernail along a concrete sidewalk and smoothed it. Now, she rubbed the end of the lipstick case cover against the concrete floor of her cell. Felt it. Yes, she'd made it rough. She tilted the cap and scraped it furiously against the floor. Success. The edges now seemed quite rough and sharp. Sharp enough to cut the rope? She could only try.

* * *

Hugh spread out the blueprints on the floor and studied them. Not, he noted, an architect's design for the building of the Manor. Had there ever been such a thing, it perished long ago, or he had not stumbled across it yet. However, what he did discover looked almost as good. Someone had done a floor plan of the house in the nineteenth century when they wired it for electricity, and it showed no dungeons or even hidden rooms. So much for that idea.

He left the blueprint where he'd found it, in a large

trunk which reminded him of the one Sabrina inherited. Hers was smaller and resided in the old nursery. This trunk was far too large to be moved, at least by him, but he decided to transfer some of the other papers to his house where he could examine them at leisure. He found a cardboard box in the corner, removed the broken lamp it contained and filled it with papers and documents from the trunk, taking it downstairs where he transferred it to his car.

His hope of finding a clue to Sabrina's whereabouts remained strong, and he had no desire to study the old papers just yet. Time for that later if she'd run off with the "bloke" Zach hinted of.

He sat back on his heels and thought about that. Sabrina couldn't have run off with anyone. She cared for him just as he cared for her. He knew it. They came close to making love, and his instincts told him she wanted it as much as he did. He'd gained a fair amount of knowledge about women by then, and this one was not only beautiful and intelligent, but sincere, outspoken and honest.

Hmmm. Perhaps that "honest" assessment needed to be rethought. He felt certain she had lied to him, or, at the least, withheld information. He didn't believe her rooms were broken into twice through coincidence. She knew something, or more likely, *had* something that someone else wanted. Her disappearance was also no coincidence. Somehow he had to find her and solve the mystery before she was hurt or killed. Because, no matter what the circumstances, he wanted her in his life.

Chapter 15

The rope frayed under the onslaught of the metal being scraped against it, and Sabrina worked like a demon, aware time was running out and she must escape before something worse happened. Her hands now close to bleeding, the lipstick cap slipped from her fingers, clanked on the floor and rolled away out of sight.

She was too tired, too angry and too frustrated to scream or even cry. She could think of only one thing left to do. Her body shaking, she stood up and pulled off her sweater. Wrapping the ends of the sleeves around her hands, she grasped the door knob with both of them, braced her feet against the wall at the side of the door and pulled with all her might. The final strands of the rope broke, the door flew open and she went tumbling backward, cracking her head first on the chair and then the floor. She lay still for a moment, assessing her body for damage. The back of her head hurt like crazy, but her arms and legs appeared intact. No broken bones. Free at last.

Well, not totally free: the open space beyond the

room she'd been locked in became another prison from which she had to escape. She rose from the floor, put her sweater back on and stuffed everything back in her purse. With the purse strap over her shoulder and the flashlight in her hand, she stepped out of the room. She surveyed the broken rope, picked up her nail file and now-ruined lipstick case and looked around.

She stood in what appeared to be an abandoned warehouse or manufacturing plant. Easily twenty feet above her, the ceiling held exposed pipes and wiring and, as it was now after six o'clock, high windows on two walls let in early daylight. She walked around the gigantic space, noting, in addition to bits of wire and lengths of rope, empty boxes of both cardboard and wood. At the far end, huge double doors no doubt led to a street beyond, but pushing on them didn't work. They were probably locked and chained from outside. She'd freed herself from one prison only to be trapped in another.

Still, she wouldn't give up so easily. She felt powerful now. If she could do the one, she could do the other. She did have one advantage on her side. Never expecting her to escape from the smaller room, her captors surely didn't expect she could get out of this one and probably took no extraordinary measures, except for chaining the outer doors, to keep her from doing so.

The windows presented her only hope. She set down her purse and flashlight and dragged one of the larger wooden boxes over to the wall under one of the windows. She stretched her leg as high as she could and managed to climb up on the box. Not high enough.

Another box. Sweating and straining, she managed to lift it onto the other one, tearing a hole in her sweater in the process. She climbed up again, then climbed onto the top box. She could reach the window. The latch opened with a screech, letting in a blast of cold air, but, although the opening seemed large enough for her to climb through, it loomed too high above to enable her to get to it. Another box. This time, she left the flashlight behind but threw the straps of her handbag over her shoulder again, not wanting to have to do the climbing any more than necessary.

Holding a smaller wooden box in her hands, she managed to climb on the first box once more, then placed the third one on top of the second and climbed up. She looked down for a moment and felt dizzy. Best not to do that. Hoping the boxes wouldn't topple and she wouldn't lose her balance, she leaned forward and made the steep climb to the top box. Opened the window. Looked out. Below her ran a narrow alley in front a vacant field. No people or cars.

She hoped to see someone so she could call for help, but apparently it was too early, even if anyone ever walked down that alley or crossed that open field.

She looked down, wondering how, assuming she could climb out through the window, she'd ever reach the ground. No accommodating wooden crates sat against the wall outside the building, no fire escape, no trees. She remained as trapped as before.

Then she heard noise, voices. Across the empty field three young boys with backpacks ran and shouted, cuffed one another playfully, apparently on their way to school. She screamed. Yelled three more times, waving and screaming from the window. They saw her and ran over to the building.

"What you doing?" one boy called up.

"I'm trapped in here," she shouted down. "Can you help me get out?"

"I dunno," said a larger boy, tugging at the cap over his longish blond hair. "That's awful high."

Sabrina remembered her purse. "I'll give you each five pounds if you can get me down."

Smiles crossed every young face. "Me dad's got a ladder," the tallest one said. "I live just over there." He pointed. "I'll get it." He dropped his backpack on the ground and ran off before she could say any more.

"How'd you get up there, lady?" another boy asked.

She decided to play on children's love of games and intrigue. "My friends locked me in as a joke. And if I get out before they come back, I'll win the game."

"Cool." They smiled, obviously enjoying being part of something like a payback scheme.

"Are you on your way to school?" she asked.

"No'm. It's summer hols. But we didn't pass the term, so we go to a tutor three days to catch us up."

The boy with the ladder appeared, and they all joined in placing it against the side of the building. However, it didn't reach high enough to do the job, unless she could get out of the window and then stretch for the top rung with her feet. She had no choice. She must try.

"Hold the ladder steady, will you?"

"Yes, ma'am." They grabbed it and braced their feet.

Sabrina turned around and put first one leg and then the other out of the window, backward, leaning against the sill to support her weight. Then, inch by inch, she slid down until at the last, she clung to the sill with her sore fingers. Pain shot up her hands and arms. She'd fall.

"Only a couple inches," the ladder-owning boy shouted. "You can do it."

She turned her head and looked down at the ladder. It seemed close. She stretched, felt her shoe hit the top rung, then let go and slid along the side of the building, her body scraping the jagged bricks.

The boys whooped and hollered. While they shouted encouragement, she searched for handholds in the grout between bricks and lowered one foot toward the next lower rung, then another. At last she leaned down, clutched the sides of the ladder and climbed the rest of the way.

Standing on the alley pavement, her legs shivered, and her voice trembled. "Thank you, thank you." She opened her purse and gave them the promised money. "You mustn't tell anyone, you know. Otherwise the joke's off."

"We won't," they promised.

"You'd better return the ladder and then get to school. I'm sorry I've made you late."

"Oh, that's all right, ma'am. We're the only ones she tutors. Can't start without us." He laughed.

Before they could run off again, she thought of something else. "Is there a taxi stand somewhere?"

The taller boy pointed. "On the street over there is some shops. A shop owner might call a taxi for you."

She thanked him and hurried across the field toward the street he'd indicated. She glanced down at her clothes. Her sweater sported more than one hole in it by then, and even her blouse and pants showed scrapes and dirt. Heaven only knew what her face and hair looked like. She could put on some of the lipstick that helped her get loose, but why bother when the rest of her appearance fairly shrieked, "refugee"?

The first shop contained a bakery and, after asking a middle-aged woman with frizzy gray hair if she would call a taxi for her, she bought a chocolate croissant and wolfed it down. She kept her remaining pound notes handy, and, when the taxi arrived, showed them to the driver just in case he doubted a person who looked so scruffy could afford the fare.

The hotel doorman also gave her a shocked look, and, as she entered the lobby, she gave one of her own to the man who rushed toward her. Hugh.

Chapter 16

The next thing she knew, Hugh's arms enveloped her and he was hugging her, kissing her and saying her name over and over. Finally he held her at arms' length and said in a husky voice, "You're alive."

She managed a smile. "Almost. But I need a bath before I decide."

He escorted her to the elevator, and, there being no one else inside, kissed her again. Once in her room, he wanted to know everything that had happened, but she headed for the bathroom, promising to tell him after she showered. She took clean clothes, including another pair of pants and a blouse into the bathroom with her and asked him to call room service and order breakfast.

"Something gigantic, with tons of sugar and fat."

When she came out twenty minutes later, she saw the "gigantic" meal spread out on a table in front of the chaise. Two plates with silver covers, plus a basket of assorted rolls, glasses of orange juice, and a pot of coffee took up the entire table top, and Hugh ushered her to the chaise and sat next to her.

"I hadn't had breakfast myself," he told her. "I

haven't been able to muster an appetite since you disappeared."

"How did you happen to be here just now?"

"I've practically lived here for the past three days. After all, your clothes were still in the room and you hadn't checked out. I spent so much time here I think they suspect me of casing the place to steal jewels like some Hollywood caper film."

His use of the word "jewels" caused a momentary flutter in the pit of Sabrina's stomach, but then she decided it was hunger and took the cover off her plate. Eggs, crisp bacon, potatoes, even hot cakes, filled every inch. She took a forkful of the eggs, thinking about what else he'd said, about haunting the hotel hoping for her return.

That and the way he kissed her in the lobby—in front of God and everybody, a most unlikely thing for a British gentleman to do—gave her a happy sensation. He did care for her.

"You must tell me everything," he said.

Between bites of food and swallows of hot coffee, she did. Beginning with finding the necklace in the first place. She determined not to hold back anything any more. She had managed to escape from her kidnappers through her own efforts, but the puzzle of the necklace in the doll still haunted her, and she didn't want to do anything more on her own.

Hours had passed, and the breakfast tray removed before she finally finished her story and answered all of Hugh's questions.

"We have to call the police," he said when she

finished.

"I suppose so." She rose from the chaise and went to the closet.

"Someone kidnapped you. Don't you see how serious that is? You might have been killed."

She returned from the closet with another sweater. "Actually, I don't think so. It seems to me those thieves were terribly amateurish."

"Just because you managed to outwit them...."

"One of them was a woman. I heard her voice before I blacked out. She probably provided the food and water, the sleeping bag and flashlight."

"You said you'd run out of food, and no one came to bring you more."

"They might have been planning to come today, but I got away first."

"Nevertheless...."

"They left my purse and took none of my money. They only wanted the necklace."

"But if it's as valuable as you say it is, that's grand larceny, and the police need to hunt them down and get it back." He stood and paced the floor, running his hands through his hair.

"The necklace wasn't mine to begin with, even if I did find it in my doll."

"Nor does it belong to whoever has it now. Remember those letters I read?"

"They indicated it was stolen from Count de Villot when the Nazis occupied Paris. How my grandfather happened to get hold of it is still a mystery, but, after all these years, I doubt Mr. de Villot masterminded my kidnapping and the theft."

Hugh stopped his pacing to stand in front of her. "You're right. If the Count, or his family, knew your grandfather had the necklace at the Manor, surely they would have done something about it a long time ago."

"Plus we don't even know for sure that the necklace I found is the same one mentioned in the letters."

"That's something I happen to believe. For your grandfather to have letters indicating the theft of a valuable necklace, and then just such a necklace—but not that one—shows up in his very own house, is too much of a coincidence." He paused. "About on the same level as your rooms being broken into twice for no good reason."

She shrugged. He had a point.

"So we must call the police." He took her hand in his. "Don't worry. I have a friend at Scotland Yard. He's been looking for you too, by the way, and he'll be very discreet. Nothing will get into the newspapers, but they know how to do these things. Trust me."

"I do trust you, but just remember, your friend hadn't found me in three days."

"That reminds me. You'd better call your father. I told him you were missing."

"You called him?"

"I needed to know if you'd gone back home."

Sabrina picked up the phone on the desk and then replaced the receiver almost at once. It was too early in Chicago and she didn't want to wake him. Besides, that could wait.

"In the first place, I don't believe my life is in danger

or ever was. Call your friend at Scotland Yard if you like. I can't stop you if you insist, but I'm not confident they'll succeed."

"Don't underestimate them."

"I don't. I read mystery novels. Inspector Lynley is a marvelous detective."

"Your joking aside, Scotland Yard can contact all the pawn shops and fences in London, and, if the thieves try to sell the necklace, they'll be caught."

"But suppose they don't try to sell it. What then?"

"What else would they do with it: let the woman who spoke to you wear it to the opera?"

"While your friend and his police force are keeping an eye on pawn shops and fences, as well as whatever else they come up with, I intend to do some sleuthing of my own."

"I think you've read too many detective novels."

"You read them yourself. You told me the other day."

Hugh took her hand again and pulled her to the chaise, then forced her to sit and took his own place close to her. "You admit the necklace doesn't belong to you, and now it's gone. So far as you're concerned, the case is closed."

"No, I must find out who kidnapped me, what happened to the necklace and, not incidentally, clear my grandfather's name."

"Even if I thought that was a good idea, sleuthing can wait a little while, can it not?" He put his arms around her and kissed her.

The trauma of the past few days evaporated under

his touch, and she held him close, enjoying the taste of his lips and the faint scent of cologne lingering on his clothes.

"Sabrina, my sweet," he murmured against her hair. "The other day...."

She remembered the day he meant vividly, thought of it often while locked up. She could almost feel his lips on her flesh and hear the pounding of her heart all over again.

He pressed forward again as he had before, but this time she resisted. Not because, as before, they'd been invited to a dinner party, but because her thoughts kept reverting to her recent ordeal. Three days of captivity, with adrenaline pumping through her body, couldn't be erased so suddenly. She'd been traumatized, and that changed her, maybe forever. Lovemaking required calm, romantic moments, and she felt anything but calm right then. She couldn't make love to him when her mind was still in turmoil. Not that men understood that. Perhaps she'd never make love to him at all. Perhaps she needed to think more of her own needs in the future. Feeling close to death had a way of doing that to you. She pushed him back and stood, trying to find the right words to convince him.

"I can't. Not now. I have to go back and find out who did this to me and what they've done with the necklace. Now, while time is on my side."

He shrugged and rose from the chaise. "You win. But you're not going to do it alone. I don't intend to let you out of my sight again. Where do we start?"

She smiled, glad he capitulated. "We need to go back

to the warehouse, or whatever it was where they hid me."

"The warehouse? Why there?"

"I want to see if someone comes to bring food or let me out."

"You are out."

"Of course, but if we go there, we may see someone coming or going and then we'll know who they are."

"Can you find it again?"

"I remember the name of the bakery shop on the next street. The name appeared on the front window and the owner was a lovely elderly lady who phoned a taxi for me. If we find that, we'll be close."

She went to the desk and picked up the telephone directory, turning to the business pages. "Here it is, 'McDonald's Muffins.'"

"Didn't I read that McDonald's in the U.S. tried to stop people from using the name?"

"That's why I remembered it. I believe the company lost the case."

Laughing, Hugh took her in his arms and kissed her. "I love it."

Sabrina noted that he'd said he loved *it,* not *her,* but had no time to dwell on it. She broke away and grabbed her handbag once more, heading for the door. "Let's begin."

"Perhaps I should go alone. Surely this is too dangerous for you."

"You just said you wouldn't let me out of your sight."

"You're right. I can't have you disappear on me

again."

"Besides, you need me. We'll talk about it in the car on the way. You do have your car, don't you?"

Apparently, either realizing he couldn't trust her to stay locked in the hotel room, or that she was right and he needed her, he escorted her to the door and they left the room.

* * *

Hugh seemed to know exactly how to get to the McDonald's Muffins' street and he stopped in front of the little bakery. "Where now?"

"Circle the block." She pointed. "The building we want is in that alley behind the empty lot."

"Alley? We don't have alleys."

"What do you call narrow roads between the backs of houses?"

"You mean *mews*." He followed her directions and turned in. "I'd call this a street or a lane."

"Whatever."

He drove slowly and she leaned her head out the car window. "There it is. See, that's the window I climbed out of. It's still open."

He stopped the car.

"Don't stop." She grabbed his arm. "This Jaguar is far too conspicuous. Park somewhere else."

"I'd park on the next street, but I don't see any place where we could observe the building without being seen."

"Then park up the, er, mew aways, just close enough

so we can see if someone goes in or out of those big doors."

He stopped the Jaguar again and turned off the engine. Silence settled around them. Nothing and no one stirred.

"We may be too late," Hugh said. "Perhaps they've come and gone already."

"It's possible, but I want to wait a little longer."

"We may be in for a long vigil." He paused. "So, tell me what's in that charming head of yours now."

"As I said before, I want to see who locked me up."

"Someone who wanted the necklace very badly."

"Depending, of course, on who really stole it."

"What do you mean?"

"Well, all the time I had the necklace, I wondered if anyone else in the family knew about it and might try to get it back."

"You suspect your own aunts, uncles and cousins?"

"They're the ones who live in the house, aren't they? They had access to all the rooms, including the attic and that trunk. Penelope may even have played with my doll after I'd returned to the States."

"You think she put the necklace inside?"

"It's possible. You know the trunk contained toys and dress-up clothes. She might have thought it was a play necklace, fake jewels instead of real ones."

"But if she played with it, why sew it up in the doll?"

She didn't answer, and he continued. "Your cousin Penelope's a woman. Was it her voice you heard before you lost consciousness?"

"No. Penelope's gone to good schools, she's one of

your upper class types. The voice I heard belonged to someone else, someone with a slight accent."

"Cockney?"

"I don't think so. Anyway, not Penelope. Maybe someone else, long after Penelope stopped playing with any of those things."

"Who else do you suspect?"

"Unfortunately, it could be almost anyone else. You know as well as I do that they're hurting for money. The Manor is about to be lost in foreclosure. If someone found the necklace and learned of its value, he or she might try to get it back and save the mansion from the bank. They all live there and they don't want to be required to move."

"Still, you're their cousin. If they thought you had it, why wouldn't they just ask you to give it back?"

"First, I might lie and say I never saw it. They couldn't prove otherwise."

She squirmed in the seat, trying to be comfortable while keeping an eye on the warehouse doors. "Second, they don't know me that well. It's been almost twenty years since my visit here, and I was a child then. For all they know I've become involved with Chicago gangsters or drug dealers."

Hugh laughed out loud. "You?"

She grinned. "You happen to like me, but that doesn't mean they do."

"I can't imagine anyone in your family not liking you."

"Except for my grandfather, you didn't know them, and he had already become senile by the time you met him. Frankly, some of them seem a very lazy lot, depending on Richard to support them in luxury."

She warmed to the subject. "Elmore has a job, but look at Uncle Philip. He's upset because he should have inherited the property, and now he won't get it. If he had the money from selling the necklace, he could pay off the mortgage and stay where he is."

"Philip is getting on in years. What are you saying?"

"Okay he's a little old for this cloak and dagger stuff, but he could have hired someone." She had another idea and turned her head for a moment. "His son Edward never seems to hold onto a job and sounded very resentful that he'd have to leave the Manor and try to make it on his own."

"I still say...."

"And then there's Zach, another freeloader, with grungy looks and a band that probably spends whatever cash they earn on drinks and women. He's built himself a music studio in the Manor that he hates to give up. Besides, his mother has nowhere else to go."

"You make a compelling case, and if it were anyone else but your very own cousins, I'd agree."

"I know what you mean. Actually I hate the idea that one of them might be behind my kidnapping, but look at it this way. They made sure I wasn't hurt and that I had food and water."

Hugh rolled down the window on his side and leaned one arm on the frame. "You know, there's something else we need to consider. So far you've just talked about them wanting to recover the necklace so they can sell it and use the proceeds to save the Manor.

What if someone wants to keep the money for himself?"

Before she could answer, Sabrina saw a man approach the doors of the warehouse.

Chapter 17

Sabrina let out a tiny gasp and Hugh gripped her arm. "Don't move," he said. "Just watch."

The man, wiry, medium height, dressed in dark clothes and a knitted cap, held a plastic bag in one hand. He bent over the padlock holding the warehouse doors closed and opened it with a key. He released the chain, and then, with a last look around, entered the building.

"Did you see him?" Hugh asked. "Is it anyone you recognize?"

"He was too far away and only turned for a second."

"Then we'll wait until he comes out."

Frustrated, she groaned. "But from this distance, I can't tell who he is. We'll have to get closer."

"I don't see how. There's no shelter for us to hide in to observe him. And we don't want him to see us."

"We have to think of something, and right now. Once he discovers I've gone, he'll probably come right back out again."

"We could bring the car up closer, I suppose."

"No, don't."

"What if we get out and stand nearer the door?"

"Then he'd see us."

"What if we pretend we're lovers out for a stroll?" He gestured, palms raised. "When he comes out, we'll go into a clinch so he can't see our faces."

"But I need to see *his* face."

"Trust me, this will work." Hugh exited the car, closing the door silently, not letting the lock catch, and helped Sabrina to get out the same way. He pulled off his coat and tie, threw them into the back seat and mussed his hair. Catching on to his idea, Sabrina removed her sweater, throwing that into the back seat as well, opened three of the buttons closing her blouse and pulled the tails out of the waistband of her slacks.

"That's better. Now hang onto me as if I'm the hottest thing since Colin Firth."

Sabrina stifled her giggles, thinking he was *hotter* than Colin Firth and then mussed up her own hair. Arms around each other, they zig-zagged up the street, pausing now and then to kiss. Each kiss made her heart pound and her knees weak, but she forced herself to keep an eye on the warehouse in between.

They'd almost reached the entrance when the double doors opened and the man came out, a ski mask over his face. He no longer held the plastic bag, but, apparently seeing the amorous pair in the street, reached up with one hand and pulled up the ski mask. Once again it resembled a knitted cap.

Hugh clutched Sabrina to him, turning her so that, if she leaned over his shoulder, she could see the man's face. He kissed her cheeks, ears and neck in quick succession, while at the same time moaning loudly as if in the midst of passion.

The man didn't watch them for long. He turned, pulled the padlock into place and closed the hasp. Then he hurried across the vacant field and walked quickly down the next street.

When the man moved out of earshot, Hugh said, "Did you recognize him? Who is he?"

Sabrina lingered a few moments in Hugh's arms. His kisses had been delightfully demanding, his mouth warm on her skin. She wanted it to go on a lot longer and almost began to wish she hadn't been so hasty back in the hotel room.

Reality intruded. "I'm not sure. He looks sort of familiar, but I can't think where I saw him before."

Hugh pulled her across the vacant lot, obviously intent on following the kidnapper. "While you're trying to puzzle it out, let's see where he goes."

Sabrina stumbled along after him. "Don't get too close."

"I won't. He's already forgotten about us. He's in a hurry to go somewhere else."

They walked for two blocks, into a section of row houses which appeared worn out and dilapidated, but might have looked better a century or two earlier. Most showed no yards in front, just dirt, broken bricks and the occasional rusted bicycle.

Other people inhabited the street, going to and from shops or their jobs, small children played noisily on the crumbling steps, and Sabrina and Hugh tried to keep their quarry in sight without getting too close.

Finally the man stopped in front of one of the

houses, where another man greeted him. They spoke together, both looking grim and concerned, and then split up, the first man going in one direction and the second in another.

"Do you recognize that one?" Hugh asked.

"No, I don't think so."

"Which one shall we follow? We can't trail both."

"Yes, we can. You do the ski mask one and I'll do the other." She started off.

He grabbed her arm and pulled her back. "No, you don't. You're not going anywhere without me. Do you want to be kidnapped again?"

She shivered at the remembrance of her ordeal. "No, but—"

"We'll follow the one you recognize."

Yet, when she looked up, both men had disappeared as if swallowed up in a non-existent pea-soup London fog. They hurried ahead anyway, glancing between houses, all the way to the next corner. They saw no one who looked like either man.

"Damn." Hugh punched his fist into his other hand.

Sabrina tried to keep her annoyance out of her voice, but wasn't sure she succeeded. "You should have let me follow one of them."

Hugh walked her back to the car. "We'll tell the police. They'll find them."

Sabrina only groaned.

"The one you think you might have seen before: he's not a relative or someone who came to the reading of your grandfather's will?"

"Definitely not an uncle or cousin, and I doubt very

much he was at the reading of the will. One of us would have remembered him."

"So much for that idea. We're no further into solving this puzzle than before."

Dejected, Sabrina sank into the passenger seat of the Jaguar and tried to think of everywhere she'd been since arriving in London. Quickly deciding she needn't go that far back, she thought only of everywhere since she found the necklace.

A memory sparked. "The necklace. When I took it to the jeweler for an appraisal, I saw another man besides Mr. Kendall, the shop owner. He stayed in the back, except he looked at me through the curtains."

"What man? The one we just saw?"

"Yes, the same large ears, and eyes that slant down at the corners. When I went back to pick up the necklace the next day, the jeweler told me he fired him and hired a different assistant."

"Where is this jeweler?"

"In Bayswater Street, a short distance from the bed-and-breakfast where I stayed at the time."

"Let's talk to him."

Grateful to be doing something to solve the mystery, Sabrina looked over at Hugh and smiled. "I'm sorry I sounded a little, er, miffed back then."

"You have a right to be, but I think your safety is more important than tracking two men who may have nothing whatever to do with the stolen necklace."

Sabrina pondered the possibility while Hugh drove toward Bayswater Street, and she put on her sweater, rebuttoned her blouse and tucked it in. Although now late afternoon, the jeweler's shop remained open.

Kendall recognized her. "Miss Gilmore, is it not?"

"You remember me."

"Remembering names and faces is good for business." He smiled. "But in this case, you visited my shop only a few days ago."

"And with a very valuable object," Sabrina added.

Kendall's smile faded. "Let me apologize once again for the delay in returning it to you. You have it safe and secure now, do you not?"

"Unfortunately no," Hugh said. "That's why we're here."

Kendall gestured them to the chairs in front of the jewelry display counter and pulled up a small stool for himself on the other side. "How may I help you?"

Sabrina paused, thinking of her recent ordeal, but decided to tell him only the necessary facts.

"The man who worked for you—the one you told me you let go——I think he's involved in stealing the necklace from me."

"The necklace has been stolen? I say, that's most unfortunate. I'm terribly sorry to hear it."

"You told me at the time," Sabrina continued, "his dismissal had nothing to do with your not being able to return the necklace to me the following day, as you promised."

"True. Bert—that's his name—only worked for me for a few weeks. He didn't have any experience with gems, but he was young and I expected to teach him everything necessary for doing his work."

"Surely," Hugh said, "you wouldn't hire just anyone

to work with jewels which might be worth thousands of pounds?"

"Certainly not. He gave references. He'd been engaged by a very fine family, but they had to let him go because of a financial setback."

"Still, you did fire him."

"He hung about with some unsavory looking companions, couldn't seem to understand the necessity of coming in on time and used the telephone for personal calls too frequently."

"So this had nothing to do with the necklace being missing for a day?"

"I don't believe so, although he might be guilty of putting it in the wrong place overnight. Unless, of course, I did that myself. As I recall, I had a great deal of work to do at the time, and, in my haste to close the shop, I may have been the one who misplaced it."

"Does Bert have a last name, an address?" Hugh asked.

"I believe I still have it. That would be in my files." Kendall rose from the stool, parted the curtains to the back room and disappeared for a few minutes. He returned with a small slip of paper on which he'd written a full name and address.

"Thank you." Sabrina took the paper and tucked it into her purse. "You've been very helpful."

"My pleasure. Call upon me again if I may be of further assistance. I do hope you can recover your property. I assume you contacted the police."

"Yes," Hugh answered. "The police have been notified."

"Then good day and good luck."

Back in the Jaguar, Hugh suggested dinner, but Sabrina rejected it. "We must go to this address and find Bert, and the sooner the better. He's already had almost three days to dispose of the necklace. He may even have sold it by now."

"But we still have no proof Bert kidnapped you or stole anything."

"I don't care. We have to find him." She pulled the paper from her purse and read off the address.

Hugh sighed and started the car.

The building they stopped before appeared even more rundown, if possible, than the buildings in front of which they'd last seen Bert.

A surly landlady assured them Bert didn't live there "no more. 'e left owin' rent. If you're a friend of 'is, you can pay it back for 'im now, there's a good chap."

"No," said Hugh, "we're not friends. In fact, he owes us money as well."

"I wish you luck then, dearie."

Nevertheless, she refused to allow them to look in the room he'd occupied, saying another prospective tenant was due to inspect it at any moment.

Hugh's smile, along with a ten-pound note, changed her mind, but she gave them only five minutes. "You won't find nuthin' there though. I cleaned up after 'im."

They climbed the filthy stairs, which reeked of tobacco smoke and urine, and went into a tiny room with one curtainless window, iron cot, washstand and battered chest of drawers. Sabrina tackled the drawers, gingerly pulling the handles to slide them out and look inside, wishing she wore those latex gloves investigators used on television crime shows. Meanwhile Hugh checked the cot, bravely pulling the mattress off to look underneath. Nothing.

Sabrina stooped to look under the bed but saw only dust elephants. So much for the landlady's cleaning.

They surveyed the room one last time and then Hugh went to a wastebasket almost hidden in the corner near the bed. He dumped out the contents on the floor and poked through it with the toe of his shoe. Empty food cartons, cigarette butts, a disgusting-looking crumpled piece of something that might be toilet paper, and a matchbook with writing on the inside.

Before Hugh could pick up the matchbook, Sabrina stopped him, took a facial tissue from her purse, and suggested he use that to pick it up. He held the item out and Sabina saw what appeared to be a telephone number.

Closing the tissue around the matchbook, she put it in the outside pocket of her purse and they left.

"Now may we have dinner?" Hugh asked. "I'm famished. We haven't eaten a bite since breakfast."

"That could qualify as brunch, if not lunch." She yawned. "Well all right, although for some reason I'm not hungry. I'm just awfully tired."

"You must keep me company at least."

All the time they drove, Sabrina yawned, the lack of restful sleep during the two nights before apparently finally catching up with her. Hugh let a valet park his car and they entered a restaurant named Le Bistro, which Sabrina figured probably was French for, "prices like a small yacht."

She yawned through the shrimp course and then nibbled on medallions of pork in a divine sauce. Hugh talked and she listened, only occasionally mustering energy to add a comment. Finally they retrieved the car and drove back to the hotel, Sabrina nodding off to sleep once or twice on the way.

Entering her room, Hugh said, "I want you to pack a few things, and then we'll go to my flat."

"I have to call my father." She sat on the side of the bed and picked up the phone on the end table beside it. She spoke to him only briefly, having no desire to give the details of her kidnapping and make him worry.

"It was just a little misunderstanding, Daddy. I'm fine, really. Listen, I'll call you tomorrow and tell you all about it. Bye. Love you."

Hugh, who had moved away, but apparently heard every word she said anyway, came to her side. "This is not some little misunderstanding, Sabrina. This is serious. Your life may still be in danger."

"Didn't your nanny teach you not to eavesdrop?" She replaced the phone and yawned again. "Anyway, even if that were true, what good would it do to tell my father? What could he do about it when he's so far away? Besides, he has no credentials to play detective."

"Nevertheless, you can't stay here alone. You must come with me."

Sabrina stretched out on the bed. "No, I can't do that. I'm much too tired, and I'll be perfectly fine right here." She closed her eyes.

* * *

Hugh stared down at her for a long time. She was asleep already. The poor thing had been through a terrible ordeal and deserved to recover. He couldn't force her to get up, pack, and go to his flat. He wouldn't even wake her so she could take off her clothes. And although tempted—his pulse skipping at the thought of seeing her no doubt exquisite naked body—he didn't allow himself to do it for her. Instead, he slipped her shoes off her feet, pulled the bed quilt over her and removed one of the two pillows, throwing it on the chaise. Next he put the night chain on the door, turned off the lights, slipped off his own shoes and settled down to sleep on the chaise.

What a woman! He couldn't believe his luck finding someone beautiful, intelligent and so resourceful she escaped from a terrifying situation unharmed. He could think of no woman he'd ever known who combined such qualities.

However, she was American. Did that have anything to do with it? Were all American women so fearless, confident, and, yes, audacious? Perhaps they were. After all, Americans left England, and many other countries, in order to build their own society free from restraints. They'd built a nation which was the envy of the world, with the highest standard of living, yet they were a compassionate people. Citizens of no other country responded to tragic events elsewhere faster than they did. Let an earthquake, fire or flood occur somewhere and Americans leapt into action, sending money, food and supplies, even their own firefighters and doctors, to help the victims. Yet perhaps, because of those very qualities, she wouldn't want to leave the United States to live there in England with him.

Wait a minute. What was he thinking? Did he want to marry her? She had a business awaiting her at home. Even if they had an affair, and he was beginning to wonder, with all this intrigue going on, when if ever that would happen, she had no reason to stay in England unless he proposed marriage. That was a serious step. He always assumed he'd marry eventually, but it would be to some English girl who'd been to the same type of school as he, and whose background and interests coincided perfectly with his. Not that she must be upper-class, he'd been honest with Sabrina about disliking the class system, but he always believed a successful union required two people as much alike as possible. And, it suddenly occurred to him, perhaps a very dull one.

Thoughts swirling in his head, he couldn't sleep, turned on the light and reached for his briefcase, in which he'd stuffed some of the papers he'd found at the Manor. He began to read old letters from past generations, and, eventually, his body relaxed its yearning to climb onto Sabrina's bed. He sighed. Knowing she was safe would have to do.

Chapter 18

"You're beautiful when you sleep," Hugh said the next morning. They were having breakfast in the hotel dining room. Sabrina had awakened early, showered and dressed before Hugh stirred from his probably uncomfortable night on the chaise.

"Thank you for staying overnight in my room. You didn't have to, you know. I'd have been all right."

He grinned. "But this way I got to see you curled up on the bed like a child, your knees up, your hand under your chin." He paused. "Not exactly the way I'd prefer to see you in bed, but we beggars can't be choosers." He paused again, giving her a sly smile. "Perhaps next time."

"Perhaps." She changed the subject, not wanting to think of how close they might have come to making love. If she gave him the slightest bit of encouragement, he might suggest they go back upstairs, or even to his flat. He'd probably want to do that anyway, if only to change clothes, having slept in his present ones.

"We need to concentrate on getting the necklace back. I'm trying to remember all we learned yesterday."

Hugh picked up his coffee cup. "Did you recognize the voice of that woman?"

"What woman?"

"The one at the rooming house, Bert's landlady. Did you recognize her voice? Could she have been the one you heard before being kidnapped?"

"Oh, no. That voice was different, with a trace of an accent. Bert's landlady has a voice like a chainsaw, and, besides, she smokes. Her clothes reeked of it. I didn't notice that smell before."

"You'd been drugged. Is it possible you just don't recall?"

"I suppose it's possible, but I doubt it. Odors are usually easily remembered." She took a sip of coffee. "Now you mention it, I noticed a scent, but of perfume or cologne, not smoke. Besides, if Bert needed someone to help him kidnap me, why would he pick his landlady and then run out on her, owing rent?"

"You've a point there."

"Today I think we should concentrate on finding Bert."

"How? Surely, we have no more leads."

"We could hang about that street where we saw him last. Perhaps he lives there now and we might see him, or his buddy." She drank the last of her coffee.

"You mean the man he spoke with?"

"Yes, I think I'd recognize him if I saw him again."

"Very well. First, however, we must return to my flat for a few minutes." He took her hand across the table. "Will you pack some things this time and move in with me? In the guest room, of course."

"No." She knew if she were to do that, no plans to use the guest room would keep them from each others' arms. And then to the love-making she wanted, but feared. She needed her own space until she sorted out her feelings. Perhaps the strong ties holding them together were simply the result of this mystery. Once they solved it—whether they found the necklace or lost it forever—she might be able to discern if their attraction could last, or remain only a brief encounter. "I don't think that's wise."

Hugh shrugged. "Well, then, let's be off."

They drove silently to his flat and Sabrina waited in the study while he changed clothes, Leonard helping him, no doubt. She couldn't see him living without a valet in her apartment or even a house they might own, doing things for himself. She chuckled, picturing him behaving like American husbands, helping with the dishes, taking out the trash. Or might he turn into one of those men whose only household chore consisted of changing the TV channel at frequent intervals?

She jumped up from her chair the moment he reappeared, freshly shaven and looking handsomer than ever. She walked immediately toward the front door, eager both to leave the premises and to begin their day's search. He stopped her.

"I've a message on my machine. The school where I teach is holding a meeting which I must attend." He looked at his watch. "I shan't be gone long. Will you stay here and wait for me?"

She felt her heart sinking. "How long?"

"Perhaps the rest of the morning. Probably lunch as

well. Leonard will fix you something."

"I'll just go back to the hotel."

"Why go there? You're much safer here, and you can do whatever you like, watch television, read."

She wondered, briefly, if she should go sleuthing on her own, but thought better of it. And if not that, she surely would just watch boring daytime television. The hotel room held no books, whereas Hugh owned hundreds, if not thousands.

"All right."

He gave her a lingering kiss on her parted lips, said goodbye and told Leonard to look out for her. After a moment spent savoring the kiss, she went back into the study and scanned the bookshelves for something interesting. Most of them held leather-bound books from bygone days, but many contained modern novels and non-fiction works of more recent years. Say what he would about not being a detective, he owned plenty of detective stories by both British and American writers. She saw titles by both Michael Crichton and John Grisham, Michael Collins and P. D. James.

Moving farther along the shelves, she saw her favorite: *Rebecca* by Daphne du Maurier. She took it down and settled into the corner of the sofa to reread it, relishing again the first scene in which the heroine, a penniless young woman employed as a lady's compan-ion, meets the handsome, wealthy Max de Winter. She couldn't miss the similarity between the novel and her own relationship with Hugh.

She wasn't poor. She owned three copy shops and, according to her accountant, she'd soon enjoy a high five-figure income after taxes. Yet her lifestyle couldn't compare to Hugh's. She didn't move in his circles, and she knew it.

A few nights before, she considered letting him seduce her, enjoy herself and then go back to Chicago, but now she rejected that. If she really loved Hugh, or even thought she did, how could she believe she could end their relationship unfazed? However momentarily exciting, an affair would only bring her bitterness and regret when it came to its inevitable end.

She tried to forget that and concentrate on the book, a mystery in its own right. Leonard, his usual half apron around his trim waist, came in, announcing he'd put some lunch out in the dining room for her.

"Not the dining room," she protested. "I'd feel as if I were in some old movie. May I eat in the kitchen?"

"Of course, Miss, whatever you like."

She followed him into the dining room and, while he carried her plate and water glass, she picked up the napkin and silver.

"Will this do?" Leonard seated her at a small table in a sunny nook off the kitchen.

"Perfect." She watched him moving things about. "Leonard?"

"Yes, Miss?"

"Where do you usually have *your* lunch?"

He hesitated too long, and she answered for him. "Right here, I'll bet."

"Yes, Miss."

"Then why don't you join me?"

"If you like, Miss." He brought a second plate and

water glass to the table.

"And stop calling me Miss. I'm Sabrina."

"I shall try to remember." He managed a smile, and she thought him quite good looking for a man she supposed was in his fifties. "As a matter of fact, Mr. Pendleton and I often have meals together right here."

"Really? That sounds, er, rather democratic."

He chuckled. "We're in the twenty-first century now, not the nineteenth. I may be employed by the man, but I don't consider myself his inferior."

She paused, thinking that over and pleased with his response. "Are you married?"

"No, Miss, er, Sabrina. I was married, but we're divorced."

"Children?"

"One. She's in university. Except not just now. She's touring the continent with friends this summer."

"Do you like working for Mr. Pendleton?"

"Very much. He's a fine gentleman, one of the best."

"Are you just saying that, afraid if you tell the truth, I'll report back to him and you'll lose your job?"

He laughed again. "Not at all. I really like him. I once worked for his family up in Durham. They're the nicest people you'd ever hope to meet, so I felt privileged to come to London and work for him again."

"Pays you well, I take it, if you can send your daughter to university and abroad."

Exceptionally well. I'm very fortunate."

"I'm glad." She ate some of her chicken salad. "Forgive me for asking so many personal questions. I'm afraid sometimes I behave like an ugly American."

"Not at all, and I like Americans, never found them to be anything but kind and polite."

"And nosy," she added with a grin.

"I don't doubt you have questions about Mr. Pendleton." He paused, then continued. "As turnabout is fair play, I shall ask *you* some questions."

"Oh, oh, here it comes."

"Are you, er, interested, romantically, I mean, in him?"

"We haven't been hiding it, I'm afraid. You've seen us kissing."

"Quite so, but your behavior is modest compared to what one sees these days. We live in a time of severely lowered thresholds of embarrassment."

"But you disapprove. You may like Americans, but you don't want him to get too involved with one. I understand."

"Not at all. I pride myself on being a rather good judge of character. Indeed Mr. Pendleton is as well, and I think it safe to say we both approve of you."

Sabrina laughed. "Next you'll say the Queen needs to give her blessing."

He grinned. "No, but I'm certain his parents will like you as well."

"Thank you."

"Of course, personally, I'd rather he has no plans to move to America. I won't leave my daughter in England and follow him."

"I don't think you need to worry about that. I like Hugh very much, but there's more than an ocean separating us."

"Have you ever thought of living here? I understand your father was born here, in Gilmore Manor. Has he ever talked about returning to England permanently?"

"No, he never has." She sipped her tea. "You know a lot about me."

"Mr. Pendleton sometimes shares his thoughts."

"While you sit here at this very table having meals."

"Occasionally."

"Well, Leonard, I like England, but I don't think I could move here."

"Pity. I think Mr. Pendleton could do a lot worse than marry someone like you."

"Thank you again."

"I am sincere, and I may even tell him so when we sit here over breakfast or lunch again. He sometimes asks my opinion." As if embarrassed to have said too much, Leonard picked up their empty plates and returned them to the kitchen. Suddenly he became formal again. "Shall you return to your book in the study, Miss?"

"Yes, thank you, Leonard."

* * *

She'd read another fifty pages before Hugh returned.

"So it's the slums again?" he asked after they settled in the Jaguar and he started the engine.

"It's not slums. The houses are a bit, er, neglected, but real people live there, some of whom, at least, are probably very nice."

"I'm sure you're right. I don't mean to sound like a

snob. I sometimes work with students who come from just such homes."

"I'm glad to hear it."

Once more they left the car parked some distance away and walked up the street on which they'd last seen Bert. After going several blocks with no sign of him or his friend of the previous day, they retraced their steps, still glancing between houses and looking closely at anyone who passed.

"There he is!" Sabrina clutched Hugh's arm and then turned toward him, hiding her face against his jacket.

"Where?"

"Just coming out of the house on the corner."

"Is it Bert?"

"No, it's the man he spoke with before they both went off. What shall we do?"

"Call the police and tell them."

"There isn't time. We have to do what we planned yesterday, follow him."

She started off at once, so Hugh had no alternative but to join her. The man in question walked two blocks and then waited at a bus stop. Hugh and Sabrina did the same, staying out of his line of sight.

Sabrina studied him as best she could. He was taller than Bert, medium-build with dark hair surrounding a bald spot and wore glasses with light-colored frames. His light-weight suit was neat and of decent quality, if not exactly from Saville Row. His white shirt and nondescript tie looked clean and neat, and his shoes were polished. He was no ruffian, and she wondered how Bert came to be connected to him.

The bus approached and, along with two chubby women who gathered in the interim, they boarded. Sabrina and Hugh chose seats behind their quarry and continued to focus their gaze on him. When he finally rose to exit the bus, they did the same, but from the back door instead of the one he used.

Trailing as far behind as they dared, they found themselves in a respectable middle-class neighborhood of well-cared-for homes and gardens. They walked behind for another few blocks before the man mounted the steps of a two-story attached house and, unlocking the door with a key, went inside.

"What shall we do now?" Sabrina asked.

"I've no idea. This is your scheme, you know."

"We must go inside and talk to him, but how?"

Hugh shrugged. "Since we're not wearing uniforms, I don't suppose we could pretend to be from the local gas company looking for leaks."

"Or," Sabrina suggested, "neighbors asking to borrow a cup of sugar."

He grinned. "Well, you might be successful with that approach, but he probably knows his neighbors."

"Not necessarily. Women generally do, but men aren't so social."

"We're selling magazine subscriptions door-to-door?"

"No, he'd simply deny any interest. I have it. We're doing a survey."

"What kind of survey? Political?"

"Television. People love to give their opinions about television programming." She opened her handbag and pulled out her pocket calendar and pen. "I'll pretend I'm taking notes, and you can ask the questions."

Hugh groaned. "I'm not much of a television watcher. I don't know what to ask."

"Just ask what their favorite program is, and we'll take it from there." She bounded up the front stairs.

After Hugh joined her on the stoop and she rang the bell, her knees began to tremble and her throat to tighten. What on earth had she gotten into, barging into people's homes, asking questions, trying to find a necklace which didn't belong to her to begin with?

A woman answered the door. Tall, middle-aged, with salt-and-pepper hair, she looked at Hugh first. "Yes?"

"We're taking a survey about current television programming." Sabrina thought Hugh played his part as if born to be an actor. "We'd like to ask a few questions about your favorite programs."

"If it does not take too much time," the woman began. She looked at Sabrina then, and suddenly her eyes widened and her face paled. "No, no, I cannot do that." She grasped the edge of the door as if to close it.

Sabrina stepped forward, knowing full well why the woman did a double-take. She recognized her, and Sabrina recognized the woman's voice. That was the person who spoke to her before Sabrina plunged into unconsciousness four days before.

Chapter 19

"I know you," Sabrina said to the woman in the doorway. "You'd better let us in or we'll call the police."

The woman's forehead wrinkled into a frown, her chin quivered, but she opened the door wider and let them enter. As soon as she did so, she called loudly, "John, come here."

The short entry hall led to a staircase and John, the man they'd been following, came down almost at once. He looked genuinely puzzled, although a bit apprehensive. "What can I do for you?" He pointed toward a sitting room on the right and they all went inside, the woman last, hanging back and putting a hand up to her face, as if trying to hide it.

"Please sit down," John said, and Sabrina wondered at his hospitality. Why invite strangers in? Did he run a business from his home, and customers often came to him unannounced? She thrust her pen and calendar back into her bag but didn't sit. "I recognize your wife."

The woman spoke to her husband in a low tone. "They said they would call the police."

"Call the police? That's ridiculous. I am John

Thompson and this is my wife Odette. We have done nothing wrong. Why should you call the police?"

Hugh gestured toward Sabrina. "Because Miss Gilmore here was drugged and kidnapped several days ago and she remembers a woman speaking to her just before she lost consciousness. The woman was your wife."

"That's impossible. My wife would have nothing to do with anything like that."

"I recognize her voice. I heard her. I'm certain of it."

"Where did this take place?" Thompson asked.

"At the Cavendish Royal Hotel."

"We have never been there."

"Someone drugged my coffee in the hotel dining room. When I became dizzy and went to the lobby, I sat on a bench, and I heard your wife speaking to me before I blacked out."

Odette Thompson still stood, a shaky hand covering her mouth, saying nothing, as if trying to minimize their opportunity to make voice comparisons.

"But hotels are filled with people," Thompson said. "It must have been someone else."

"The woman who spoke to me had an accent, just like your wife."

"Many people have accents. That doesn't mean she spoke to you, or that we are guilty of anything."

Hugh spoke directly to Mrs. Thompson. "Where were you last Saturday morning?"

"She doesn't have to answer that," Thompson said. "We are respectable citizens." He rose and came forward, as if he'd remove them by force if necessary.

Although, since Hugh towered over him, that seemed improbable.

Sabrina tried to think of what to say next to learn more from them. "This happened because someone wanted to steal what I was carrying that day, a very valuable necklace. When I woke up hours later, it was gone."

Thompson shook his head vehemently. "We know nothing about that. We have no stolen necklace here."

Hugh looked over at Sabrina before answering. "We could have the police come and question you."

Thompson pointed to the door. "Then you may leave now and send the police. They will find nothing."

Sabrina wanted very much to search the house, but Hugh ushered her to the front door. With a last glance inside, he turned and helped Sabrina down the steps onto the sidewalk. The door closed noisily behind them.

"I know she's the one," Sabrina said immediately, tears of frustration forming behind her eyelids. "I remember that voice."

Hugh steered her down the street. "You could be mistaken, you know, because of the drug, the trauma. Hundreds of people stay in hotels, and many of them might have accents."

"There's more. Remember I said the person who spoke to me didn't smell of smoke, but wore perfume or cologne? Well, this woman wears the same fragrance."

Hugh stopped walking and stared at her. "You're sure?"

"Of course I'm sure."

He frowned. "Let me just play devil's advocate for a moment. Suppose this woman *did* approach you as you lost consciousness. Perhaps, as a concerned citizen, she tried to help, keep you from falling off the bench, but had nothing to do with your subsequent kidnapping."

"In that case, why didn't she admit it just now?"

"Your telling her what happened next might have frightened her. People don't like to get involved in anything illegal or dangerous." He began walking again, but more slowly.

"But surely, if she was as friendly as you think she was and saw me like that in the hotel, she wouldn't have just left me. She'd have done something, called someone to come and help."

"Perhaps she did, and then Bert came up and carried you off."

"Then she could have said that. No, she's involved. I know it. Look how frightened she became when I said we'd call the police. An innocent person wouldn't behave that way."

Hugh took her arm again to walk over to a taxi stand. "It's hard to know how people will react, innocent or guilty. We'll just have to tell my friend at Scotland Yard and let them investigate further. At least we have a name and address, something for them to go on."

Inside the taxi, Sabrina lowered her head into her hands and tried to think. She'd been so sure they'd finally made a breakthrough, only to have it become a dead-end.

"What next, Podner?" Hugh gave it a John Wayne drawl, as if trying to cheer her with a bit of humor.

"I don't know. There must be something more we can do."

He took her hand in his. "Look, Sabrina, just let Scotland Yard handle this and try to forget all about it."

"Don't you want to know what happened to the necklace, too? Don't you want to get to the end of this mystery? That's the important part. Nobody reads a book to get to the middle."

"Perhaps, but we don't need the necklace. If someone in your family has it, and they use it to save the Manor from foreclosure, that's commendable."

"Not if it really belongs to some French family and they know it."

"Probably they don't know it. I only found out because I translated those old letters." He paused, staring out the taxi window. "And if that person just keeps the proceeds for himself, well, you probably don't want to know."

"I don't see how it could be anyone in my family, not now. I think Bert saw me in the jeweler's shop that day, saw the necklace and decided to steal it. He followed me. Remember I told you my feeling of being followed. Later he broke into my rooms and finally he called me to the telephone in the hotel so he could put something in my coffee. Then he kidnapped me and stole the necklace."

Hugh's look turned into a frown. "Why did he keep you locked up for days? Why not just steal it and run?"

"I don't know. Perhaps because it takes time to sell

such things and he wanted to be sure I didn't raise the alarm too soon."

"I guess that makes sense, but I don't see where the Thompsons fit in."

"They helped him. John Thompson and Bert took me out of the hotel. Mrs. Thompson provided me with food and water until I could be released."

"You're guessing, and, even if that were true, I'm afraid we have no evidence of it and no more clues to follow."

"I know." Sabrina felt tears sting again and pulled a tissue from her bag. In doing so, she remembered something.

"The matchbook!" She dug into the open side pocket and brought out the matchbook they'd found in Bert's room. Although no matches remained, she saw numbers scrawled on the inside. "This looks like a telephone number."

"So what?"

"Stop the car. We have to call this number right now."

Hugh, apparently realizing Sabrina's need to do something to end the suspense, told the taxi driver to stop near a telephone box. "I've left my mobile phone in my car, so we shall have to use this."

"Maybe not. I have my cell phone. It should work now."

Hugh took the phone from her and told the driver to wait. He took the matchbook from her and pressed numbers. Then he returned the phone to her.

"Here, you listen, in case it's Bert. Would you

recognize *his* voice?"

"I'm not sure. I doubt if I ever heard it."

Sabrina listened to silence, then strange sounds and finally ringing. More silence. Then a male voice. She snapped the cell phone cover down and stared at Hugh.

"Sabrina, what's the matter? Did someone answer? Did you recognize a voice?"

"I think... I mean... Where did we call?"

"Long distance, I believe."

"What long distance? How far away?"

Hugh studied the numbers again. "I say, now that you mention it, that's a foreign country code."

"Which foreign country?"

"France."

"Then that explains it."

"Explains what?"

"The person who answered the phone said, "Monsieur de Villot.""

Chapter 20

"De Villot?" Hugh repeated. "Are you certain?"

"Yes. He answered the phone saying, 'Monsieur de Villot.' Well, actually," she explained, "there was more. I only recognized that much. Isn't that the name of the French people from whom the Nazis stole the necklace in the first place?"

"That's what I read in those old letters to your grandfather. Nevertheless, this couldn't be the same person. That happened so long ago."

"He might be very old, but so was my grandfather, and he fought in that war. Or perhaps this is the original owner's son or grandson."

"Why would Bert have their telephone number on a matchbook?"

"Perhaps he didn't find out about the necklace when I brought it to Mr. Kendall's shop. Perhaps he knew about it all the time. Maybe this Monsieur de Villot sent him to all the jewelry shops in London to try to find it."

"That's a bit far-fetched, like looking for a raisin in a coal mine, especially after all these years. Why would he even assume the necklace is in England instead of

France or Germany or anywhere else?"

"He might have people looking in other countries as well. Anything's possible."

"Possible, yes. Probable, no."

"Shouldn't we at least find out if this de Villot has the necklace?"

"If he does, then it's been returned to its rightful owner, and the case is closed." He paused. "That should be easy to verify. We have his number. We can call him back and ask."

Sabrina didn't need to think about it very long. She hated that the necklace had been stolen from her, to say nothing of the ordeal she endured when locked in the warehouse. And, if the rightful owners got their property returned, she wouldn't worry any more about the circumstances. She handed the cell phone to Hugh.

"You speak to him. My high school French flew out of my head years ago, but I know most Brits speak it well."

"I'm not positive mine is up to the challenge, but I'll give it a try."

Hugh asked the taxi driver to remain parked, while he and Sabrina got out of the back seat and stood on the sidewalk. Sabrina watched him press the numbers and waited. She recognized the French words, *"Voulez-vous"* something and then she heard more rapid French, followed by silence while Hugh frowned, followed by more rapid French.

Finally Hugh turned to her. "Are you up for a quick trip to Paris?"

"Yes," she said instantly. Her adrenaline pumping,

she didn't know why they should go to Paris, but she didn't care. The plot had thickened, and she wanted to follow it to the end.

Hugh asked for her calendar and pen and concluded his conversation with the Frenchman by writing something on one of the address pages in the back of the book. An address in Paris, she assumed.

They got into the taxi again, and, on the ride to the airport, Hugh asked her if she was sure she wanted to go.

Her curiosity kicked in. "Why does he want to see us?"

"Because he knows about the necklace."

"He knows I found it, and someone stole it from me?"

"Not the details, no. I didn't get a chance to tell him. He's Nicholas de Villot and he's the son of the original owner. He refused to tell me more on the phone."

At the airport, Hugh bought two first class tickets to Paris and called Leonard to tell him where to find the parked Jaguar.

Then, their flight ready to depart, they boarded and took their seats in the plane. Sabrina fell silent, thoughts swirling in her head. First, that she loved the idea of just hopping on a plane at a moment's notice. Having a lot of money, as Hugh obviously did, made travel so much easier and more pleasant.

After she ordered a soft drink from the flight attendant, she returned to the subject which was the reason for their sudden decision to fly to France.

"The necklace disappeared so many years ago. What

did you say to him? Did he know the necklace turned up again?"

"Yes, he knew. But at first he refused to discuss it with me and became very angry. I tried to explain how we happened to get involved, but he didn't want to hear it just then. Finally he asked me to come to his home at once. They have an apartment in town."

"I'm glad you agreed." She grinned. "Being locked up for three days was no fun, but flying to Paris is exciting. Chasing down Nazi loot is a lot more interesting than replacing the toner in my copy machines."

He laughed, then turned sober. "I just hope we're not placing ourselves in danger."

"What could be dangerous about visiting a nice French family?"

"We don't know if they're nice at all. Besides, his story may be a pack of lies."

"Yet the name is the same."

"For all we know, that may be a common name in France. These people may not be the rightful owners. Or, if they are, they may decide we stole the necklace and call the gendarmes. I don't fancy spending the next twenty years of my life in a French jail."

She gave him a skeptical look. "You're being pessimistic. I'm sure everything will be fine." A smidgen of worry traced its way up her spine anyway.

The flight took only an hour, but when they landed at Charles de Gaulle Airport, and took a long taxi ride into the city, the sky was beginning to darken.

The taxi driver—as if getting ahead of everyone else on the street assured him a place in the next *Le Mans* auto race—plunged into the roundabout at the Arc de Triomphe and then cut off several other vehicles in order to exit.

He turned down a tree-lined street and jerked to a stop in front of a large ornate building with a black wrought-iron fence and gate.

After paying the driver, Hugh helped Sabrina out of the taxi.

When he rang the bell, a servant opened the door and Hugh gave him their names and the reason for their visit. Almost immediately, Monsieur de Villot himself appeared. He was a tall, slender man with graying wavy hair, deep-set blue eyes and rather more than his share of nose. From the wide sumptuously decorated entrance hall, he ushered them into a library and the servant closed the double doors behind them.

De Villot spoke in heavily accented English. "So you are Monsieur Pendleton who telephoned me."

Sabrina wondered why their host didn't welcome them to his home and offer them a seat. Or better still, invite them to dinner. She was beginning to get hungry, and she loved French food.

"Yes," Hugh answered. "As I started to tell you on the telephone, we learned about—"

De Villot interrupted him. "You have the necklace, do you not?"

"No, as I said, it was stolen from Miss Gilmore." He pointed in her direction.

"Do not think I am naive. I know you either have it or know where it is. You must turn it over to me at once, or you will find yourself in very deep trouble."

Hugh looked as surprised as Sabrina felt, and she said nothing. An icicle of fear slithered down her back.

De Villot moved to a small desk in the room and apparently pressed a button or something which would summon the servant, because the double doors opened again, and, this time, two French policemen entered the room.

One of them stepped in front of Hugh and spoke in forceful rapid French. Sabrina's limited, all-but-forgotten knowledge of the language was enough to reveal what he said, even if Hugh hadn't translated it immediately into English.

Her mouth dropped open and she repeated the words loud enough to be heard in Montmartre. "We're being arrested?"

Chapter 21

At police headquarters, or wherever they'd been taken, Sabrina was ushered into a small separate room, all wood with glaring overhead lights, and asked to wait. She sat in one of the two chairs near a medium-sized table, and a woman police officer sat in the other but made no attempt at conversation. Not that Sabrina wanted to try her limited French at that moment anyway. She was still in shock from being ushered into a patrol car and hurtled through the streets of Paris like a notorious long-sought fugitive.

Meanwhile, where was Hugh and what was happening to him? Even in her worst nightmares, she had never been in such a predicament. Yes, she had been kidnapped for three days, but by amateurs and had managed to escape by herself. This time she was arrested by actual authority figures in a foreign country and her companion taken from her for questioning or possibly torture. Well, maybe not torture. She seemed to remember reading somewhere that France abided strictly by Geneva Convention rules. Nevertheless, why did the police arrest them? Why did Monsieur de Villot think they still had the necklace when she and Hugh were convinced it had been returned to the Frenchman?

The door opened suddenly and a young man came in bearing a tray with sandwiches and a glass of wine. He set it on the table in front of her and left as quickly as he had appeared.

Sabrina glanced at her guard, but the woman merely waved a hand, as if she was not interested, or not permitted to fraternize with a prisoner. Sabrina shrugged and ate one of the sandwiches. Not the gourmet meal she'd been hoping for, but not bread and water either, and who knew when she'd be offered food again? She hoped Hugh was also being plied with goodies.

After she ate, she squirmed on the hard wooden chair she'd been provided and tried to puzzle it out. Her naturally optimistic spirit wouldn't let her believe that she'd be confined for very long. Hugh would rescue her. He spoke excellent French and was an educated upper-class British citizen. He would explain everything and they would be released. Wouldn't he? Her palms wet, she stroked them on the sides pf her slacks and took several deep, calming breaths, telling herself not to panic. She glanced at her watch and noted the time.

Exactly two hours had gone by when the door opened and Hugh rushed in. Sabrina leaped from the chair into his arms, and he held her close for a long moment.

"It's all right," he told her. "Everything has been straightened out, and we're free to go."

"Go where?"

"They're taking us back to de Villot's house. I'll

explain it all to you later."

His hand at her back, he led her out of the building and into a patrol car. Sabrina's pulse jumped again at the thought of returning to the home of the people who had them arrested, but Hugh took her hand in his. He squeezed it gently, renewing her confidence that he knew what he was doing and would protect her. After the vehicle made a more sedate return to the mansion, de Villot ushered them into a spacious and luxurious drawing room where a mature woman of slender build and silver hair sat in a blue brocade wing chair. He introduced her as Madame de Villot.

He and Hugh spoke in that same rapid French, then de Villot switched to English. "Forgive me, Mademoiselle." He made a little bow. "I did not realize you were not proficient in French, so I will repeat what we have just said. I have apologized for the reception I gave you earlier this evening, and Monsieur Pendleton has been gracious enough to accept it and forgive me."

Sabrina wasn't sure what to say, so she simply smiled.

They all sat, she and Hugh on a sofa covered in the same blue brocade as Madame de Villot's chair. Miles of matching fabric swathed the windows facing the street, and the plush carpeting, if it had been white, could have hidden golf balls.

"We will have a drink, no?" Their host went to a cleverly concealed bar and poured red wine into glasses. Sabrina said, *"Merci,"* one of the French words she remembered.

Seated finally in another wing chair, de Villot placed

his glass on the table next to him, made a tent of his long fingers and began. "We have always known about the thefts from the days when the Nazis occupied our house during the war. My father had hidden most of the jewelry, but the German officers discovered a few pieces and took them. They also stole many valuable paintings, but most of those have since been recovered."

"And your house as well?" Hugh asked.

"Yes, but we do not live there now. We prefer the city." He paused and turned to Sabrina. "And now it is your turn. You are Mademoiselle Gilmore and you know something about the de Villot necklace."

Hugh nodded to Sabrina. "Perhaps you should tell him how you happened to find it."

Sabrina set her glass on the coffee table in front of the sofa and cleared her throat.

After she said her first complete sentence, de Villot interrupted her. "You are an American?"

"Yes, I live in Chicago and went to England to visit cousins. My father, David Gilmore, was born in England."

"I see. Continue, *s'il vous plait.*"

She told the story almost the way she had told it to Hugh, but without the details of her awful ordeal in the warehouse and the way she shinnied down a brick wall to get out. "I escaped, and since then Mr. Pendleton and I have been trying to discover who stole the necklace and what has become of it."

De Villot rose from his chair and scurried to a box on a corner cabinet, opened the lid and brought it to where they sat. Inside lay a jeweled necklace.

"It's been returned." Sabrina looked up. "Then why did you accuse us of having it?"

Hugh didn't wait for an answer. "Now that we know, we can leave and not trouble you any further." He frowned. "Perhaps you could have told me this when we spoke on the telephone. Instead you asked us to come here and then had us arrested."

De Villot reached in and pulled out the necklace, dropping it unceremoniously in Sabrina's lap. *"Regardez.* Do you see a necklace worth a million francs?"

Sabrina looked. And looked again. Holding the necklace up, she saw it was not the one she'd found in the doll. This one contained the same color, size and approximate number of stones in a similar setting, but it was a fake. She knew nothing about gems, but she did know this was not the necklace she possessed for a few days.

"Where did you get it?" Hugh asked.

"From a gentleman who assured me of its authenticity and to whom I paid a large sum." He paused. "Not to worry on that account. I shall stop payment. Furthermore, I did not give him all that he wanted."

Sabrina almost chuckled out loud and gave Hugh a look meaning, "What did I tell you: amateurs."

"I promised to pay the balance when I received the necklace," de Villot continued. "I never saw the original myself, being a child when the Nazis occupied Paris, but, as you yourself have seen, this is an obvious counterfeit."

"Then why did you want to see us?" Hugh asked.

De Villot turned in his direction. "Because I believed

you might be behind the deception. I thought you had the necklace copied and persuaded your accomplice to try to sell it to me. I am not a fool."

"No, and we're not accomplices. As we told you, we've been trying to find the real necklace so we could return it to you."

Sabrina said, "I think I know when someone copied the piece. I took it to a jeweler for an appraisal, but he couldn't return it to me the next day and gave me no good explanation. Probably his assistant, Bert, took it out of the shop that day and had it copied."

"By whom? Where?"

"I don't know." She looked at Hugh. "Do you suppose John Thompson might be involved somehow?"

"Possibly. Look," he said to their host, "you know we're not the thieves."

"Yes, I know that now. The commissioner telephoned me from police headquarters and assured me that everything you told them is true."

"I showed them my identification, suggested they call my banker." He paused. "In addition, I have a friend in Scotland Yard who knows all about this."

Sabrina thought Monsieur de Villot smiled sheepishly again before he spoke. "It has all been verified. I have a friend in Interpol, and as I'm sure you know, they have checked your identity with Scotland Yard. It is settled now, and I apologize once more for having put you through such an ordeal."

Sabrina put the imitation necklace back in the box and looked over at Madame de Villot.

She waved a thin, multi-veined hand. "My 'usband

is very, er, cautious. You must forgive him."

"It was natural for him to be suspicious," Hugh said, "but now you know we are who we say we are."

De Villot continued, smiling again. "We will discuss that in the morning. It is late and you must be tired from your journey. You will be our guests tonight."

"Stay overnight?" Sabrina got to her feet. "But we can't. I mean, we're not prepared. We rushed over here without packing anything."

"That is no problem." Madame de Villot rose from her chair and strode to the wall where she pulled a cord and a man servant appeared almost immediately. "Georges will show you to your rooms and Collette will bring you anything you need."

Hugh looked at her and shrugged, and then all of them left the room and followed Georges up a curving white and gold staircase where they separated into different rooms. Sabrina's room, splendid in pale green, boasted antique furniture, a poufy looking bed nearly swallowed in white tulle, and another carpet so thick she felt disrespectful to be wearing shoes.

Collette brought a satin nightgown and matching peignoir, and, leading her into a nearby bathroom, pointed to a new toothbrush still in its box, soap, lotions and cologne that smelled like Chanel No. 5. She said *"bon nuit"* and left, and Sabrina decided she liked being surrounded in luxury once more. Having been mistaken for a jewel thief, even briefly, apparently had its advantages.

* * *

A strange noise woke Sabrina and caused her to be disoriented for a moment. As memory returned, she got up, slipped into the peignoir, went to the door of the room and looked out. Except for a night light glowing softly from the bathroom next door, she saw nothing but darkness, and intent listening didn't reveal the source of the sound she'd heard.

Her mouth dry from sleep, she tiptoed silently into the bathroom, closed the door gently and poured a glass of water. She drank quickly, then opened the door and headed back to her room. Suddenly a strong arm went around her shoulders and a scream caught in her throat.

Chapter 22

"Shh." Hugh's voice. "It's only me. What are you doing?"

"I was thirsty. What about you?" she whispered back.

"Couldn't sleep. I miss you." His hands slipped between the peignoir and nightgown and he caressed the smooth fabric over her back and waist.

Delicious sensations traveled up her spine, and she shivered with desire. He pressed her to him and kissed her, and she wrapped her arms around his neck, smoothing his hair. He kissed her more passionately, his lips forcing hers apart, while his hands reached lower and cupped her *derriere*.

She broke away. Her voice shaky, she whispered, "We mustn't. What if they see us?"

"Let's use the bed in your room."

"No." Every part of her body ached to do as he asked, but propriety won the battle. "No, please. It's not polite to do that in someone else's home. Go back to sleep."

She hurried away before she could change her mind

but heard his last whispered words, "As if I shall sleep now."

She had felt his own desire through the thin fabric of the nightgown but forced herself to close the door and go to bed. Sleep took a long time returning to her as well.

* * *

In the morning, over a buffet breakfast that could have satisfied the first class passengers on the Titanic, Nicholas de Villot again apologized for his doubting their intentions the day before. His friend in Interpol had contacted sources at Scotland Yard and verified Hugh was not only a respectable member of English society, but had reported the stolen necklace some days before.

"While the local police trace the box this false necklace arrived in, we will conduct our own search for the genuine one here," de Villot said. "If you will be kind enough to do the same in London, we will post a reward."

"We intend to continue our search for the necklace," Hugh assured him.

"And you must keep me informed of anything you learn."

"I'll be glad to do that."

Breakfast over, Hugh and Sabrina thanked their hosts, said goodbye and stepped into a waiting taxi. As they rode, Hugh asked, "Have you been to Paris before?"

"Yes, once years ago. After college, some of my girlfriends insisted we take a tour of Europe: France, Germany, Italy."

"One of those nine-cities-in-five-days tours?"

She grinned. "Something like that."

"The Eiffel Tower?"

"Of course."

"Notre Dame?"

"Yes."

"Did you take the funicular up to Montmartre, to Sacre Coeur Cathedral?"

"Even that."

"Would you like to see it all again, this time with me?"

"It's very tempting." Tempting hardly expressed her feelings, but unfinished business always nagged her psyche, making her put duty first. "Perhaps another time. I think we need to go back to London and finish what we started."

She wondered if they would ever return to Paris together, ever act like lovesick tourists at those historic sites. She doubted it. She remembered what he had started the night before, and her heart did a little waltz. However, they'd known each other only eight days, and, much as he might want to take her to bed now, he'd forget her a week after she returned to Chicago, as she must do soon.

He took her hand. "Then at least let me take you back on the Hovercraft. I'm not afraid of flying, but it's such a hassle these days: crowded airports, tedious waiting, and uncomfortable seats. The Hovercraft is less cramped and one can walk about."

"Doesn't it take longer?"

"Traveling to the airport, checking in, security screening and waiting for the flight, then reverse the process on the other end takes almost as much time as going by boat. Please."

She couldn't deny him that small request, especially after last night. "All right."

They went to Calais and boarded what looked like a large ferry boat perched on huge black pontoons. Which it was. She knew how it worked: that air pressure pushed the craft upward so that it floated just above the water of the English Channel, a very smooth and fast ride. The attendants even called it a "flight."

Inside the ferry's spacious cabin, Hugh bought coffee for her and tea for himself and they took their cups to a small table near the windows.

"I wish we'd stayed in Paris," he said. "I'd have taken you to the Moulin Rouge, and even for a night boat ride on the Seine. Remember that film with Cary Grant and Audrey Hepburn where they did that?"

"*Charade*. It's one of my favorites. I watch it every time they show it on television. At least the first five minutes."

"Why especially the first five minutes?"

"That's where they meet at a ski lodge, introduce themselves and he asks if they'll see each other again. She says, 'I have a great many friends, so unless one of them dies...' and he says, 'Well, let me know if anyone goes on the critical list.'"

He laughed. "So you have seen it rather a lot, often

enough to memorize the dialogue."

"And the rest of the movie is the two of them solving a mystery: who killed her husband and why." She remembered also that the three men who threatened Audrey Hepburn also looked for something valuable: stamps, however, not jewels.

"The film ended happily, as I recall."

"Hollywood likes happy endings, at least most of the time." She also remembered that at the end Cary Grant's character proposed to Audrey Hepburn's, but she didn't remind Hugh of that.

"Let's go out on deck. The weather is perfect." He found a deserted area near the railing and, as they stood looking out, he put his arm around her waist.

She leaned against him, enjoying their closeness. "In spite of the fine weather, there aren't many people on board."

"I suppose most people take the Chunnel these days. We shall have to do that some time."

Another "some time" that would never happen. "I'm glad we didn't. It's too lovely a day to cross the channel under an ocean of water."

"My feelings exactly." He nuzzled her neck, then kissed her. "I wish last night hadn't ended the way it did."

She decided to be noncommittal. "I thought it was for the best. I don't believe it's a good idea to, er, give in to passion in other people's houses, especially people one hardly knows."

"But France is, after all, the home of *l'amour*. They probably expected it."

"Then I'm sorry to disappoint them, but we're not French."

He grinned and traced her lips with his fingertip.

The Hovercraft sailed smoothly on its way, and Sabrina wished the trip would never end. She loved being alone with Hugh, felt more connected to him every moment they spent together. The ordeal of her kidnapping was gradually receding in her mind, and she realized that—had that not happened—they might be further along the road of a romantic adventure, rather than a dangerous one. These quiet moments together had been missing from their relationship, and she relished them now.

She reached up and pulled his face close to hers again, kissed his chin and brushed his hair, that the breeze had tousled beguilingly, away from his eyes. If only they could spend many more hours, many days, many years, just being together, at peace with each other and the world.

Her common sense told her it would never happen and, as the craft drew near the English coast, she took a deep breath and changed the subject. "What shall we do first when we're back, see the Thompsons?"

"First we land in Dover, then, if you want to change clothes, we go to your hotel. And, finally we go to my flat so I can check my messages. I'm expecting to receive word about another meeting I shall have to attend."

"I hate postponing our search. The longer we delay, the more likely it is the thief will have sold the necklace and run off with the proceeds."

"I suppose we could visit Thompson first, if you prefer."

"Yes, please. Your last school meeting took you away for half a day, and I don't want to wait that long." She paused. "Unless I go on my own, that is."

"You know I don't want you to do that, so you win."

"Good." She smiled, but it was a small victory.

* * *

Both Thompsons were at home when Hugh and Sabrina arrived at their house, but they were reluctant to let their visitors come inside. "We told you before that we know nothing about any kidnapping or missing jewels," Thompson said. "Leave us alone."

Before he could close the door, Hugh stuck his foot into the opening. "We have information that may clear you."

Sabrina thought it more likely what they learned made them appear more guilty, but she kept silent, pretending an assurance she didn't feel.

Hesitating, Thompson finally agreed to "a minute," and ushered Hugh and Sabrina into the sitting room.

"What do you do for a living?" Hugh asked.

Apparently taken off guard by the unexpected question, he stuttered. "Why, I'm, that is, I'm a metal worker."

"In a manufacturing plant?"

"No, free-lance."

"What kind of metal work?'

"See here, what has this to do with Miss Gilmore thinking we stole her valuables?"

"We've recently learned," Hugh said, "that a copy of the stolen necklace we've been looking for has turned up."

"So, what has that to do with me?"

"Someone made that copy, someone who knew Bert, and we think that person could have been you."

"I did no such thing." He rose from his perch on the edge of a chair. "There, you have your answer. Now go."

Odette Thompson, who might have been listening outside the sitting room door, came into the room. "Tell him, John."

"I just did."

Her voice strengthened. "No, tell him the truth."

"We didn't do, er, what he says."

"If you have nothing to hide," Hugh said, "why don't you listen to your wife and tell us?"

"I will tell you." Mrs. Thompson, wearing an apron over a plain brown dress, came into the room and sat in a chair by the fireplace. "You are correct, Miss Gilmore, you heard my voice. But I did not steal your necklace."

"Let me explain." Her husband sat again and took up the narrative. "This person, Bert, called and asked me to help him. He would give me a job to do."

"And what would that be?" Hugh prompted.

"I work free-lance sometimes for jewelers, putting gems into different settings."

"Then you admit—" Hugh started.

"No, hear me out. We were to meet in the lobby of a hotel. My wife went with me, thinking she might do some shopping while we were in town." He ran a hand across his bald spot.

"We waited together. He said someone else would come with the gems. Then Miss Gilmore appeared out of the dining room. She was staggering, as if very sick, and nearly fell. That's when my wife spoke to her."

Mrs. Thompson nodded.

"Bert told me that this person had the jewels, and he asked me to help her into the back seat of his car. He took the parcel she carried, and inside was a rag doll, and inside that was a necklace. Bert said he wanted me to copy it."

Sabrina cringed at his calling Amy a rag doll, but she stifled a sarcastic response. "Did you copy it?"

"No, Miss, I did not. I thought it looked very suspicious, the necklace being hidden in a doll like that."

"What happened next?" Hugh asked.

"He jumped into the car and drove off. That's all."

Sabrina's voice rose. "You let him drive off with me?"

"I thought you knew him, and he would take care of you."

"If you suspected something, why didn't you call the police?"

"And tell them what? I knew nothing except that I turned down a job from someone whom I also didn't know."

Silence filled the room for a moment, and then Hugh said, "Just a minute. That's not the end of it. A few days later we saw you talking to Bert on the sidewalk on Temple Street."

Thompson's brow furrowed. "Oh, yes, now I remember. I'd been to visit my younger brother who lives in a rooming house there. The boy is on drugs, I'm afraid, always in need of money."

"And Bert spoke to you."

"Yes. I was surprised to see him. He must have followed me there, or else he had other reasons to be in that neighborhood."

"What did he say to you?"

"He asked me to forget what I'd seen, said he found someone else to copy the necklace."

"And you still didn't tell the police about it?"

"I confess that crossed my mind, but I feared that, if it *was* something illegal, he might involve me somehow. I don't need that kind of trouble, especially with a brother who might be, er, dealing, you know."

"I understand." Hugh looked over at Sabrina. "I'm satisfied that could be the truth. And you?"

She turned to Mrs. Thompson. "Then you aren't the one who saw to it that I had food and water while I was locked up?"

"I never saw you again until yesterday when you came to our door. I am truly sorry for what happened to you, but you must believe we had nothing to do with it." She pulled a handkerchief from the pocket of her apron and touched it to her mouth.

"Yes, I believe you."

Hugh stood. "Then we'll be going." He and Sabrina said their goodbyes and Thompson closed the door behind them.

As they stood on the sidewalk, Hugh asked, "What now? This case has more dead ends than a street under repair."

"Kendall," Sabrina said. "Bert must have had help getting me into that warehouse. Perhaps Kendall knows the names of other men Bert might have associated with. He said Bert spent a lot of time talking on the telephone."

"You're right." Hugh sounded enthusiastic again. "As well, Thompson told us that Bert said he found someone else to copy the necklace. Perhaps there are records of the telephone calls to and from Kendall's shop that might provide a lead."

He helped her into the waiting taxi and, once again, they headed for Bayswater Street.

Sabrina settled into the back of the taxi, clutching Hugh's hand, the future of their relationship in doubt. If only some benign fairy godfather would appear and solve everything, she'd vow to send gifts to his children for the next fifty years.

Chapter 23

Kendall greeted them warmly, but they had to wait twenty minutes in his shop, which smelled of pine-scented room spray, while he displayed and then sold an engagement ring to a young man for his fiance. While they waited, probably looking, Sabrina thought, as if they, too, wanted rings, she glanced over the many sparkling items displayed in the glass cases. Necklaces, brooches, earrings, and, especially hundreds of rings, lay in neat rows.

Hugh stood at her side. "Aren't these nice? Which do you like best?" Sabrina felt as if her heart had leaped into her throat. Was he thinking...? Would he...? No.

"Actually jewelry has never interested me." She shrugged and spoke in a quiet tone, not wanting to offend the shop owner. "I know that makes me a strange sort of woman, but there you are." She really had no reason for her lack of interest in wearing jewelry, except possibly that she'd always preferred simplicity to ornateness.

"Never?"

"When Peter and I became engaged he offered to

buy a ring, but I told him I'd prefer a solid gold wedding band instead, something a bit wider than usual, perhaps with a design on it."

Hugh continued to scrutinize the wares, but Sabrina sat in one of the little padded seats and waited for Kendall. Talking about engagement and wedding rings made her uncomfortable, and her eyes misted. She wanted to be married some day, and she feared that this London vacation would never bring that goal closer. Perhaps it would even push it further away.

Finally the customers left with their purchase, and Kendall turned to her with a smile. "What may I do for you today?"

"We want to talk about Bert again, if you don't mind."

"Not at all. I only hope I may be of some help."

"We've learned that the original necklace belonged to a family in France." She refused to admit her grandfather might have stolen it. "Apparently, the Nazis stole it during the occupation, but somehow it ended up in my grandfather's house and I found it, quite by accident, in the doll I once owned."

"Quite so. I remember the doll."

"You must also remember that I brought the necklace to you for an appraisal, and then it disappeared from your shop."

"Only temporarily misplaced, my dear lady, only temporarily misplaced."

"No." Hugh came forward. "We know now that someone took it from your shop and had it copied." He paused as if for dramatic effect. "Unless, of course, you copied it yourself."

"I? I would never do such a thing."

"I don't think you did," Sabrina said. "But it could only have been you or Bert, who worked for you at the time."

Kendall frowned. "I know I returned the genuine necklace to you, not a copy."

"I believe that too. In fact, we saw the copy that someone made. It's an obvious forgery."

"You have this copy? May I see it?" Kendall asked.

"I'm afraid not," Hugh said. "It's in Paris. Bert, or an accomplice, tried to sell it to the French family who owned the original. Probably it's now in the hands of the French police. Or Interpol."

"I still don't understand," Kendall said. "How can I be of help in all that?"

"Tell us more about Bert. Did he leave any personal effects behind, papers with names or telephone numbers?"

"No, I don't believe so."

"Did you overhear any conversations he had either in person or on the telephone?" Hugh asked. "Any names you might remember?"

"You said he spent too much time on the telephone," Sabrina added. "Surely there's something you remember."

"Yes, he made many calls, but I'm not the kind of person who listens in to conversations that are none of my affair." He sounded a bit insulted that they would think he'd eavesdrop. And he did look so proper with his almost old-fashioned attire and upper-class accent.

Sabrina hurried to explain. "Not intentionally, of course, but accidentally. Any scrap of information you might have heard."

Kendall shook his head. "I think he called his former employer once or twice, but that's all I know about."

"Do you have a list of telephone calls, perhaps from your monthly bill?"

"This month's statement hasn't arrived as yet. You're welcome to look at the last one, however." He went into the back room and returned with a portion of his telephone bill, duly marked with the number and date of the check with which he'd paid it. "Here it is."

He scanned the list, telling Hugh and Sabrina whose numbers they were. "As you see, none are unfamiliar to me. I'm terribly sorry. Perhaps next time." He pointed to the date on the paid bill. "I expect another bill should arrive any day now."

"Thank you." Sabrina smiled. "Will you call us when it comes?"

"Of course."

Hugh gave him one of his cards, and they left the shop. On the sidewalk Hugh said, "You know, we don't have to wait for the telephone company to send him a bill. The police can get those numbers instantly. I'll call my friend and ask him about it. They can trace all the numbers too."

"Assuming," Sabrina reminded him, "that Bert even made any incriminating calls from that shop. Perhaps he has a cell phone."

"You mean a mobile telephone? That's something

the police can probably check as well. Technology is always one step ahead of law enforcement, but I believe it's possible."

He hailed another taxi. "And now, my dear Miss Gilmore, we're going to my flat. I must check my own messages."

* * *

At Hugh's flat, Leonard seemed pleased to see them. "Shall I prepare something for dinner?"

"Yes, please." Hugh turned to Sabrina. "I'm just going up to my office for a moment. Make yourself comfortable anywhere."

After freshening herself in the downstairs lavatory, Sabrina went into the fragrant-smelling kitchen to see Leonard. She already liked him very much. She often thought that if you had no one in your life you liked talking with, then your life was unfulfilled, superficial.

"Did you miss us?"

"Indeed, Miss... er, Sabrina. However, Mr. Pendle ton often disappears for a day or so without telling me. Says I'm not a wife he must report to." He gave her a sly smile.

Sabrina's mind supplied the inference: and probably doesn't want one. "May I do anything to help?"

"Good heavens, no. You're a guest. You may sit and watch me if you like. I'm not one of those fussy cooks who becomes flustered at someone looking over his shoulder."

"I'll sit quietly in a corner then."

"Not quietly, I hope. You must tell me where you and Mr. Pendleton went. Days or even weeks may pass before he tells me, and I have a more-than-usual share of curiosity."

"We went to Paris."

Leonard turned to her with an expectant look on his face. "The city of lights and romance?"

"Not much romance. A little touching, some kisses."

She stopped. Why had she felt free to admit that to him? Why did she feel so close to him, as if he were a girlfriend to whom she could confide the events of her latest date?

"I'm beginning to wonder if Mr. Pendleton is truly, er, I mean, if Paris doesn't stir romantic urges, what will?"

"Oh, he's fine. I'm the one who put Parisian-style romance on hold."

"Not for too long, I hope. Soon you'll be returning to America."

"I know. I just hope we solve this mystery by then."

She told Leonard all about their sleuthing: the talks with Kendall, the Thompsons, Nicholas de Villot, and how they happened to spend the night in his ultra posh Paris apartment.

"Fancier than this?" Leonard asked.

"As fancy," she said, not wanting him to feel outclassed.

Hugh found her there and took her back into the study. She noticed he had changed clothes, wore a navy blazer over grey slacks and a shirt open at the throat. "I have good news and bad news."

"The bad news first."

"I have to go to that meeting tomorrow and it will

last two days."

She groaned. "The good news?"

"It's being held in Durham and, inasmuch as my brother and his family live there, I can stay with them overnight. At any rate, I haven't seen them in ages."

She pretended to be annoyed. "Good news for you, perhaps. What about me?"

"You can come with me."

"No, I can't do that. They don't know me."

"How will they get to know you if you don't come? Besides, it's not just my brother and his family. Although my father has died, my mother still lives there too." He paused. "You'd like each other."

The thought that he wanted her to meet his family made her pulse quicken. Unless of course, he made this invitation only on the spur of the moment, and he expected her to decline.

"But you'll be in meetings the entire time. I'll simply be in their way, a stranger they're forced to entertain."

"I'll be back every evening. At least I'm fairly certain I will."

She frowned. He was hedging already. "No, it's out of the question. I'll wait in the hotel."

Leonard came in and announced dinner. Knowing he'd had such a short time to prepare, Sabrina marveled at the variety and quality of the dishes he served. They enjoyed Cornish game hens with wild rice, a mixture of carrots and zucchini in a buttery sauce, as well as a mouth-watering peach pie, which Hugh called a "tart."

When they were again settled in the study, Sabrina asked, "When do you leave?"

"Tonight."

Her voice rose in pitch. "Tonight? When tonight?"

He glanced at his watch. "In about an hour, I should say." He pulled her to him and kissed the side of her neck. "We have time," he whispered.

She knew what he thought they had time for, but if they were ever going to make love, it would not be in less than an hour with him eager to dash off and leave her.

"I think I'd better go now." She scooted off the sofa and left the room. "Would you call a taxi for me?"

He followed. "No."

"No?"

"You must stay here while I'm gone."

"I'm not going to do that. I'm a grown woman and perfectly able to take care of myself. The necklace has already been stolen, so no one is going to need to kidnap me again." She paused. "I'll even call hotel security and ask them to station a man outside my door, if that will please you."

"You are a very stubborn woman."

"You don't have to be concerned about me. This was never your problem, you know." She hoped the tone of her voice belied somewhat the testiness of her words. Yet, on the other hand, if they quarreled, they could eventually part with fewer regrets.

He grinned, obviously not taking her seriously. "Touché. But I won't call a taxi. Leonard will drive you and make sure you at least get into your hotel safely."

"All right."

In the end, he went with her. They sat in the back

of the Jaguar, kissing and holding one another, but he didn't get out at the hotel's *porte cochere*.

"If I take you upstairs, I shall miss my train."

"You said it doesn't leave for awhile."

"I know, but I'd make love to you for hours."

Yes, she wanted hours or nothing. She stepped out of the car, waved to him and Leonard and let the doorman open the door for her.

In her room, she pulled off her clothes, flopped across the bed and called her father.

"Are you all right?" he asked. "You promised to call me back yesterday, but you didn't. Your hotel front desk didn't know where you were either."

"I've been to Paris."

He didn't answer at once. "Alone?"

"No, with a man."

"It's about time you did something like that, Sabrina. Who is the man? Will I ever meet him? Will I get to walk you down the aisle before I need a wheelchair?"

"Nothing happened in Paris. I think I'm falling in love with him, but he's British and has a position he loves and a mother and brother and, well, he'll never want to live in the U.S."

"Your mother was American and I followed her here, so it does happen."

"You loved her. I don't know if he loves me at all."

"So," he went on, "come home and find someone here. I want a grandchild or two that I can spoil rotten."

Find someone there? After Hugh, would anyone in Chicago, or the entire United States for that matter, thrill her so much?

"Hold the thought. I'll call you again in a day or so."

She hung up and turned over in the bed, staring at the ceiling. All she really saw was Hugh's face, his wonderfully blue eyes and fair hair, that would look adorable on a child, their child. But that was fantasy. Probably Hugh didn't love her. And even if he did, would he want to do as her father had and move to Chicago to be with her? She felt certain the answer was no. She rolled onto her side.

If he wanted to marry her, and that remained a big doubt, could she give up her life and move to London? For a moment, she indulged in thoughts of living in his elegant flat with servants, taking glamorous vacations and having no business she must run. Wealth made a strong incentive. Yet, she knew she wasn't falling in love with Hugh because of his financial position. She'd been attracted to him when she imagined him a low-paid librarian.

On the other hand, could she leave her father? He'd gone to the U.S. as a young man and made himself quite at home, with an excellent career he apparently loved. Besides, he had raised her after her mother died, and, even today, when she had her own apartment, they lived close to each other and spoke and visited back and forth often. No, she couldn't do that to him. She felt tears slide from her eyes and slither across the sides of her face into her hair.

Chapter 24

Hugh spent the night at the family home in Durham. His brother William had picked him up at the train station and his mother and sister-in-law, Helen, had both waited up for him. On the other hand, Bill and Helen's two children had been tucked into bed at their customary hour.

"I say," Bill told him, when they'd made their greetings and relaxed in the sitting room with glasses of wine, "you're looking fit. You must be enjoying your holiday from teaching."

Hugh couldn't help grinning. "Very much."

"Traveling, are you?"

"Well, I did go to Paris for a day."

"Only a day? No mademoiselles there who interested you enough to stay longer?"

Hugh set down his half-full glass. "You forget I'm not the swinging bachelor sort. Actually I went with a young lady, and she is neither French nor English. She's an American."

"How did you meet her?" Obviously interested in the new information, Helen leaned forward, letting her blond hair swing around her face.

"Do you remember my telling you about Richard Gilmore?"

His mother answered, her voice firm and cultured as usual. "The owner of Gilmore Manor?"

"The same. I met him a few years ago, and we talked about books."

"What else?" Bill chuckled. "You live, eat and sleep for books."

Hugh ignored his gibe. "Unfortunately Mr. Gilmore has died and, knowing of my interest in such things, it turns out he left a few centuries of old papers and manuscripts to me."

"Just what you need in that flat of yours," Bill said. "More dusty papers."

"That aside," Helen said, "what has it to do with the American girl?"

"She's a granddaughter. Her father David is one of Richard's sons and she came to the reading of the will."

"If she's a granddaughter," his mother asked, "how does she happen to be American?"

"Her father married an American lady and moved there. To Chicago, in fact, where he's a commodities broker."

"How interesting," Helen said. "And what about this young woman? What does she do?"

"She owns three printing shops."

Bill raised his glass, as if in a toast. "I say, that sounds rather impressive."

"Is she one of those no-nonsense businesswomen, all tailored suit, shingled hair and horn-rimmed glasses?"

Helen asked.

Hugh couldn't help grinning. "Far from it. She's not only beautiful, and has a figure any actress would envy, but she's also intelligent, witty and clever."

Silence reigned for some moments, while his family members glanced around the room at one another and eyebrows rose.

His mother spoke next. "You seem to know rather a lot about her already."

Hugh took a deep breath and recited how they'd met, their several meetings—he didn't call them dates—and then launched into a short version of her kidnapping and the mystery of the stolen necklace. It had taken longer than he expected, especially as he was interrupted many times with questions from his family.

"So you've been plunged into a mystery," Bill said.

"It sounds rather dangerous," Helen added.

"When may we meet Sabrina?" his mother asked. As usual, she had gone straight to the heart of the matter.

"I had hoped she'd come with me tonight and stay here while I'm at my meetings."

"Of course she should have done," Helen said. "You did insist we'd love to have her, didn't you?"

"I tried, but she thought it would be an imposition, inasmuch as I'll be in meetings all day. She didn't want to inconvenience you."

"You see," his mother said to the others, "I told you Americans have good manners. You must be more forceful next time."

He sighed. "She's leaving to go home on Sunday."

"Oh, no." Helen seemed clearly disappointed. "I was

so hoping you were about to tell us you're engaged."

Bill gently chided his wife. "What an optimist you are. Hugh lets eligible women get away all the time."

"Eligible or not," Hugh said, "this one lives in America, has a widowed father and a business to consider."

"Not that we need to give our approval," his mother said, "but I do think you should make every effort to bring her here. Once she gets to know us, she may want to stay."

"Didn't you say her father went to America to marry her mother? Maybe you could do the same."

"Trying to get rid of me, are you?" Hugh said it with a chuckle, but it wasn't as if he hadn't thought of that already.

"It's time you were married," his mother said.

"Don't wait as long as I did," Bill warned. "Marriage is wonderful. You'll like it."

Hugh raised his glass again. "Here's to a very supportive family. You haven't even met her yet, but you think I should marry her."

"You have impeccable judgment," Bill said. "If *you* love her, I'm sure we will too."

Hugh took a swallow of his wine. "Don't get your hopes up too high. Even if I love her, I'm not sure she loves me."

"This is Kismet," Helen said. "I feel it." They all laughed.

"But you must persuade her to live here," his mother said. "If she loves you, I'm sure she'll want to. After all, married women generally live where their husbands prefer, don't they?"

"Not anymore." Bill put his glass down. "These are modern times."

"However," Helen said, "her father chose to live in America and that was a long time ago." She glanced upward. "He must have loved her very much to do that."

"Hugh," Bill said quietly, "you're my brother and I love you, but you need to think of your limitations before you go running off to America."

"I suppose you mean I'll lose my job and wouldn't be able to go on teaching over there. But I wouldn't need to work, you know. Or, if I wanted to keep occupied, I could help Sabrina run *her* business."

"No, what I meant was that you're somewhat, well, selfish. Wives require some attention. I can't really see you giving up not only teaching but your preoccupation with books, your entire way of life, for someone else."

"We'll see."

After the others retired to their bedrooms, Hugh pondered Bill's comment about his selfishness for a long time. He could be right. Lying in bed awake, he relived memories of growing up in that very house, of school, of happy holidays and playing games with his brother. Then he pictured Sabrina in that setting. Of course, they wouldn't live in Durham, but in his London flat. At least until children arrived. He stopped himself. Doubt fluttered in his gut. What if she wouldn't?

* * *

After breakfast in the hotel dining room, Sabrina returned to her room, wondering how she would ever survive two days without Hugh. She realized now it had been a mistake to insist on coming back there. Had she stayed in his flat, she could have talked to Leonard or read a book. She'd lived on her own for a long time and didn't need to be with people all the time. Books took their place.

Furthermore, she and Hugh had followed up every lead in the mystery of the stolen necklace, talked to everyone who might be involved. True, they had never found Bert, but perhaps he'd long since fled the country. She could do nothing more.

She sat on the chaise and stared at the blue trunk in the corner of the room. She remembered her first day in London, listening to the reading of the will, finding Amy, her long-lost doll, meeting Hugh, their putting on the dress-up clothes from the trunk and dancing to an old record on the gramophone. An ache started up deep inside.

Even if her feelings for him were genuine love, he didn't love her. As she told her father the night before, Hugh would never leave England to settle in the U.S. as he had. Nor had Hugh asked her to stay in England with him. This adventure was over, and the sooner she accepted that fact the better.

Her two weeks' vacation would end soon anyway. This was Thursday and she planned to go on Sunday. Perhaps she should go home right then, before Hugh returned and they had an affair that ended with her heart broken.

She got up, went over to the trunk and sat on the floor in front of it. She lifted the hasp and pulled out the dress-up clothes, then the old books. She loved books, especially these, which reminded her of the summer in England, and she would take them home with her. Hugh had said some of them might be first editions. They might be worth something, should she ever want to part with them. They were her inheritance, after all. She only wished Amy could go home with her as well, even without the necklace. But she would never have kept the necklace in any case, didn't need it. If she'd never known who the rightful owners were, she would have sold it and used the proceeds to help pay off the mortgage on Gilmore Manor.

She made a pile of the books on the floor at her side. Too many to take on the plane, she'd have to have them shipped back. She scrambled to her feet and picked up the phone, asked the accommodations desk if they could arrange for that. They gave her the telephone number of a shipping company, and, when she called, they promised to come the next day to pack and ship them.

As for the clothes and the trunk itself, they would always be too much of a reminder of Hugh. She'd leave them there, back at the Manor. Perhaps one of her aunts would want them. She decided to return the trunk that very day. In any event, she needed to say goodbye to her relatives.

The decision to do something brought her a measure of comfort. She always liked being active, getting things done. She phoned for a bellman to come and carry the trunk downstairs. When he arrived, she followed him and returned to the lobby where the doorman hailed a taxi for her. The driver loaded the trunk inside, they drove to the Manor, and he placed the trunk on the doorstep.

Thomas opened the door for her, and he lifted the trunk and placed it in a corner of the echoing, empty hall.

"They've all gone, Miss."

"All of them? I had hoped to say goodbye. I'm going back home tomorrow."

"Mr. and Mrs. Philip have moved to a flat."

"Is that...?" Sabrina began.

"Yes, Miss, a home for, er, retired folk. Mr. Edward is staying in a hotel for the moment."

"What about Aunt Charlotte and her son?"

"Gone as well, left an address on the cork board in the kitchen should you need it."

"The house is deserted then."

"I'm afraid so, Miss. A great pity, losing it this way. Can't be helped, I suppose. Costs a pound or two to keep up a place of this size today."

"And where will you go?"

"I'm happy to say I've lined up another position, and I was just going myself. You shall have to let yourself out when you've finished."

"Thank you, Thomas. Good luck."

"And to you, Miss. Give my regards to your father."

"I will."

Thomas picked up the two suitcases behind the door and went out, heading for the garage, once a stable, where perhaps he kept a car. Sabrina closed the door behind him, wondering what to do next.

Some ancient, heavy furniture remained in the large entry hall, but, as she moved quietly though the first floor rooms, she saw that very little else remained.

She climbed the staircase and looked into all the bedrooms. Here and there a particularly large piece of furniture remained, something no one wanted or could accommodate in their new quarters. Unfaded places on the carpets spoke of beds and desks which had now been removed.

On the top floor, she looked into the nursery where the gramophone still sat, then hurried out for fear the sight would overwhelm her and set off a fresh bout of tears.

She opened another door and found herself in what must have been Zach's music room. The walls and ceiling glittered with some shiny material that she assumed was an acoustical fabric to keep the noise of his playing from disturbing everyone else in the house. The carpet had suffered some abuse, but no instruments or other furniture remained.

The attic occupied the entire back half of the third floor and it almost overflowed with boxes and trunks containing the memorabilia of centuries of Gilmores. The thought of all that family history being destroyed upset her. The bankers would have no use for it. Probably the mansion would be turned into some sort of school or a nursing home where patients would be pulled, pulsed and patched. Or, and this was truly unthinkable, it would be torn down to make way for a shopping mall.

Yet, she couldn't prevent that from happening. Even if she sold her business and used every penny of the proceeds—which might or might not provide enough to save the house—she couldn't pay for its upkeep. She sighed, better not to fantasize over the impossible.

She settled for taking a last look at the heirlooms stored there. After all, she had nothing else to do that day. She opened trunk after trunk of clothing, knick-knacks, old school reports and toys from the many children who had grown up in the house over the centuries. Plus piles of letters fastened with faded, decaying ribbon or twine. One trunk contained stacks of bound records and ledgers, what passed for financial spreadsheets in bygone days. Years before the steam engine, surfboards and mind-altering drugs.

Then she remembered Hugh had said he inherited all the old papers belonging to her grandfather. Surely, he should have these as well. Most of them might be worthless, but she couldn't make that determination on her own. He would have to have them, and soon, before someone from the bank came in with a bulldozer and destroyed them all.

The shipping company. She had written their number in the back of her pocket calendar and arranged for them to pick up her books and ship them to her home. Why not ask them to pack up these boxes and send them to Hugh's flat? She pulled out her cell phone to call them, only to discover it had no life. She'd forgotten to recharge the batteries. How could she remember such mundane things when her life was in turmoil?

She wondered if the mansion's telephones still worked, and went down to the next floor, to the room she knew had been Richard's office. The desk, chair, bookcases and files had been removed. Perhaps Hugh had already taken all the papers from the room. A telephone sat in lonely splendor on the floor, and she picked it up. What luck, the service was not yet terminated.

She asked the shipping company to come as soon as possible and remove all the boxes of papers to Hugh's flat, then hung up, grateful she'd accomplished something. Next she returned to the attic and refolded the tops of the cartons. Using the black felt-tip pen in her purse, she wrote Hugh's name on the top of every one. Then she decided to call Leonard and tell him to be on the lookout for them.

She went back to the office, picked up the phone again and listened for a dial tone. Instead, she heard a man's gruff voice.

Chapter 25

Hugh's mobile telephone rang in the middle of a meeting. Fortunately, he had set it to vibrate so as not to interrupt the proceedings. Fortunately, as well, he sat near the back of the room and could slip out with a minimum of disruption.

Once in the hall outside the meeting room doors, he pressed the Send button and held it to his ear. "Yes?"

"Mr. Kendall here."

His mind on the subjects being discussed in the next room, Hugh required a moment to remember who Mr. Kendall was. "Oh, yes, the jewelry shop."

"Quite so. I'm sorry to disturb you, but you did ask me to inform you if I learned anything."

His pulse quickened. "Yes, what did you learn?"

"It's not so much what I learned as what I remembered."

"And that would be?"

"I feel quite terrible about it. I should have thought of it earlier."

"Thought of what?"

"You see, my mind sometimes, well, you know how

it is when one gets older."

If the man were standing in front of him, Hugh thought he'd be tempted to throttle him. Although that particular action would hardly solve the problem. "What?" he almost shouted.

"Well, sir, you remember I said that Bert had occasionally telephoned his former employer?"

"Yes, I remember."

"I should have thought of it, the name being the same and all."

"What name?"

"Gilmore, of course. The young lady who came into my shop with the necklace was Miss Gilmore."

"And?"

"And Bert had formerly been employed by someone at Gilmore Manor."

* * *

Sabrina almost put the phone back in its cradle. She never listened in on conversations. But, wait, Thomas had said she would be alone in the house, because everyone else had already gone. Who could be using the telephone? And, if an incoming call, why had she not heard it ring? She remembered she'd been in the attic most of the time, so that probably accounted for her not hearing it.

She picked up the receiver again, carefully, quietly.

"No, you're not to come here. I've put your share in the box, as I said I would do."

Sabrina recognized the voice as one she'd heard

before, but her brain refused to register its owner.

"How do I know you really done that?"

That voice, harsh, a lower class accent, didn't sound familiar.

"Bert, listen to me."

Bert? The missing Bert was on the other end? But who was speaking to him from the house? Or was she mistaken and Bert was in this very house now? Her knees weakened and she slumped onto the carpet, still holding the receiver to her ear, but missing some words because of the thumping of her heart.

"Everything worked the way I planned, did it not? I promised you half before, and you got it, right? So trust me. You'll get the rest."

Finally Sabrina realized whose voice she heard: her cousin, Elmore Manville.

She continued to listen to the telephone conversation, clutching the instrument tightly, as if it might leap from her hand at any moment.

"You better not mess up, 'cause I could go to the coppers, y'know."

"I know that, but it might be your word against mine, and who would they believe?"

"I got facts."

"Calm down, Bert. I don't want the coppers snooping around any more than you do. Not that you deserve it, after what you did. But I put your share in the box, just as I said I would do. And I'm leaving the country so I can sell the necklace and recoup my costs."

"If you're lyin'—"

"You're the only one who lied. You nearly wrecked

the whole scheme with your stupid idea."

"I needed to protec' m'self, just in case you wasn't square with me."

"But I am square with you. Now do as I said, and lie low for two months."

Silence for a long moment, then Bert said, "A'right."

The receiver clicked into place, and Sabrina put hers down as well. Still sitting on the floor, she tried to put the pieces of the puzzle together. Bert had stolen the necklace and had turned it over to Elmore, perhaps without telling him how he acquired it. Yet, why did Elmore talk of leaving the country to sell it? And how had he come to know Bert in the first place?

She remembered the comment about Bert's "stupid" idea. Could that possibly mean trying to sell a copy of the necklace to Nicholas de Villot? If, when Bert worked for Kendall, he saw the necklace come into the shop, it was perfectly possible he "borrowed" it for a day to have a copy made. Not by Thompson, but someone else. Then he returned it, and from then on he had followed Sabrina in order to try to steal it back. Finally, of course, he had. However, what connection could he possibly have with Elmore? How did Elmore gain possession of it?

She got to her feet and went cautiously to the door. She'd obviously been listening on an extension and decided that Elmore—not Bert, thank goodness—had used another one. But which?

She'd never lived in the house except for the one summer so many years before and had no idea how many telephones existed and in which rooms. Besides the one in that office, perhaps a bedroom or two had others. The kitchen most likely, even a study or other first floor room. She peered into the hallway and saw nothing. Creeping along the passage, she peered into every bedroom on the second floor. Through the open doors she saw a telephone on the floor in two of them. No Elmore.

Her heart banging as if a drummer sat inside, she slithered along the wall to the staircase, looked down. Nothing. She stopped. She needed to do something, but what?

A sudden doubt crossed her mind. Suppose there was some other explanation for the telephone call? Go back to the beginning. Bert worked for Kendall and saw the necklace. He heard her name: Gilmore. Perhaps he'd heard about the Gilmore family—it was, after all, prominent in that part of England—and called Elmore telling him about what he'd seen. Perhaps he thought Sabrina had stolen it from the Manor and he wanted a reward for returning it.

Yes, that made sense. And Elmore had given him half the reward already and put the other half in a box somewhere for Bert to pick up. Nothing sinister in that. Except, why did he need to leave the country in order to sell the necklace? Another thing: did he know it really belonged to Nicholas de Villot? Perhaps his leaving the country meant that he intended to go to Paris to return the necklace and hoped for some sort of reward from the Frenchman. That would explain everything.

Confident now that, although she had been kidnapped, no other crime had been committed, she marched down the steps and went into the kitchen. No Elmore. She had to cross the hall to get to the study, but on her way she spotted some things she hadn't seen there before: a large black suitcase and a brown leather briefcase. In addition, on the massive oak table that still resided against the wall, she saw a set of car keys, a pair of glasses and a folder such as the airlines provided to hold tickets.

Elmore appeared from the back of the staircase, where a closet held boots and mackintoshes. "Sabrina!" he said loudly, obviously surprised to see anyone else in the house. "What are you doing here?" He wore a suit and tie, carried a light-colored raincoat over his arm.

"I came to say goodbye. I'm going back home tomorrow, but there was nobody here but Thomas. He let me in."

"Just now?"

"No, I've been here about an hour."

"What were you doing?"

"Looking about. I thought we ought to save those family papers in the attic for Hugh Pendleton. He did inherit them, you know."

Elmore pursed his lips, as if thinking about what she'd said. "Yes, good idea." He paused. "Well, I'm off. I'm leaving tomorrow as well."

"You don't live here now, do you? I see the furniture's all gone."

"No, I'm staying at a hotel until I can relocate." He seemed to realize that didn't answer her question. "I just came back to pick up a few things."

"Then it's all right that I called a shipping company

to come and remove those trunks full of papers in the attic?"

"What? Oh, yes, of course."

"I was just about to make another call when I heard you on the phone and realized I wasn't alone in the house."

"You heard me on the telephone?"

"Yes, you were speaking to Bert. Did you know he drugged me and locked me in a warehouse for two days so he could take the necklace?"

Elmore's face went through a veritable cornucopia of expressions. Finally he settled on one, his lips a firm, thin line, his eyes narrowed into slits. He spoke in a harsh tone. "I didn't tell him to do that. No one was supposed to get hurt."

"You're going to return the necklace to Nicholas de Villot, aren't you?"

He said nothing, only moved slowly toward her.

Sabrina's mind worked feverishly to sort out the new information. Elmore knew all about the kidnapping. Her first suspicions had been right. She should have trusted those instead of blurting out everything she knew. What a fool she'd been. She backed away from him.

So quickly she couldn't comprehend it until too late, Elmore threw the raincoat over her head and knocked her down. She fell heavily onto the stone floor. Dazed only momentarily, she struggled to free herself from the garment, but Elmore dropped on top of her and forced her onto her stomach. He grabbed for her hands and pulled them to her back, tied them with the sleeves of the coat.

He pulled her roughly to her feet and the coat slipped from her head. "What?" she gasped out.

"Shut up! Let me think."

"What are you doing? What's going on?" Those were stupid questions, but what does one say in such a situation, except maybe, "Damn, I've gotten myself captured again"? She should have listened to Dr. Phil, who said, "Never miss a chance to shut up."

"You shouldn't have come here, barging into things that are no concern of yours."

"I didn't barge into anything. I found the necklace hidden in my doll."

"It doesn't belong to you."

"I know that. I started to return it to your office when this, this Bert drugged me."

"I don't know anything about that."

"Yes, you do. He must have told you."

"You're free now, aren't you?"

Now there was an ironic question. She had been free until a moment ago and now *he* had captured her. "Why are you doing this?"

"For money, of course." He pushed her in front of him into the drawing room. Next to the fireplace hung a long wide piece of cloth—another of those old fashioned bell pulls—and he tore it from its mooring and tied the end around her hands, then removed the raincoat.

She flexed her wrists. He'd been wise to switch. She might have got loose from the coat, but not these tight knots.

"Why do you need the money?" Another foolish question. Everyone wanted more money than he had. No one was ever satisfied or thought he had enough.

"To get away. To live the kind of life I should have had if grandfather hadn't been so incompetent."

"You have a good job."

"You know nothing about me."

"And the necklace doesn't belong to you, either."

"I know that. It belongs to a Frenchman. Someone wrote letters to grandfather about it, but I never dreamed he really had it, that he hid it somewhere in the house."

He looked around the room, as if trying to find something else with which to tie her up, finally settled on the raincoat again. This time he forced her to sit on the hearth and wrapped the coat sleeves around her ankles, tying the ends into a thick knot.

"There. That'll keep you from running out, at least for a while. I'll have Bert come and get you."

And lock her up as he did before? The very thought made her muscles shake with fear.

"Why are you doing this?" she repeated.

"If you must know, I have no intention of returning the necklace to the Frenchies. It's mine now."

"They'd probably pay you a reward for returning it. You could use that money to save the Manor from the bank."

He laughed. "A reward? Save this crumbling mausoleum? If they gave me the whole bloody thing, I wouldn't save this place."

"But—"

"Get this, I'm no Gilmore. Never was."

"Uncle Philip adopted you."

"Treated me like a poor relation. Always catering to his own children, that stupid Edward and his sister Penelope. They're getting what they deserve. Let the mansion fall to the wreckers. Serve them right. I have other plans for my future."

He quickly pulled a cell phone from his pocket. Pressed some numbers. "Bert? Come over right away. I've got a job for you."

Sabrina forced herself not to scream or cry. Once again she'd done the wrong thing. She could have been in Durham at that very moment, drinking tea with Mrs. Pendleton, instead of about to be locked up again by Bert. Or even killed.

Chapter 26

Hugh hurried from the building, at the same time dialing Sabrina's hotel number on his mobile telephone. Waited while they rang her room. No answer.

He ran to his brother's Bentley, which he'd borrowed that morning, and leaped in. Before starting the engine, however, he dialed his own flat. Leonard answered.

He didn't bother to identify himself. "Leonard, is Sabrina there with you?"

"No, sir." He sounded puzzled. "We dropped her at the hotel last night."

"Has she called?"

"No, sir."

"She's not in her room. Do you have any idea where she might have gone?"

"Shopping? Ladies like to do that, you know. I shouldn't worry if I were you. You might leave a message."

"You could be right, I suppose."

"Perhaps she's visiting her cousins at Gilmore Manor."

His voice cracked. "That's what I'm afraid of."

"Afraid? Surely she's safe with them."

"You don't understand. I just learned that Bert, the man who kidnapped her, once worked at the Manor."

"I don't follow," Leonard said.

Hugh tried for a calmer tone. "Bert made a copy of the necklace and tried to sell it to Nicholas de Villot. How did he know it once belonged to him? I only found out about it myself because I translated some old German letters."

"You think...?"

He explained. "Someone at the Manor must also know about the French connection, and he must have told Bert."

"How could this put Miss Sabrina in danger? I confess I'm rather confused."

"So am I, but I need to find out. What if Bert is at the Manor and he kidnaps her again?"

"Why would he do that if he already has the necklace?"

"I don't know. I only know I need to get there right away." He spoke his thoughts aloud. "I'll fly home, maybe rent a helicopter. You must drive the Jaguar to the airport and wait for me."

He started the Bentley and sped to his brother's home. He'd rather have gone straight to the airport, but, in spite of his urgent need to return to town, he didn't want to leave the car there in the event his brother might need it.

Although he always thought it a bit reckless to drive and talk on the telephone at the same time, he did it then, called the airport and arranged for a helicopter from Durham back to London.

He cursed himself for leaving town in the first place. He should never have left Sabrina alone. Still, to be fair, he hadn't known that someone in her very own family knew Bert, perhaps ordered him to steal the necklace from her. They had seemed to reach a dead-end in their search, had followed every lead and probably ought to give up. At least he thought so.

However, he reminded himself, perhaps he overreacted. Just because Bert once worked at Gilmore Manor—perhaps as a gardener, chauffeur or mechanic—didn't make any of her cousins co-conspirators. Nevertheless, he couldn't take a chance.

He next asked himself why. Why did he have this overpowering need to protect her, whether she needed protecting or not? Yes, she'd been kidnapped once, but, as she herself insisted, she was probably no longer in danger. The real reason wriggled its way from his subconscious mind. He was in love with her. He couldn't bear the thought anything might happen to her. He wanted her with him always. Always? Surely that implied marriage, because unless he intended to offer a permanent arrangement, she would no doubt return to America and he'd never see her again. She was too independent, to say nothing of too desirable, to settle for something less. He must make a commitment.

Perspiration formed on his forehead. Marriage. It was time, he knew, no matter how many British men before him postponed such a step into their forties. Just the night before his brother had urged him not to wait.

Even his mother seemed ready to accept whatever wife he chose. But should he marry Sabrina, an American he'd known just under two weeks?

Yet, assume they truly loved one another, and they could be happy together. How could that work? His roots were there in the U.K., where his family had lived for hundreds of years. How could he leave it and go so far away? Plus Sabrina wouldn't want to leave Chicago and live in England. She had a thriving business, and a father who lived nearby to whom she was devoted. But he couldn't—at least he didn't believe he wanted to—live in America, however much he admired its people.

Yet, he mustn't forget Sabrina's father had emigrated to her country in order to marry her mother. Yes. He knew now that he loved Sabrina enough to do that as well. How bad could living in Chicago be, especially if Sabrina were there? She had said she might sell her business, and if she did, they could move to another city, maybe San Francisco, which both of them admired. And her father? Well, she had said he was thinking of retiring from the commodities exchange, so he could come with them. Yes, he'd propose to her. If only he wasn't too late.

* * *

As Sabrina sat on the hearth, the chill of the stones underneath seeped into her body. In fact, every part of her became cold, yet she suspected she shivered more from fear than the temperature in the old house. Bert had been summoned and would soon arrive. What would he do to her next? Take her back to that awful warehouse, this time making sure she had nothing to help her escape from that little room?

She remembered the terrible darkness. What if he left no flashlight this time? Worse, what if he left no food and water? He might even leave her bound and gagged, unable to eat or even move, much less explore her surroundings and find a way out.

A noise came from outside the drawing room. Elmore had left the room after his brief call to Bert, and she listened for his footsteps on the floors which were now barren of their Oriental carpets. She thought she heard him in the hall. Perhaps he'd gone back to that closet under the stairs, looking for a piece of rope or something else with which to tie her more securely than the sleeves of the raincoat. Given enough time, perhaps she could wiggle her legs out of its folds. If she could manage to stand up, she could certainly do so.

She wondered if she should even try to stand right then. Would it be best to let him think her helpless, and then, when an opportunity arose, leap up and surprise him? Surprise him how? She had no weapon and her hands were tied behind her back.

Still, she had to do something. If she hadn't worked against all odds in that warehouse, she might be imprisoned there now. At least she must try. First, she should attempt to stand up. She'd feel less vulnerable if she were standing.

She should probably do it before he returned. Failing to find something in the closet, he might go out to the garage and look there. Garages often held ropes or wires, or a dozen other things he might use to bind her feet and legs.

But standing when her arms and legs were tied presented a formidable challenge. She had no leverage, nothing to push against. Behind her yawned the fireplace opening, in front and on each side, nothing. She rocked her body back and forth until she slid off the hearth onto the floor. Now what? She lay down, rolled onto her side and tried to get up from that position. No luck. She struggled back to an upright sitting position, noticing with relief that her action had loosened the raincoat a bit. What should she try next? A wall.

Rocking back and forth again, like a child scooting along on her behind, she maneuvered over to the wall next to the fireplace. She pressed her back against it, pulled her knees up as far as possible, then tried to get them up and under her. That didn't work either. Next she tried turning her knees to the side to gain some leverage.

By that time, the major part of the raincoat had fanned out over her legs, only the sleeves still tightly tied around her ankles. Her feet were covered by the coat. But she wore her flats that day. An idea floated up to her consciousness. It might not work, but she had to try. She lifted her feet under the coat, wiggled them, flexed them up and down, twisting and turning to pull the coat down. At the same time, she flexed her knees as much as she could. The coat began to move downward, and then, with a mighty thrust of her legs, it loosened and collapsed. She pressed her back harder against the wall, brought her legs up and stood.

She'd done it. She almost laughed out loud, then assessed the situation again. Okay, she could stand, and perhaps she could run out of the house before Elmore returned. But with her hands still tied behind her and the raincoat tangled around her feet, she'd have to be very careful not to trip and fall. And what about the outside door, no doubt closed? How could she turn the knob to open it? She'd worry about that later.

As she maneuvered her way forward, loud noises came from the hallway and, moments later, two men entered the room. First Bert, and behind him a very tall, burly man with a beard, bushy hair and eyebrows the size of rats.

Bert stared at Sabrina and sneered. "Looks like we got 'ere just in time."

Chapter 27

Back in London, Hugh took over the wheel of the Jaguar and handed the mobile telephone to Leonard. "Call the hotel, ask to speak to the front desk, find out what they know."

Leonard did so, then reported back. "They say she asked to have a shipping company collect some books to be shipped to Chicago. But she hasn't checked out yet."

"Talk to the hosts or hostesses in the dining rooms, have Sabrina paged if necessary."

Leonard did. "She's still not answering."

"Try again every five minutes."

"Yes, sir."

"What about the bellman or doorman?"

Leonard asked to be connected and listened some more, then said, "The bellman took a trunk out of her room and helped load it in a taxi for her. However, he doesn't know where she went with it."

Hugh said nothing else, his mind a whirlwind of possible places Sabrina might have gone. If she took the trunk with her, it made sense that she'd gone to the

Manor. But, what if, after he dashed off to Gilmore Manor like a deranged man, she hadn't done so after all?

He would feel like a fool, but that didn't alarm him nearly as much as the thought she had gone somewhere else, somewhere he'd never find her.

Yet, she wouldn't just run away to Tahiti or someplace. Not this intelligent, responsible woman who'd left someone reliable in charge of her business for two weeks. She'd have gone home, or at least phoned her father to say she was coming. He glanced at his watch. Not too early to call her father in Chicago. He gave the number to Leonard. "Try this one."

* * *

Sabrina stared at the two men coming toward her. She had struggled to untangle her legs from the raincoat, even to stand up, all in vain. She escaped from the warehouse because she was alone, with her arms free and no one to stop her. What could she do now?

Bert stepped forward. "It's Miss Gilmore, isn't it? So we meet again." He gave her a grin that revealed poor dental hygiene.

She didn't bother to answer, only backed up toward the fireplace, wishing it were a door instead.

"You pick her up," Bert said to the other man. "You're stronger'n me."

"Maybe we should tape 'er mouth. Don't want 'er screamin' now, do we?"

"Ain't nobody about as can hear 'er screamin'. Manville says they all left yesterday."

Sabrina had backed up to the fireplace as far she could, her feet still entangled in the raincoat so that she almost lost her balance. Although her wrists remained bound, she reached out backward with her hands to brace herself and keep from falling.

Her fingers touched the fireplace tools. A plan catapulted into her mind. She stretched her hands back as far as she could and grasped something heavy, with a smooth long handle. Like a fireplace poker.

As Bushy Hair reached out for her, she turned her body around sharply and swung the poker as hard as she could. She heard it connect with a loud thud, then heard crashing, screams and curses.

She turned to look. The poker had struck Bushy Hair squarely in the middle of his stomach, he fell backward and knocked Bert over as well. Both men lay in a heap on the floor, Bushy Hair on top of Bert, clutching his belly and screaming like a jungle hyena.

What luck that her one blow had felled both of them. But then, she was overdue for a little luck.

She dropped the poker, kicked the raincoat from her feet and ran. Into the hall. Saw the front door closed, no exit that way. And no time to turn the knob and open it, even if she could.

She ran to the back of the hall, where the curving staircase concealed a built-in closet. Where Elmore had found the raincoat he'd tied her with and no doubt looked for a rope. A closet, which the British called a "cupboard," where twenty years before, she and her cousins had sometimes hidden during their games of hide and seek. She dashed inside to hide once more.

She crouched into the dark corner behind a tall Oriental jar that held umbrellas, wondering for a moment why her aunts and uncles had not taken those things with them when they moved out. She knew that the jar didn't conceal enough of her, knew full well she'd be found sooner or later. Bert and Bushy Hair would look everywhere for her and eventually they'd discover the closet. She could only hope they might go upstairs in their search, and, provided Elmore didn't return from wherever he'd gone, she'd have a few minutes to open *some* door and get out of the house.

She heard the two men, still yelling and cursing, come into the hall, their footsteps noisy, hasty.

Bushy Hair called. "You can't get away from us. Might as well give up 'fore you get hurt."

The two men spoke together in lower tones, and Sabrina couldn't make out the words, but soon after Bert called to her.

"Come out now, peaceful like and we won't hurt you. We just want to put you somewhere for a little while." Pause. "Somewhere safe, like before. With food and water and everything." Pause. "We don't want to hurt you."

Like she'd believe that.

She didn't move, hardly dared to breathe lest she reveal her hiding place. If those men had never been in the mansion before—and she could think of no reason to believe they had—they probably didn't know that the closet existed. Unless you stood at the back door behind the staircase, itself hidden from view, you couldn't see the closet door. You simply assumed it to be an innocent wall holding up the staircase.

Unless they exhausted every other possible hiding place and finally discovered it.

Footsteps, sometimes loud, sometimes soft, told Sabrina the men were searching the first floor rooms, all of which opened onto the enormous front hall. Then she heard them approach the staircase. She held her breath.

They went up the stairs. Now she'd make her move. She gave them a minute to have reached the second floor, to begin searching in the bedrooms and lavatories, then crept out from behind the umbrella jar and pushed the closet door. It squeaked.

She froze. No, they hadn't heard it. She tiptoed to the back door. That entrance was seldom used, she knew, except by servants. It led to the kitchen garden, the garage and the stables. When a member of the household needed to go somewhere, he or she simply asked a chauffeur—when they had one, otherwise Thomas—to bring the car around to the front.

She backed up to the door, hoping her hands, with their wrists inside their knots, could turn the knob. And why not? After all, they had grasped the fireplace poker, hadn't they?

Yes, the knob turned under her fingers. She whirled around, dashed through the now open door and collided with Elmore.

Chapter 28

"Where do you think you're going?"

She didn't answer, couldn't. Tears of frustration welled in her eyes. She wanted to scream.

Elmore had indeed found a rope in the garage or stable. Roughly, he turned her about and pushed her back into the house, staying close behind. In the hall, he did something to her arms and she realized he had thrust the rope between her hands, so that it went around the bell-pull he'd tied them with earlier. Then he dragged her, shuffling backward behind him, toward her trunk, which still sat innocently in a corner.

"Bert!" he called as he went, but the two men were probably on the third floor by then and couldn't hear him. She didn't want them to—they frightened her.

"Why are you doing this?" she asked. "Have you no sense of decency, no compassion?"

"None whatever."

Keeping one hand on the rope, he stooped down and lifted the hasp of the trunk, reached inside and pulled out the fancy dress clothes, leaving them in a heap on the floor.

"Take off your shoes," he ordered.

"I can't, remember?" She wanted him to do something, anything, that might give her an edge.

He didn't buy that. "Kick them off. They're not tied."

He was right. She wore flats, and she had no choice—unless she risked his doing something worse to her—but to use one foot to press on the heel of her other shoe and release it. Then the other shoe came off the same way.

"Get inside the trunk," he barked.

"Please don't do this. I won't stop you from running away."

"How can I be sure of that?"

"I promise not to do or say anything until you're safely out of the country. Just don't lock me in there."

"Sorry, I don't trust you. Get in."

Still she hesitated. "I'll suffocate and you'll have a death on your hands. You don't want that, do you?"

"No you won't. This old trunk is far from airtight. Besides, after Bert takes you out of here, I'll tell him to open the top so you can breathe."

"Don't leave me with them. I'm your cousin, remember?"

"I told you, no. I don't want to hurt you, but I will if I have to. Get in by yourself or I'll knock you out and dump you in."

He looked angry enough to do it, but Sabrina was too angry to give him the satisfaction. She pretended to stretch one leg over the edge, then swung around with all her might and knocked him off balance. Recovering quickly, he shoved her down hard, and she found herself lying in a heap inside the trunk.

He yelled at her. "Put your legs together." She didn't, so he grabbed her knees and forced them in position.

Elmore pulled the length of rope free from behind her hands, leaving the bell-pull still tightly bound around her wrists. Kneeling on the floor next to the trunk, he used the rope to tie her feet together. From a back pocket he pulled a large piece of dirty cloth, no doubt something he'd also found in the garage or stable, and leaned forward as if to tie it over her mouth.

She twisted her head away. "Please, no. I won't be able to breathe."

"Yes, you will." Nevertheless, he stopped.

She had a moment's hope that he'd reconsidered it, but the hope died quickly. He pulled a clean handkerchief out of his pocket, and, struggle though she did, he stuffed it into her mouth, then tied the rag over her face, tying it behind her head.

"There, that's so no one will hear you if you scream. We don't want the boys to have any trouble, now do we?" He got to his feet. "Bert will take you some place safe, some place with food and water, like before, and day after tomorrow he'll let you go. By then, it will be too late and I won't care what you do."

Sabrina grunted, wriggled and tried to get out, but he put a hand on her head and pushed her down into the trunk, then lowered the lid and she heard the lock engage.

Although the trunk had a few feet of depth, its

length didn't allow her to stretch out, so her legs were bent at the knees, while her head and feet touched the ends. It was also as dark as the inside of a cave.

The memory of the darkness in the little room in the warehouse returned, causing her heart to pound, and the wad of cotton in her mouth brought nausea. She told herself not to think of that, to breathe through her nose, and to try to stay calm. If she couldn't scream, at least she could pound on the end of the trunk with her feet. But, without shoes, her kicking made little sound and hurt her toes, while trying to bang on the trunk lid with her bent legs only hurt her knees.

She tried to look on the bright side. Elmore had spoken of food and water. Possibly he accompanied Bert when they put her in the warehouse, and that's why she had those necessities. Perhaps Bert would obey his instructions and provide them again, as well as release her in two days. But, she finally decided, why should he? With Elmore out of the country, no one would know if he released her or not, and he would be far better off if she never turned up to tell her story and to identify him.

She lay still in the dark, listening for noises that might tell her what was happening outside her tiny prison, trying to formulate a plan. After all, she had escaped before. She'd just have to do it again. This time, she feared she had little hope of success. She might die there in the trunk, already so much like a coffin.

She thought back over her life, its lack of real accomplishment. The world would never remember or care that she'd been a successful business woman.

Worse, she'd never been married, never had children. She thought of Hugh, wished they'd made love at least once. Instead she would die without it ever happening. Tears threatened to choke her, and she had to will herself to stop thinking of that and just keep breathing. In, out, in out, until whatever would happen happened.

* * *

Hugh drove up the curving gravel driveway in front of the Manor and got out of the Jaguar.

"Stay out here," he told Leonard, "and if you see anything suspicious, sound the horn."

He mounted the steps to the door and rang the bell. Nothing. He tried the knob, found it turned easily and the door opened. He went inside.

Bathed only feebly in light from the open door and the high windows on either end of the two-story hall, the few remaining pieces of furniture looked forlorn. A small piece of worn and faded Persian carpet covered a bit of floor, but flags and pennants still flew from high rafters and here and there an ancient sword or shield still adorned the stone outer wall.

He paused and listened, heard faint voices from somewhere above. He debated calling Sabrina's name, but something told him not to. A chill that had nothing to do with the cold dank air in the nearly deserted house crept up his spine.

He glanced at the table near the door, saw a set of keys, eyeglasses and a folder with airline tickets. Carefully, he used his fingernail to lift the flap of the folder

and read the destination name printed there: Mexico
City. For a fraction of a second, he wondered if Sabrina
planned to go to Mexico, but dismissed it. She needn't
go that far to get away from him if she wanted to.
Furthermore, he didn't believe the car keys belonged to
her. She had no car in London, unless she rented one.
And hadn't the hotel doorman told Leonard she'd gone
off in a taxi? Finally, she didn't wear glasses.

Beneath the table stood both a suitcase and a
briefcase. Someone planned to leave town. If not
Sabrina, then who?

He turned and walked slowly down the hallway.

A voice came from behind him. "Who are you?
What do you want?"

Twisting his head, he saw Elmore Manville, Sabrina's
step-cousin, dressed neatly in suit and tie, a raincoat
over an arm. A slightly soiled raincoat.

"Oh, it's you, Pendleton. What can I do for you?"

"I'm looking for Sabrina."

"She's not here. No one's here. We've all moved out,
as we said we would do."

"Except you're still here."

"Just picking up a few last items, don't need to let
the bankers have everything, you know." He tried for
a chuckle but didn't quite manage it. He seemed nervous, his lips jerked into a caricature of a smile.

"So everything's gone then: people, furniture."

"Everything." Elmore moved toward the table, then
turned about as if suddenly remembering something.
"Oh, if you're wondering about the old papers and
records Richard Gilmore left you, they're gone. Sabrina

said you wanted them and she had them shipped to your flat. Before she left."

"And that would have been?"

"Yesterday, I think."

"You didn't see her today?"

"No, she didn't come today."

Hugh's gut tightened. The man lied. She'd been with *him* all day yesterday. Nor had he ever told her to have the remaining papers shipped to him. She'd been there that very day, but where was she now?

He'd have to search the house. He continued the walk he'd started before Manville appeared, crossed the floor toward a shadow in the corner.

Manville stepped forward as if to stop him. "I say, you must leave now. I'm instructed to lock up the house."

Hugh ignored him, moved faster. The shadow in the corner turned into a large trunk, a trunk he recognized. On the floor next to it lay a heap of clothes. He reached down and picked them up. He knew them. One was the coat he had put on that day in the nursery when they'd danced, the other the lace dress Sabrina had worn. Why were they on the floor instead of inside the trunk? Was it possible something else was in the trunk?

Two more black shadows lay on the floor: women's shoes. Could they be Sabrina's? He didn't recognize them, but who else could they belong to? Everyone else had moved out. Had they locked her in that trunk? Every muscle tensed, his breathing escalated.

He heard faint sounds, like someone thumping from inside, but before he could investigate further, louder noises came from behind him. Two more men bounded down the staircase. He recognized one as Bert, the man they had seen coming out of the warehouse, but not the other. That one looked like his worst nightmare: big, burly, with bushy hair and the nastiest expression since Hannibal Lechter.

Chapter 29

Three against one. Hugh had done his share of boxing at university, kept himself in shape as much as possible, but three men—one who looked as if he could bench-press lorries—were more than he could handle. He would have to try diplomacy until he could think of something clever as an alternative.

He walked back toward the open front door. He could run out, jump into the Jaguar and be gone in sixty seconds, but that left Sabrina in their clutches, an unacceptable option.

"Elmore." He addressed the most likely-to-be-reasonable of the trio. "Let's negotiate this. I won't stop you from leaving if you just release your cousin. You may keep the jewels. I only want Sabrina."

Elmore smirked. "You have no bargaining power. I have both Sabrina *and* the necklace. You have nothing."

"Money?" Hugh offered. "I'm not a poor relation like the rest of the Gilmores."

"You may have pots of cash, but it's not on you, is it?" He sauntered over toward his two henchmen. "I'll just let my friends here take care of you. Like they did Sabrina. Keep you, shall we say, under wraps for a bit."

"But she is here in the house, isn't she? In that trunk?" Even the thought of it made his blood run cold.

"Whether she is or not is no affair of yours. Just now you need to be sensible and let Bert lock you up somewhere safe." He turned to the smaller man. "Go out to the stable and find some more rope."

Back to Hugh. "Nigel here will see you don't run off before he gets back."

Nigel? This bushy haired gorilla was named Nigel? But at least that narrowed the opponents down to two. Yet Bert didn't move right away.

"Out that way." Elmore's tone showed impatience, his hand pointing off to the side. "The door behind the staircase." Bert, with a last worried look around, did as instructed.

By now Hugh had surmised the men had no weapons. If so, they would have turned a pistol on him to keep him from moving. Fortunately, as well, the men were amateurs.

Nigel, however, looked indeed big and strong enough to hold him down if he got close enough, and, even as he thought of it, the thug moved toward him. Again, the thought of simply running outdoors came to him. Leonard waited there, sitting in the Jaguar. They would be two against two, a more even match.

Then he had another idea. Backing up near the table again, he stooped down and picked up the suitcase, hefted it and, straining against its weight, threw it at Nigel. He'd always had good aim and the suitcase struck

Nigel in the chest, knocking him down. Hugh picked up the briefcase and plunged through the door. To the Jaguar. He opened the back, threw the case inside, slammed the door and yelled. "Go!" He would not get inside. He would not leave Sabrina.

Leonard, who sat in the driver's seat, apparently understood immediately. Hugh didn't look to see, but heard the car start and wheel out of the drive, its tires throwing up a spray of gravel.

Hugh had no idea if the briefcase held the necklace, or even the cash from its sale. One or the other might be in the larger suitcase he'd thrown at the men. Or even in a safe deposit box somewhere or already transferred to the Caymans or some other foreign nation that sheltered ill-gotten gains.

Elmore and Nigel rushed out of the house then, yelling, and Elmore chased the Jaguar for several yards before apparently deciding to abandon the idea. Hugh didn't wait for them to capture him. He stooped down, grabbed handfuls of gravel, and threw it at them, aiming for their heads.

Elmore slowed down, his hands in front of his face to protect it, but Nigel ignored the sharp gravel that struck him and rushed ahead. He clutched Hugh's arms to his sides in a fierce bear hug. Hugh managed to put one foot behind Nigel's ankle, forcing him off balance, but lost his own balance and crashed onto the driveway with him. He struggled to regain his feet, while still pummeling Nigel with his fists.

Nigel moved fast for a man of his exceptional size, pinned Hugh's arms behind him and pushed his face into the sharp stones. Hugh resisted the pressure as much as possible, but thought his neck would snap from the effort. He twisted his shoulders and hips until at last he got his knees under him. He stood, but Nigel swung a beefy arm at him. Hugh ducked, and both men threw punches, most of Nigel's landing in tender parts of Hugh's body. He stifled an X-rated oath. Yet, he noticed with some satisfaction that Nigel showed signs of suffering a few injuries from Hugh's blows as well.

Hugh tried to keep far enough away so as not to be caught again, grabbed handfuls of gravel every chance he got and threw them in Nigel's face. Elmore, apparently deciding the time had come to join the fray, rushed in and attacked Hugh from behind, just long enough to distract him and give Nigel an opportunity to land a serious blow. Hugh went down, and this time Nigel sat on his back, ground Hugh's chin into the dirt and stones. Pain shot up his face. He tasted blood on his lips.

In spite of everything, a jarring sound penetrated his hearing, came closer, louder.

Elmore yelled, "Stop!"

Nigel let go of Hugh's neck, climbed off. A police car, siren wailing, careened into view, stopping inches from where Hugh lay. Uniformed officers jumped out. Elmore and Nigel sprinted toward the side of the house, perhaps toward their own parked car, the officers close behind.

In spite of his aching muscles, Hugh dragged himself to a sitting position and put a hand to his bleeding mouth. Behind the police car, the Jaguar reappeared.

Leonard got out and helped Hugh to his feet.

"I know it must have been you who called the police," Hugh said. "But they arrived so quickly."

"When you went inside, I took the liberty of doing a bit of investigating on my own, saw another car parked at the side of the house. I thought you wouldn't mind if we had some reinforcements."

Although his face hurt to do it, Hugh grinned at him.

Chapter 30

The hasp of the trunk opened and light hit Sabrina's eyes. Before she could adjust her vision, Hugh's voice came to her ears, and then his strong arms went around her and he lifted her to a sitting position.

"Sabrina, darling, are you all right?"

As if realizing he'd said a foolish thing—her mouth still sealed tight with the dirty rag—he reached behind her head to undo the gag. She spit out the handkerchief.

"I am now."

While he untied the bell-pull from around her hands, she thought of his calling her "darling." That had a nice ring to it. Even better, once he untied the ropes around her ankles and lifted her effortlessly out of the trunk, he held her tightly, pressing her body into his, running one hand over her back, the other over her hair. "Dearest Sabrina," he murmured.

She held him as well, the anguish of the past few hours slowly receding. She was safe at last, the nightmare over. Soon he'd take her somewhere and they'd tell each other everything.

He took her by the shoulders and searched her face as if for signs that she was as happy to see him as he was to have found her.

"Hugh! Your face!" She reached up and touched his mouth with her finger. "You're scratched, bleeding." Then she noticed his clothes looked as if he'd been mashed in a garbage compactor. "What happened?"

He tried for a grin, but winced. "You should see the other guy."

"You were fighting? Who's the other guy? Bert? Or that gorilla?"

"The gorilla. The police have him now."

"And Bert?"

"Yes, and your cousin Elmore. The two of them worked together."

"I know. I overheard him on the telephone talking to Bert, and I realized he was behind the theft."

She paused while Hugh took her in his arms again and planted tender kisses on her lips, cheeks and forehead.

"It's all right. You're safe now and it's all over." He pressed her even more tightly into his embrace.

Without moving from the exquisite shelter of his arms, she whispered against his cheek. "But how did *you* know? You went to Durham for that meeting."

"I'll tell you all about it, but first let's get out of here. Leonard is just outside in the car. We'll go back to my flat." He released her a bit, but she clung to his arm and didn't protest. She didn't want to be out of his sight again.

They stopped first at a small hospital where Hugh's

face, and a few other cuts and bruises, were attended to before going on to Hugh's flat. After he changed clothes, and while Leonard prepared dinner for them, Hugh told his part of the story: how he'd learned that someone at Gilmore Manor might have been behind her kidnapping and the theft of the necklace, how he'd flown back and discovered Elmore, then the trunk with her shoes next to it.

"Poor Elmore. I never liked him very much, but...." She repeated what Elmore had said, about not feeling like part of the family, and intending to sell the necklace and keep the proceeds for himself.

"I'm afraid his greed will land him in prison for a long time," Hugh said.

"I expect the courts will be hard on him, even though he probably didn't want anyone to get hurt. I'm almost sure he was the one who left the food and water for me."

"We'll see. At any rate, he wasn't as vicious as Bert's friend Nigel." He told her how he had thrown the briefcase into the Jaguar and told Leonard to drive off with it, how he'd fought with Nigel, and nearly lost, until the police arrived.

"But you could have escaped," she told him. "You were already outside, at the car. You should have jumped in and got away."

"And leave you? Not a chance." He grinned at her. "I love you, Sabrina."

His words made her tremble, her face became hot. Then her own words tumbled out before she even knew she said it. "I love you too." She threw her arms around his neck and they kissed with a deeper passion than before, their mouths pulsing with desire.

Finally, reluctantly, she broke the kiss. "What do we do next?" Her chest heaved, and her breathing came in gasps.

He looked longingly at her. "Do you mean about us? I think we need to talk."

"Not now." Suddenly afraid of what he might say, she didn't want to think that he might let her leave the country in two days and she'd never see him again. She remembered the reason for their recent ordeal. "What about the necklace? Where is it?"

"I'm pretty sure it's in the briefcase Elmore was about to take away. The police have that now, but, if the necklace is in there, I'll see that it's returned to Paris, to Nicholas de Villot."

Sabrina realized he spoke as if he knew she would be leaving soon, had perhaps made up his mind that the talk he suggested, if it ever took place, wouldn't change the reality of their eventual parting. He'd said he loved her, but that didn't necessarily indicate a commitment. She thrust that aside, unable to bear it.

"However, the necklace is yours," he said. "That is, if you'd rather keep it."

"No. It's true I found it, but now that I know the real owner, I can't do that." She shrugged. "I don't need it anyway."

"You're forgetting the reward he promised. That belongs to you."

"And you. I'd probably be dead right now if you hadn't rescued me."

"Well, I certainly don't need the reward."

Leonard interrupted them to say dinner was ready, and they went into the dining room. A large tureen of thick vegetable soup, a giant bowl of green salad and a platter containing chunks of French bread awaited them. Leonard must have read her mind to have prepared such comfort food for them.

"Leonard, how did you know we'd want something just like this?"

"I decided it's what *I* wanted to eat tonight. I had rather an adventure myself."

"You were indispensable, as usual," Hugh said, "calling the police even before I knew we'd need them."

"A good servant anticipates his employer's wishes." After a sly grin, he added, "I think I saw that in a film," and returned to the kitchen.

Sabrina remembered the film, *Gosford Park*. She watched him go, and sat down to eat.

"As I was saying, perhaps you could give the reward money to some charity."

Sabrina took some bread and butter. "I'd like to use it to save Gilmore Manor from the bank, but I doubt that will be enough. I just hate the fact that I can't stop the foreclosure."

"Surely, it's not your problem."

"As a Gilmore, I feel that it is."

"But you live in Chicago."

Her heart sank. There it was again: his decision that she must leave.

"I know." A thought crossed her mind. "What if I sold my business? I've had a very generous offer, you know. That might be enough."

"You're not serious."

"Yes, I am." He wanted her to go. Okay, she'd survive that too. She just couldn't let herself think about it. "I can do something else, get a different job. My apartment is paid for. All I need is enough to pay the property taxes and supply me with food and clothes."

"You'd do that just to save an old house over here?"

"Yes, I would. Rather than let it go out of the family. I just hope what I can scrape up will be enough."

"In that case, why don't I help you? If whatever you manage to acquire isn't sufficient for the task, I'll supply the balance."

For a moment she felt a surge of hope, but then rejected it. "Oh, no, you mustn't. It's not your problem. I couldn't accept anything from you."

"All right then, not a gift, a loan. You can have a mortgage with me instead of the Bank of England."

She smiled at that, and her heart fluttered. "You're wonderful to offer." She pushed aside her bowl. Minestrone had never tasted so good, but she'd lost her appetite. "I'm afraid I've been dreaming."

"What do you mean?" He rose and came close to her chair.

She checked the tears that threatened to come. "I can't run the Manor from Chicago. Oh, I suppose I can come and visit every now and then, not wait for another twenty years."

"You don't have to stay here and run the Manor." He put a hand under her chin and tilted her face so she could look into his eyes. "I meant what I said. I'm going to do just what your father did, move to the United States and marry the woman I love."

Sabrina's tears flowed then, tears of happiness. She let him pull her to her feet and they embraced again. "Oh, Hugh," she said between kisses. He put his arm around her, they climbed the stairs and went into his bedroom.

"Are you sure you're all right?" She gently touched his bruised face. "It won't hurt you to...?"

"I assure you the part of my anatomy I plan to use is perfectly fine."

Chapter 31

In the morning, Sabrina lay in Hugh's arms and remembered them making love several times the night before. He was an excellent lover, strong but gentle. He had rained kisses everywhere on her naked body before pulling her toward him to caress the most sensitive areas and bring her to the peak of desire. His touch, his scent, his deep, mellow voice in the dark blocked out everything but the yearning for those moments never to end.

Eventually, they had slept, and now, cosily entwined with him, she sighed deeply and stroked his chest with her palms. Until Leonard knocked on the door and asked if they wanted breakfast before he'd be forced to feed it to the disposal.

Hugh stirred then and kissed her passionately, then freed her mouth. "Shall we go down to breakfast?"

"I am hungry, but, now that we've made love, I seem to want to go on doing it."

He chuckled. "There's always later."

"But I have no nightgown or robe, only the clothes I wore yesterday."

Hugh rose from the bed and gave her one of his silk

dressing gowns. "This may not be quite proper, but Leonard won't care." He pulled on a pair of slacks and a smoking jacket and they went downstairs.

The pungent smell of bacon and eggs had never thrilled her as it did that morning, knowing she'd share it for the first time with her lover. She tried to hide a silly smile that kept creeping onto her face. Leonard served them at the small table in the kitchen nook, never saying a word, although he seemed to stifle a grin now and then. He even sighed rather loudly when they finished their cinnamon toast and went back upstairs to make love again.

Later that day, Leonard drove Sabrina to the hotel, where she packed her things and checked out. Hugh declared he had work to do, disappeared for a few hours in his office, and later went off in the Jaguar. He gave Leonard the night off, took Sabrina to dinner at a fine restaurant and then to a revival of *Oklahoma!*.

He grinned. "I might as well get used to American culture."

At breakfast on Sunday morning, while they drank their coffee, Hugh said, "I have a wedding present for you." He went to the sideboard and returned with a fancy wrapped box.

"A pre-wedding present," Sabrina said, "we haven't even set a date." She paused before opening the box, her face tingling at the thought of his buying something for her. "And just when did you have time to go shopping?"

"Yesterday, of course. Come upstairs now and open it there."

She put her arm around him and they ascended the stairs to his bedroom. Flopping on the bed, she tore off the ribbon and paper. Inside lay a doll, *Amy, her* doll!

"Hugh, I can't believe this. Where did you find Amy?"

"Leonard found her the other day, in a pile of trash outside the Manor."

She hugged Amy to her chest and noticed something hard inside the doll's body. She looked up at Hugh. "Not the necklace?"

"No, of course not."

"Then what?" The doll's back was open as before and Sabrina's probing fingers pulled out a small velvet box. Inside was a gold wedding band. Not plain and narrow, but a wide one with intricate raised edges, a vine design and cut-outs. Her breath caught at the sight of it.

"I know you don't care for jewelry," Hugh said, "but—"

She threw herself into his arms. "I will love and wear this as long as I live."

They kissed and then Sabrina's thoughts turned to something more serious, that had popped into her mind several times already. "If you're going to live in Chicago with me, then perhaps I ought to reconsider trying to save Gilmore Manor."

"What do you mean? Don't you want to sell your business after all?"

"Of course I do. Especially now when I want to spend all my time with you, not running a business. But it's occurred to me that perhaps the income won't be enough."

"Even if I help?"

"Even if you help. Because it's not enough just to pay off the mortgage and own the house again. Such a place requires a tremendous upkeep. The roof leaks, I'm told, and probably there's plumbing and wiring and heaven-only-knows what else needs to be done. I'd want Uncle Philip and Aunt Frances to be able to live there again, and they'll need a cook, a housekeeper, a gardener. They're not used to doing those things themselves, even if the house weren't so enormous."

He squeezed her hand. "You are a marvelous lady."

She brushed aside his compliment. "I wish I could make a miracle so that, after all these years, my generation didn't lose it."

"Not your generation, really, your grandfather's. He apparently mishandled the family's finances."

"Poor grandfather. Uncle Philip said his father was never the same mentally after the war."

Hugh put his hand out as if to stop her. "After the war, your grandfather...." He got up from the bed, stood for a moment without moving.

"What's the matter?"

"I just remembered something." He struck himself lightly on the side of his forehead, then winced again. "Why didn't I think of this before?"

"Think of what?"

"Come with me." He stretched out his hand.

Sabrina took it, wriggled off the bed and let him lead her into his office.

He spoke rapidly. "The papers. I mean, yesterday,

while you were gone, the shipping company delivered those boxes of documents from the Manor that you marked for me."

"So?"

"So I looked into them and found something interesting."

"Among the old ledgers and bills? Imagine them keeping paid invoices for more than a century. I was afraid you'd hate me for saddling you with them."

"You did the right thing, whether you knew it or not." They entered the office where he flicked on a lamp and sorted through the stacks on his desk. Finally he stopped searching and pulled a sheaf of documents from the twentieth century piles.

"See here. Your family didn't own just the house and the land it sits on. They owned—they still own, I believe—the land that's under half of the nearby village."

She stared at the documents. "They owned the village?" She had never heard of someone owning an entire village.

"You see, a long time ago, the land was probably given to your family by a prince or duke or someone. I'll know more when I can examine the rest of the papers."

She interrupted. "It was when I picked up the telephone to tell Leonard that I had the shipping company send them to you that I heard someone on the line and realized Elmore was in the house."

"Talking to Bert," he finished for her. "Those papers from the attic may give us the history, but what I do know is that Richard Gilmore owned the land under part of the village, and the shop owners who built their shops on it paid him rent." He grinned.

What he was saying began to sink in. "A lot of rent?"

"Not much in the 1930s, but I daresay rent on retail establishments amounts to considerably more today."

"Then where is that money? Did Richard lose it all? Did he gamble or something? I never heard anyone say so."

"No, it appears what happened is that, when the war started, your grandfather stopped collecting the rents, perhaps told the shopkeepers that they needn't pay it during the war."

"That was very generous of him, but surely they paid it afterward."

"I don't think so. See." He flipped several pages, his fingers running down columns of dates and amounts. "There's no record of those payments after 1939. I think he forgot. Everyone seems to agree he became very confused when he returned. His experiences during the war had damaged his mind."

"But why didn't the shopkeepers pay the rent anyway?"

Hugh shrugged. "Would you? If no one came around to collect rents, perhaps they just forgot about it themselves. The shops may even have changed hands in the interim, and the present owners just assume they own the land." He paused again. "This could amount to hundreds of thousands of pounds."

Sabrina dropped into the desk chair. "Surely I can't ask them to come up with all that back rent now, more than seventy years later."

"You don't have to, although I suspect you'd have the law on your side if you did. What you *can* do is ask them to start paying rent now, at today's rates. That could be enough to maintain the house and the grounds and even taxes."

The reality began to sink in. "If they would. Do you think they would?"

"I really think it's probable. Anyway, it's worth a try."

"Hugh, you're a genius. You've solved everything."

Hugh took her in his arms again. "While you're feeling so grateful, why don't we...?"

* * *

Later, once again basking in the afterglow of their shared intimacy, Sabrina said, "We must call my father."

"Isn't it a bit early?"

"He won't mind being wakened for our news."

"He'll get a shock. He doesn't know me. What if he doesn't approve of our marriage?"

"He will. He's been nagging me to get married for years. But I don't care if he doesn't."

She picked up the telephone beside the bed and made the call. Her father had been sleeping, but became instantly awake when she told him the news. He also wanted to know where she'd been when Leonard telephoned two days before. He'd been worried and had called the Manor only to learn those phones had been disconnected.

Sabrina explained as much as she could, leaving out being locked in a trunk, then told him that Hugh had decided to move to America to be with her.

"Really?" He paused. "You know, Sabrina, when you told me about going to Paris with a man, I had a strong premonition that you'd fall in love and want to stay over there. And I'd miss you terribly."

"But now you won't, because I'm coming home and bringing him with me." She grinned over at Hugh and snuggled into his arms. She held the receiver between them so Hugh could listen as well.

"But you see," her father continued, "I began to think that perhaps I should return to England instead. I was born there, you know, would never have left except for your mother. But she's been gone so long." His voice weakened momentarily. "And I might take early retirement. I'm allowed to. I'll still get a pension. And with what I've invested over the years I'll have more than enough to live on."

"Daddy, what are you trying to say?"

"That you and your young man don't have to live in Chicago on my account. I'll live in England again."

The inference sank in. She visualized living in Hugh's flat, or anywhere else in the country she'd come to love. She looked at Hugh, who, although he'd been willing to move across the ocean to be with her, now wouldn't have to make that sacrifice. "Did you hear that?"

"Yes. I think it's a splendid idea."

"Daddy, are you sure?"

"Yes, I believe I am. I've actually thought about it

several times over the years, but I didn't want to uproot *your* life. When I went to England three weeks ago for your grandfather's funeral and stayed those few days in the Manor, I began to feel that the time was right. Just thinking about it now makes me as eager as a schoolboy."

"Oh, Daddy, we're going to save the Manor and you can live in it just as you used to, with your brother Philip and his family and your sisters close by."

"But what about you? Will you live in England too?"

"If it's all right with Hugh." She laughed. "Perhaps he's always secretly wanted to live in Chicago."

Hugh shook his head, then leaned into the receiver and spoke to his about-to-be father-in-law. "You and your daughter have made me the happiest man in the world."

* * *

David Gilmore listened for a long time to the silence on the other end of the line, assumed it meant Sabrina was being thoroughly kissed. Or could they have dropped the phone and...

"Sabrina? Sabrina?"

THE END

IF YOU LIKED THIS BOOK . . .

Visit the author's website and check out her other romance novels: www.phyllishumphrey.com

COLD APRIL - A love story set on the Titanic

THE ITALIAN JOB - An Italian backdrop for a novel of romance, jealousy, and old questions that need to be resolved.

NORTH BY NORTHEAST – On a sightseeing train trip, a jewel heist and a kidnapping give a school-teacher and a mysterious passenger more excitement than they bargained for.

ONCE MORE WITH FEELING – A female San Francisco stock broker deals with a handsome new client, his eccentric twin aunts and an insider trading scandal

SOUTHERN STAR – Written with co-author Carol-ann Camillo, the novel takes the reader on a yacht trip in the Bahamas, where anything can happen. And does.

STRANGER IN PARADISE – The manager of a Hawaiian hotel is about to lose her job because of a handsome stranger. And then a tsunami strikes the island.

FREE FALL – Can a woman who's afraid of heights fall in love with a skydiver?